ONWARD CHRISTIAN SOLDIERS

by
Mary Wallinger

DORRANCE PUBLISHING CO., INC.
PITTSBURGH, PENNSYLVANIA 15222

Copyright © 1992 by Mary Wallinger
All Rights Reserved
ISBN # 0-8059-3221-6
Printed in the United States of America

First Printing

I dedicate
this book to "Charles" — despite whose
efforts it has been written, and in the hope
that he leaves the next one alone!

ACKNOWLEDGEMENTS

Many people have helped to make this book possible, and I thank them all, patients and colleagues alike.

Although I have changed most of the names, it has been impossible to alter the characters. Had I done so, this book would have been a work of fiction. I can only say that if you recognize yourself, it is because you made a lasting impression on me.

My special thanks go to Sue and Alan, for unearthing the Nightingale Pledge, and to Squirrel for his technical advice, and for jogging my memory.

INTRODUCTION

I started training to become a nurse in 1965. The hospitals of today bear little resemblance to the hospitals of the sixties. We had no Intensive Therapy Units, no machines, and very few disposable items. Organ transplants were still at the planning stage, and many of the modern drugs, that we now take for granted, were still in their infancy.

Florence Nightingale, as everyone knows, went to Scutari, the barrack hospital of the Crimea, and became a legend – The Lady With the Lamp.

On her return from the Crimean War, Florence Nightingale established a nurse training school at St. Thomas' Hospital in Lambeth. The nurses that she trained went out and founded their own training schools.

I was perhaps fortunate, or perhaps not, in starting my training in one of these "Old" training schools. "Flo" had started teaching nurses in 1860. One hundred and five years later, we were still doing things much as she had done. Changes were resisted with the cry "Miss Nightingale would not have approved."

Whether those days can be called the good old days, or whether they should be described as the bad old days, I do not know. All I know, is that having worked for 20 years in the NHS I have seen many changes. Despite the hardships, the pain, and the sorrow, I am proud to call myself a nurse.

Undoubtedly, many of the changes have been for the good of the patient and have made the work of the nurse a lot easier. The one thing that has remained constant is the unrest within the profession. Then, as now, we were complaining that we were overworked and underpaid.

Today, student nurses spend more and more time in the classroom, and, with the implementation of Project 2000, will spend less than twenty percent of their training on the wards.

They will emerge as qualified nurses, well able to fill in forms and understand the machinery that is now a vital part of any ward, but there is more to nursing than watching a heartbeat on a screen.

I am afraid that we will be so busy watching the screens that we will lose sight of the patient.

Nurses, true nurses, are rapidly becoming beings of the past.

Miss Nightingale would most definitely not have approved.

FLORENCE NIGHTINGALE PLEDGE FOR NURSES

I solemnly pledge myself before God in the presence of this assembly to pass my life in purity and to practice my profession faithfully.

I will abstain from what ever is deleterious and mischievous, and will not take or knowingly administer any harmful drug.

I will do all in my power to elevate the standard of my profession, and will hold in confidence all personal matters committed to my keeping, and all family affairs coming to my knowledge in the practice of my calling.

With loyalty will I endeavour to aid the physician in his work, and devote myself to the welfare of those committed to my care.

CHAPTER ONE

My announcement that I had decided to become a nurse caused my family and friends a great deal of amusement. I must admit that they did have good reason.

There were several points that bothered even me. I had frequently been in trouble at school because of my hatred for any form of authority, and for my refusal to conform. I was well known for my ability to avoid anything even vaguely resembling hard work, and I literally rolled over at the sight of blood.

After twenty-five years of hard labour I have outgrown the taunt that I am idle, although at home I am often accused of being into energy conservation. Mostly mine.

Over the years, I have spent many an hour on the carpet of various Matrons' Offices because of my refusal to conform, but I remain anti-authority.

The blood problem is still with me, and apart from the time that I spent on the operating theatre, it has not proved to be too much of a handicap. There is, in fact, very little blood let loose on the wards. Mostly it comes in bottles, and that I can cope with.

I still don't really know why I decided to become a nurse. It was not my life-long ambition, merely a spur of the moment thing. I needed to work. I wanted to leave home, and I wanted to do something that was worthwhile, at the same time gaining some sort of qualification.

The choice was rather limited. There was nursing, teaching, or the police force.

As I had spent many a long winter in hospital as a child, and had been very happy, I thought, "Why not go back there and work." At least I knew what it felt like to be on the receiving end.

Having made the all important announcement, the family's mirth spurred me on. My parents said that I would never cope with the discipline, and that I would either get thrown out or give up because the work was too hard. There has been many an occasion when both of their prophesies have been perilously close to coming true, but I have survived so far.

I managed to convince a Matron that I was a hard-working and well-behaved girl, and thus was accepted to start the three year training required to become a State Registered Nurse. I was given a list of things to bring with me when I started, and sent on my way.

I'm not sure whether it was my acting ability or her staff shortage, but I was in. That was all that mattered.

I duly presented myself at the Nurses Home attached to the Preliminary Training School, with a case containing a two week supply of underwear, three pairs of black woollen stockings, two pairs of flat black lace up shoes, and a second set of clothes to wear off-duty, all clearly labelled with my name.

My parents had said that they expected me to be home by the weekend, and Grandfather had given me the money for the train fare. Such was their confidence in me.

The P.T.S. Home was a large Victorian house, about a quarter of a mile away from the hospital, and was to be both home and school for the next three months.

Home Sister answered the door herself, and showed me to my room. I was to share a room with two other girls, and to prevent any bother over who was having which bed, she had stuck a label on each one. She explained that it was possible that we might wish to change beds, but her permission had to be sought first.

"Because I must know where you girls are sleeping." she said.

I didn't know whether she was trying to be funny or not.

By the side of each bed was a cupboard and a chest of drawers. Not a mirror in sight.

I was told leave my case by the bed, and the maid would unpack for me whilst Sister took me round the house. I was rather pleased at the thought of having a maid to unpack for me. Had I known that the maid would inform Sister P.T.S. of the contents of my case, I would have insisted on unpacking my own things.

The ground floor was all classrooms, the middle floor living rooms. There was a kitchen with a sink, a kettle and a gas ring, a dining room, and a sitting room full of armchairs that looked as if they had come from a clearance sale in a junk shop.

The rest of the house was bedrooms; two bedrooms, a loo, and bathroom on each floor. One did not have to be a mathematician to conclude that six girls into one bathroom did not divide, especially as the only mirror on each floor was in the bathroom.

There were eleven other girls, and with one exception, we were all just eighteen years old. Beryl, the exception, was nearly twenty. To the rest of us she seemed very old, and we treated the poor girl as a mother figure.

We spent our first evening getting to know each other, and we rapidly came to the conclusion that the only thing that we had in common was the fact that we were all going to start training the next day.

We had not yet learnt to be honest with each other, and were all trying to prove that we had wanted to be nurses since we came out of nappies. Strangely, the one girl that had *really* always wanted to be a nurse gave in her notice at the end of our first week on the wards, her reason being that it was not what she had expected!

I was the first to leave the sitting room. I had left home very early and I was tired. As I left, some of the others decided that they too were tired, and followed me out. I was getting ready for bed when my two roommates came in. They had been chased out of the sitting room by the maid, who had told them that we were supposed to be in bed by 10:00 P.M.

We sat on our beds, there being nowhere else to sit, and related our life histories. Sue came from Manchester, and Wendy was from London. Neither of them had ever been near a farm and were interested to hear that my father was a farmer. They both had a very idealised impression of farms, and neither of them could understand why I had chosen to leave the farm to become a nurse.

Our conversation was ended abruptly by the maid. She didn't even knock. She just opened the door, came in, switched off the lights and went out.

Despite being tired, it took me ages to get to sleep. The bed was as hard as nails, and the clock on a nearby church chimed every hour. I was used to the sounds of the countryside, and that did not include a church clock.

Monday morning saw us all in the classroom well before eight o'clock, the one and only time that we were all early. We had been woken at 6:30 A.M. by Mildred, the maid, banging on our doors and telling us we had to be up and dressed by seven. Like fools, we all believed her. When she repeated the exercise the next day, not one of us stirred.

Bang on the first strike of eight, Sister P.T.S. arrived. A tall, very pretty woman, with a calm, almost etherial quality. She would have passed as a nun anywhere. She also had the patience of a saint.

We were told to sit in alphabetical order, starting at the desk at the front left hand side of the classroom. Chaos reigned for a while, as we only knew each other by our Christian names. Sister P.T.S. solved the problem by reading out our names and we duly sat at the appropriate desks.

Once we were all settled, Sister announced her plans for our first week. The first day was to be fairly easy. In the morning we were to sort out books, be measured for our uniforms and white coats, and learn the hospital rules. After dinner we were going to be taken to a local technical college to learn how to cook. Work would start in earnest the next day.

We started with the rules. As Sister read them out I was appalled. The list was endless. Each sentence started with "Nurses do not" or "Nurses shall not." We did not run, shout, or stay out after 10:30 P.M. We did not have visitors in the Home unless Home Sister was present, and we were not allowed to visit each other's rooms. Sister ended her reading of the "Commandments," then read out a list of articles that the maid had removed from our cases whilst she was unpacking them. As we had all been told what we should bring, anything not on the list was unnecessary, and would be parcelled up and given to us when next we went home.

It appeared that so far we had broken nearly every rule that it was possible to break in the twelve hours that we had been in the Home. Sister listed each misdemeanour, and as she did so, we all developed a hatred for the maid. Of all the sneaks I have met, she was the champion. If one of us went to the loo more often than she thought necessary, she reported it to Sister.

Apart from the breaking of petty rules, all of which we had been unaware, our main sin was that we had been calling each other by our Christian names. Henceforth, they did not exist. We were to address each other as Nurse, or by surname only. If we had cause to refer to a third person, she would be Nurse Bloggs.

It appeared that if we called each other by our Christian names, the patients would do the same, ward discipline would cease to exist, and riots would ensue.

We nearly had a riot when it came to the issuing of white coats. They came in three sizes, short, average and tall. If you were short, you were thin. Medium height equalled medium build, and if you were tall you were naturally fat.

Eventually, the long-suffering lady from the linen room had us all decently clad, even if some of the coats had more hem than body. It was the first example that we met of refusal to make changes.

When Florence Nightingale started training nurses, they had obviously come in three shapes, so we had to, like it or not. The fatter girls were told to diet, and the thin ones that they had to put on weight. It was easier to get us to fit the coats, than to get the coats to fit us. I was not very impressed by the length of the coats either. The hem had to be at least two inches below the knee.

We had each been given a cloak, and again these came in three lengths; long, longer, and even longer than that. The hem of mine was three inches off the ground. The cloaks were wonderfully warm and were dark blue outside with red linings. They also had large hoods to protect us from the rain. Unfortunately, we soon found that we could not use the hoods, as the fans of our caps were in the way.

Having been issued with our coats and cloaks, we then began the saga of our caps. We were each given a large square of starched white cotton and showed how to form it into a cap. Then, while Sister watched, we tried. I could manage to get the front bit looking presentable, but I could not get the tail to form a fan. However hard I tried, I ended up with something that looked as if I had slept in it.

I never did master the art. I relied on Sue, one of my roommates, to do it for me. We were all given two white hair clips to anchor the caps, one clip on each side at the back. The clips were not supposed to show. Even that wasn't easy. My cap had a tendency to slide slowly backwards, then fall off. I was lucky because I had long hair, and I soon learnt that I could hold my cap very firmly with a hatpin stuck through a pleat of hair.

Once she had us looking more or less like embryo nurses, Sister handed us each two small books. One was a syllabus, the other a record of instruction.

The syllabus, she informed us, was to be used as a guide, so that once we left P.T.S. we could study on our own. It bore the words, "Revised in 1952" on the cover. It must have been one of the few things in that hospital that had.

The record book had a nice plastic cover, and inside it was my name, the date of my entry into training and my index number. Sister explained that these books were our own record of our progress. Each time we were taught something, the appropriate column would be signed by the tutor. We were to hand them to the ward sister when we went onto a new ward, and as we became proficient in any of the procedures, the sister would sign her name.

They were, Sister informed us, known as Schedules. Thus was I introduced to the greatest bugbear of my training.

The most welcome sound that morning was the sound of the church clock striking twelve. Dinner time. We were allowed forty-five minutes for dinner.

Most of our meals were served in the P.T.S. Home, but for dinner we had to walk to the main dining room. The wind lifted the tails of our caps and tried to blow them off. Then, when we let go of our cloaks to hold onto our caps, the wind whipped the cloak about. By the time we arrived, we had more or less mastered the art of holding our cloaks together with one hand, and our caps in place with the other.

A dining room maid met us at the door and told us to collect our trays, then pointed to a table in the centre of the room. That, she informed us, was the P.T.S. table. Having eaten, we returned to the sanctuary of the P.T.S. sitting room. None of us had enjoyed being stared at by our seniors.

Sister P.T.S. had told us not to return to the classroom after dinner. We were to wait in the hall for the bus that was taking us across town to the college. As we stood waiting in the hall, a decrepit-looking vehicle drew up, and we joked about it being our bus. We stopped joking when we saw Sister beckoning us aboard. As the bus bounced down the road, there were several remarks passed as to whether or not Miss Nightingale had even ridden in it. It certainly looked old enough.

Sister P.T.S. shepherded us through the college until we came to the Domestic Science room. It was a big airy room, and it smelt vaguely of food. Our teacher introduced herself as Mrs. Davis, and explained why we were there.

We were to learn the theory and practice of invalid cookery. She was going to teach us to plan, cook, and serve meals that would tempt even the poorest of appetites.

We spent the afternoon learning how to prepare a breakfast tray. First we cut a grapefruit in half, using a grapefruit knife. Then we loosened the segments so that a weak patient could manage to eat them. After that, we cut wafer thin pieces of bread and made rolls of butter. The meal, we were told, was to be presented nicely, so that the patient would want to eat.

Having decorated the trays with paper napkins and doilies, we were told that we could eat the results of our efforts.

I wondered at the time if I would ever have occasion to cut up a grapefruit for a patient. I was right. I never have, nor have I ever seen a grapefruit knife on a ward. The only bread I have ever buttered was ready cut, and that can't be made to look appetising, especially when it has started to curl at the edges!

Having cleared away the results of our labours, we were escorted back onto the "bus" and driven back to the Home. Our first day as nurses was over, and we hadn't learnt anything that was going to be of any use to us.

After supper, Sue and I decided to go for a walk round the town. As we went out through the front door, we were accosted by Mildred. The door, she informed us, would be locked at 10:00 P.M.

The more I saw of that woman, the less I liked her.

CHAPTER TWO

The next day, we were all seated in the classroom before Sister arrived, but only just. The enthusiasm of the first day appeared to be lacking.

Sister drew our attention to a frame on the wall. It contained a copy of the Nightingale Pledge, ground rules laid down by "Flo" for the good of the patient and the profession. Sister explained that at the end of our time in P.T.S., we would be expected to know it by heart, and would not be allowed on the wards until Matron had heard us recite it. We were to regard the pledge as our own version of the Hippocratic Oath.

The first hour was spent outlining our programme for the next three years. Each year we would spend a block of three months in the classroom, three months on night duty, five months on day duty, and a month on holiday.

Holidays, we were told, were allowed at Matron's discretion. Even if we were due for one, should Matron decide that she was short of staff, or that we were behind in our training, then the holiday would be cancelled.

Each week we would work four split shifts, going on duty at 7:30 A.M. and working through to 8:30 P.M. with either the morning or the afternoon off. One day we would work from 7:30 A.M. until 5:30 P.M. and we would have one and a half days off each week.

Should the ward be busy, we would be expected to work through our off duty period. Sister assured us that it was rare for a nurse to work overtime.

Our progress would be closely watched by Matron, and should any of us prove to be unsuitable, we would be asked to leave.

At the end of our first year we would sit for our Preliminary State Exam, and if we passed that, Matron might invite us to stay and complete our training.

It was made to sound as if only the prefect were allowed to finish their training. In practice, what really happened, was the useless ones were given the push before taking "Prelims." That way, the hospital achieved a one hundred percent pass rate.

The lucky ones would do two more years training before sitting for the Final State Exam to become a State Registered Nurse. We would then be expected to work as junior staff nurses for a year, "to gain experience," at the end of which we would each be given a hospital badge and a silver buckle. The chosen few would be asked to stay on and join the staff.

Failure to complete the extra year meant that you did not get your hospital badge, nor the buckle.

Whilst in P.T.S. we would have every evening and weekend free, although we had to be in by ten-thirty every evening, except Sunday, when it was ten. Should we wish to sleep away from the hospital at the weekends, we had to see Matron and ask her permission.

I wondered what went on in the town between ten and ten-thirty on a Sunday night that made it so dangerous? Maybe they were afraid we might panic and catch the last train home if we were not locked in. I came very close to it on several occasions.

I was sure that Sister had told us the day before that we were allowed out during the week until ten-thirty, but Mildred had told Sue and I that she locked the door at ten. Having heard her say it again, I was ready for a fight with Mildred. As far as I was concerned, Sister made the rules and not her.

I wasn't concerned with their plans for us over the next four years. I just wanted to get the next three months over, and get on with being a proper nurse. I rather fancied the thought of ministering to the sick.

Sister eventually got round to outlining our P.T.S. programme. Monday mornings we would be given written, and sometimes practical tests, to see what we had retained from the week before, and Monday afternoons we would spend learning to cook. The previous afternoon had just been an introduction.

The announcement that we were to learn to cook was greeted with groans, but we were assured that it stated in our syllabus that part of our preliminary exam was on invalid cookery. Had we read our syllabus, as had been suggested, then we would have known.

I was a bit worried about learning to cook. I could make a cup of instant coffee, and sometimes my toast was edible, provided one did not mind the odd bit of charcoal.

My Mother had long since given up trying to teach me how to prepare a meal, on the basis that it was too traumatic. I was apt to put a pan on the cooker, and then pick up a book. By the time I remembered what I should have been doing, the kitchen was invariably full of smoke.

I need not have worried. The whole exercise was a waste of time, although I am still very proud of the certificate awarded at the end of the course. It says that I am proficient in invalid cookery.

Miss Nightingale must have been concerned about her patient's diet, and decreed that nurses should learn to cook. So, learn we did.

We scrambled eggs, boiled eggs, and even coddled eggs. Fish was steamed and boiled, (and then, I suspect, fed to the cats.) In fact, we spent ten Monday afternoons learning how to feed patients in an ideal situation.

When we eventually got around to feeding real patients, the bread was all medium cut, the eggs put in a pan in the middle of the night and left to simmer for a couple of hours, and the fish came from the hospital kitchen in the final stages of dehydration.

Even with the certificate, I still can't scramble eggs.

The rest of the mornings would be spent in theory, and the afternoons in doing practical work. The first week was the exception, as we had to learn the basics of anatomy.

My heart sank. I had spent the last two years at school doing little else. Now I was going to have to sit through four days of boredom while the rest of the class learnt things I already knew.

There was a general stir as we prepared pencils and paper, and tried to look pleased at the prospect of bones and things. We covered every system in the body during those four days, at a speed and depth that left us reeling. I had no idea the body was so complex. No wonder it kept going wrong.

If that was basic anatomy, thank goodness we did not need a comprehensive knowledge. Sadly, most of it was wasted on us, as it was very little use on the wards. I never had a patient tell me that he had a pain in the area of his Ptotolemy's ligament. He was more likely to say that his stomach hurt when he stood up!

Friday evening saw us all rather depressed. We had expected to learn to become nurses, but all we had done was to grapple with books full of the most complicated diagrams. We had been training for a week, and apart from dinner times, we had not even been near the hospital, never mind a patient.

The thought of the Monday morning test did nothing to lighten our depression. Sister had told us that if we had not managed to grasp the basics, then we would have to go through the lessons again until we had.

Gone were any plans of spending the weekend relaxing. Saturday and Sunday saw us all pouring over our books, determined to pass the test.

The Monday tests served two purposes. Obviously it was important for Sister to know how much we had actually learnt, but they also made us work together as a team. We gradually became a "set," rather than twelve individuals, and we learnt the importance of the group. The bonds that we formed during P.T.S. remained throughout our training, and in many cases, beyond.

It gave one a very comfortable feeling, knowing that there would always be at least one member of the set to whom one could turn for help. It was rather like being a member of a large family.

By supper time on Saturday, we had all exhausted ourselves studying, so we decided to go to the cinema. The film ended at ten-fifteen so we would be able to get back to the home before ten-thirty. We had ignored the fact that we had all been told by Mildred that she locked the door at ten.

We arrived back at 10:20 P.M. to find the door locked, and the Home in darkness. It was a freezing cold night, and rather than stand around ringing the door bell in an attempt to wake Mildred, we elected to go straight over to the hospital, and ask someone to come and let us in.

It was a wise decision. As we went in through the doors it was only just ten-thirty, and Night Sister was preparing to lock up the Main Home. Beryl, being the eldest, had been elected spokesman, and she explained that we had been locked out. She also explained that there was some confusion over locking up times. Sister P.T.S. had told us ten-thirty, but the maid had said ten. Beryl added,

"We should have realised that the door would be locked at ten. After all, Mildred is in charge of the Home."

Her last remark was a stroke of genius. Night Sister rang Mildred and made her get up and unlock the door. We learnt later that we were the responsibility of Home Sister during the day, and Night Sister at night. Mildred only slept in the P.T.S. Home. She was not in any way responsible for us.

From then on the Night Porter was responsible for locking our door. He, like all the other porters I have worked with, was a true gentleman. Before he locked the door, he would ring the bell and enquire, "Are all the young ladies in?"

If, as sometimes happened, they were not, he merely dropped the Yale latch. He had done his job, the door was locked. All we had to do was unlock it. The last person in was responsible for making sure the catch was dropped.

We might have won that battle, but we paid for it later. Mildred increased her spying activities, and hardly a day went by without one of us having to apologise to Sister for committing some minor offence. The most frequent one was that of not drying the bath after we had used it!

The next few weeks progressed without any major incident. Having all managed to pass our first test, we were introduced to the Clinical Tutor and began our real training. As far as we were concerned, the paper work was all very well, but it didn't get us any nearer to the patients.

Sister Schmidt was the only Sister to be addressed by her name. All the others were known by the name of their wards. Schmidt was bad enough, but Sister Clinical Tutor was too much of a mouthful.

She taught us how to make beds, beds, and yet more beds. It seemed to me that here were as many different ways to make a bed as there were patients to fill them.

The fun really started when we came to bed baths. The Practical Room was arranged like a small four-bedded ward. Two of the beds were occupied by aged dummies, known as Dolly and Mabel. Dolly was fine, but Mabel was apt to lose her head. One never knew when it would fall, and it used to do it at the most unlikely times. Having to chase across the room after the rolling head helped to liven up the proceedings.

When we were judged proficient at baths, we were taken out in twos to the wards and allowed to bath a real patient. Sister Schmidt took Sue and me to the Female Medical Ward, and supervised while we blanket bathed a huge woman. Our patient was very nice. It was just that there was so much of her, and as she was recovering from a stroke, she was unable to move herself. It did not take us long to realise that there is a vast difference between the classroom and the ward.

Lifting a dummy, or a fellow student is entirely different from lifting a patient. It was our first and last excursion to the wards.

For the rest of the time we practiced on the dummies. One memorable day, we were being taught how to lay out a body. The morning had been spent in learning what was to be done, and why. The need for respect was stressed. After all, a life had ended, and the nurses carrying out the last offices would be making the body ready for the relatives to pay their last respects.

I was chosen to work with Sister Schmidt, which I did not enjoy, as mistakes could not be hidden. As it was such an important procedure, Sister P.T.S. would be supervising. Mabel had "died" before we went to lunch. I had helped to lay her flat, and then covered her in a clean white sheet.

Once that was done, she was to be left for an hour. Leaving a body alone for one hour was a rigid rule, and one of the few that I have neither broken, nor seen broken by others. It took, we were told, an hour for the soul to leave the body.

We laid up a trolley with the Last Offices box, and all the other things needed. I was to do the work, and Sister would assist me. The classroom was quiet. Every one was overwhelmed at being in the presence of death, even if it was only Mabel.

I was doing fine until I started to brush her hair. Then, off came her head. It jumped across the bed, bounced onto the floor, and shot under the screen. Once there it stopped, stuck between the bottom bar of the screen and the floor. The eyes, which we had so solemnly closed, were now wide open, staring fixedly at me.

I did the only thing possible; I screamed.

I have since laid out countless bodies, but I will never touch their hair. The memory of having to pull out Mabel's head from under the screen haunts me still, even though one would have to search hard to find a less realistic-looking dummy.

It took a long time for Sister P.T.S. to forgive me, and I had to work hard to make up for ruining the atmosphere that she had worked so hard to create.

I managed to take temperatures and blood pressures without incident, and the years I had spent at chemistry came in useful when learning to test urine. I must be one of the few that mourn the advent of the urine testing sticks.

Sister P.T.S. was just getting over the Mabel incident, when I blotted my copy book for all time. We had reached the stage of learning to give injections. As it was not possible for us to practice on patients, and no one would volunteer to act as a guinea pig, we had to use oranges. Orange peel is similar to skin, or so we were told.

Whoever decided that must have had very odd skin, or else he had never seen an orange.

The skin is pinched to form a fold, and the needle pushed into the top of the fold. To make sure that the needle was not in a blood vessel, a little fluid was pulled back into the syringe. So far, so good. We had been given oranges that had red specks in them (they used to be called blood oranges), and as I pulled the plunger back, the syringe filled with "blood." I fainted.

It was some time before I came to, and a lot longer before I was forgiven. I was treated to a long, and public, lecture on my stupidity. It was also a long time before I ate an orange; the smell of orange peel still turns my stomach.

Suddenly the final week was on us, and we all managed to pass the final P.T.S. exams. I somehow managed to achieve second place in the class, which surprised everyone, me most of all. As Sister handed us our marked exam papers, she returned our Schedules. It must have taken her hours to sign her name against each of the procedures that she had taught us, yet she did not complain. She was one of the few sisters that didn't, and yet she had more to sign than any of the others.

We had now to face the real world, or at least the real hospital. The Change List had gone up. Our fates were sealed. I was to go to Ward One, a men's ward that took minor surgical emergency cases, and casualties that needed admission.

We spent a morning being shown round the hospital, and were even taken to see one of the wards, although we were only allowed as far as the doorway.

The hospital had been built in the early thirties, and was in the form of a hollow square. The wards formed three sides and the Nurse's Home the fourth.

Most of the wards were L-shaped, the doors being at the corner of the L. Sister's Office was next to the door. The sluice, bathrooms and clinical rooms were at one end, and the kitchen at the other.

There were three newer wards; the Radiotherapy ward was the newest. The other two had been added at the end of the thirties, and were both very long, straight wards.

On our last day in P.T.S. our uniforms arrived from the linen room. We each had three blue and white short-sleeved striped dresses. The idea was that we wore one dress, had one at the laundry, and one spare. There were, however, fourteen detachable collars. We would at least look clean, even if we smelled. Our belts and aprons would be given to us by Matron before we went on duty on Monday, and we spent hours being groomed for the ceremony. By the time we went to dinner, we all knew exactly what to say, and how it should be said.

Our final afternoon in P.T.S. was spent learning how to behave on the wards. We learnt that we should stand up straight with our hands behind our backs when being addressed by a senior member of the staff. That we should never run, unless ordered to do so, and that we should never question any order.

Matron was to hear us recite the Nightingale Pledge, after which we would be free for the weekend, once we had emptied our rooms. We had great hopes of finishing early. Matron thought otherwise.

She sat for over an hour, telling us that, although the hospital was not the most modern in the country, the training that we were receiving was second to none. We were all very lucky girls to have been accepted for training. So commanding was her presence (she bore a distinct resemblance to Queen Victoria) that we all believed her implicitly.

At last she stopped talking. Our moment had come. Solemnly we stood and recited the Pledge. Having sworn to uphold the honour of the profession, we were dismissed for the rest of the day. Matron made it sound as if she was giving us the afternoon off. In fact, we left the classroom only five minutes earlier than usual!

There was nothing left for us to do but to pack up our belongings, and move. Our next home was to be Number 9, another Victorian house, but this time only a few hundred yards away from the hospital.

Home Sister welcomed us to our new rooms, and showed us which table to use in the dining room.

At last, I was on the way to becoming a nurse.

CHAPTER THREE

It felt strange to be in uniform. At last we were real nurses. Well, that's what we thought. At 7:30 A.M., we had the dining room to ourselves, as the rest of the day staff had already started work, and the night staff had not yet arrived for their suppers.

Breakfast was a strangely quiet meal. We were all scared, more I think of going in to ask Matron for our belts and aprons than of starting work on the wards.

Sister P.T.S. arrived to collect us, and marched us, in alphabetical order, to Matron's Office. Being at the end of the line, I had to wait for what seemed hours.

I think that was the first time that I questioned the sanity of the system. There we were, twelve girls, dressed up in blue striped dresses, worrying in case Matron said that we could not have our aprons and belts. If she did not intend to let us loose on the wards, she would hardly have gone to the expense of having the uniform dresses made for us.

I was considering what would happen if I went on the ward without my apron, when Sister P.T.S. woke me up,

"You next, nurse. You know what to do?"

"Yes Sister."

The door opened and in I went. Hands crossed behind my back, all as rehearsed.

"Please Matron, may I have my apron and belt?" So far so good. Only an idiot could have got it wrong.

Matron nodded and held out what looked like a sheet of cardboard and a piece of old dress material. I took them from her and thanked her. She looked so regal, enthroned behind her desk, that I had to resist the urge to curtsy.

I left her office clutching my apron, and went to see Miss Grey, the Assistant Matron, to try on my uniform. The apron was as stiff as a board, and the waist settled over my hips. The belt was even worse. It hung down like a cowboy's gun holster.

Miss Grey pulled and pushed to try and make them fit. In the end she gave up and said, "You must have lost weight, child. Come here while I pin you up."

On her desk there was a pile of nappy pins. I can't have been the only one that had lost weight. Eventually I was dressed to her satisfaction, if not mine, and sent off to my ward.

My belt was pinned at the front. There was a lump in the middle of my back where it covered the pin in my apron. The worst part was the apron bib. As the waist of the apron had been made smaller, the cross over straps were now too long, and the bib hung down in front. I would have needed a forty inch bust to have filled it.

I collected my cloak from the hooks outside Matron's Office and put it on. I didn't have far to walk, but I still wore my cloak. It helped to cover all the lumps and bumps in my uniform. All too soon I reached the ward door.

Opening that ward door and walking through it was one of the most difficult things that I have done in my life. It took ten steps to get from the door to Sister's Office, and I aged a year with every step. I was sure that all eyes would be watching me as I walked down the ward. I needn't have bothered. The patients were all busy eating their breakfasts.

I was saved the trauma of knocking on the office door as it opened just before I reached it, and Staff Nurse came out to meet me.

"Hello. You found your way here then. Come with me and I'll show you where we hang our cloaks."

When I had hung up my cloak, Staff looked at my apron.

"I really don't know why the linen room can't manage to fit uniforms properly. Come back to the office and I'll find you some pins."

With the aid of two more pins, the straps on my apron were shortened and I was made presentable. I did not feel very comfortable. There were too many pins under my belt for that, but at least I didn't look such a freak as I did before.

I followed Staff back into the ward. Two nurses were clearing away the breakfast things, and another was taking round urine bottles.

"Sister will be busy for a while yet," said Staff, "While we are waiting for her, we can start to make the beds."

In the next half an hour we made twenty beds. Here, there was none of the finesse of P.T.S.. The bedclothes were thrown over a chair, the bottom sheet put in the dirty linen billy, and replaced with the one that had been on the top. By the time the last bed was made, I was shattered. How was I going to get through the next nine hours?

"Sister will be back now." announced Staff. "Take the linen trolley out to the flat and leave it there, then come back to the office. I'll introduce you to Sister."

As I pushed the linen trolley out to the "flat," (the area outside the ward doors that contained all the cupboards) I had a chance to admire the newly made beds. We had covered up the red "night" blankets with clean starched white counterpanes. The beds looked very smart, and I hoped that the patients would sit in their chairs all day and not mess up the beds.

Sister Ward One was very small, and very Irish. Her hair, although now grey, had obviously once been red. I was soon to learn that she had the temper usually associated with red hair!

As soon as I walked into her office, Sister started talking.

"Nurse, I have very few rules on this ward. I expect my patients to be comfortable and happy, and the ward to be clean and tidy. If not, then God help you. Staff, call the nurses in for the report. You, child, can stand there and wait. On the board behind you is the off-duty list. For your time on this ward you will be Nurse Four. I don't have time to keep fiddling about with the off-duty rota. There it is, and there it stays. We are now in week three."

She hardly paused for breath. I turned round to see the list. It was marked, Sister, Staff, Nurse One, Two, Three, and Four. The weeks were headed One, Two, Three, and Four. It was a fantastic system, allowing one to plan a social life for weeks ahead. Many years later, I adopted the same system, although I did not call my nurses by numbers!

The other nurses followed Staff back into the office. There were three more students, and with them came the Ward Maid. It surprised me to see the maid come in for the report, but as I sat and listened, I realised why she was there.

Sister went through the Kardex, a flip-up file with a card for each patient. As she went, she read out what the night staff had written, then waited for comments from her nurses. The maid was able to contribute as much as any of the others.

One of the most valuable lessons I learnt on my first day, was that patients talk to the maids far more than they do to the nurses. Having listened to the reports, Sister issued orders for the patients' care during the day.

There were twenty men on the ward, and it took over half an hour to go through the report. As she closed the Kardex, Sister looked at me.

"You will work with Nurse Three for the next two days. In that time I expect you to learn where everything is kept, the ward routine, and the names of the patients. You may all go."

Out we went. Nurses wearing aprons, (now, of course, they wear overalls, and look like loo cleaners at London Underground stations) don't appear to walk, they glide. This is because the starched apron acts as a splint, and the only part of the leg that can move is the bit between the hem and the floor. It took me months to perfect the glide. For the moment, I just shuffled off after my mentor, down the ward to the sluice.

One, I was to learn that day, went *down* to the sluice, but *up* to the kitchen. Since the floor did not appear to slope, I would have thought that one could just as easily have gone *along* the ward to either. Scutari must have been built on a hill, and Flo located the kitchens at the top and the sluice at the bottom!

The sluice was a small room with two large white sinks, an array of shining brass taps, and an enormous metal barrel-shaped "thing" on the wall.

"All you need to know," said Nurse Three, "Is how the washers work, how to clean bottles and bedpans, polish the brass and copper, and damp dust. Oh, and you need to know about the washer, it's temperamental. If the door isn't closed properly you get drenched. Have you ever seen one like it before?"

I had been on the ward for an hour, and not opened my mouth. Now I was being asked a direct question. All I could do was to shake my head. I most certainly had not seen anything like it before. The one that we had in P.T.S. was new and shiny. All one had to do was put the pan in the rack, close the door and push a button.

"Right, what you do is this." continued Three. "You pull down the door towards you, slide the pan onto the rack, slam the door shut, then turn the taps on and count to ten. The pan should be clean by then. If the door is not properly shut, the water jet forces it open and you get the water all down your front. You try it."

The barrel thing had a metal plate in the end that folded out. I pulled the handle, and it obligingly opened. The inside of the door had two pieces of bent metal welded to it, roughly in the shape of a bedpan. I pushed a pan on to these, lifted the door and slammed it shut. The door was secured by levers, I pushed those down and turned the taps. All was well. I remained dry.

Next came the bottle washer. Men, bless their hearts, (and their anatomy) can pass urine into a bottle. One of the sinks had a metal prong sticking up from its base, and a waste hole about six inches across. One by one, the bottles were upended over the prong, and the taps turned on. It looked very simple. However, adjusting the force and the temperature of the water took considerable skill. Too hard, and the bottle was lifted into the air, too soft, and the thing did not get cleaned. Too hot, and the bottle cracked, too cold, and the men complained!

Nurse Three explained,

"If a patient asks you for a bottle, take one off the drying rack, cover it with one of those square sheets and take it to him. Don't empty it. Just leave it on the side there with his name by it, in case it has to be measured.

"Right, now you know where to find the tools of our trade. We'd better get on with the work. It doesn't pay to upset Sister on a Monday."

I was beginning to feel that I was in danger of losing the use of my voice. I had to say something, so I plucked up courage. After all, this girl was only a few months my senior.

"What is your name?" I asked.

"Page," she replied, "but round here I answer to Three. The old bat can't be bothered with names, so she calls us after the place that we occupy on the off-duty list. You had better get used to being called Four. She even has the patients at it."

I had found it hard enough to cope with becoming Nurse. Now I was going to have to suffer the indignity of becoming Four!

Our first job was the damp dusting. All the beds from one side of the ward were pushed into the middle. Then the window ledges, bed ends and bed side lockers were wiped over with a wet cloth. The idea was to remove all the dust that making the beds had generated. To make sure that there were no bugs lurking about, the cloth was soaked in a solution of Carbolic. When the first side was done, the process was repeated on the other side.

As the beds were pushed back into place, the wheels had to be tidied. That meant that they all had to face the same way. The wheels on the left of the door had to point away from it, and this continued round the ward, so that the wheels of the bed to the right of the door pointed towards it.

The wheels only needed a nudge and they shot out of line. As the ward junior, it was my job to keep them straight. I found this a difficult and time consuming process. I could never see, then or now, what the point was of that exercise.

When the beds were all back in position, the patients had their coffee. Page and I were sent to the bathroom to clean mackintoshes.

In this instance, a mackintosh is not a thing that one wears in the rain. It is a long, thick, red rubber sheet that covers the mattress, the idea being to keep the mattress clean. To further protect the bed, and as far as I could see, ensure total discomfort for the patient, a smaller, or draw mac, was put across the bed where the patient sat. When a patient had been discharged, the macs were taken off the bed and cleaned, a process known as carbolising.

A large board was placed over the bath, the mac laid on the board, and then scrubbed with carbolic. When it had been scrubbed clean, it was put onto an old-fashioned drying rail and hauled up to the ceiling to drip dry. One rapidly became adept at dodging the drips.

There must have been a mass exodus from the ward, because there were piles of the things to be scrubbed. But, as Page commented, we were well out of the way. Sister, I was told, had only a vague idea where the bathroom was. It was the one place that she never poked her nose into. I didn't blame her, the smell of carbolic was enough to have knocked her over.

Eventually the dryer was hauled up to the ceiling for the last time. I smelt of carbolic for the rest of the day.

As we walked back up the ward, Sister met us.

"Three, you and Four are to go to first dinner. Get back early please, and start on the beds."

Bliss. Food, and a chance to sit down. She couldn't really expect us to cut short our break, could she?

Page and I hung up our cloaks and aprons, and joined the queue. For the first time in three months I didn't bother to look to see what was on offer. I just collected my tray and sat down. There were five of the others already there, and they looked as numb as I felt.

"I hate to admit this" said Sue, "but my mother was right. Nursing is not a job for a young lady. I've done nothing but clean and scrub."

We had all done much the same. No one had even spoken to a patient, let alone smooth a fevered brow.

I had just taken a sip of my coffee when Page appeared.

"Come on, if we are not back by half-past she'll go barmy."

As I staggered to my feet, I thought of the next five hours. Would I survive, or would I be the first nurse to collapse halfway through her first day. I was past caring.

Staff was on her own in the ward when we reported back. Sister had disappeared.

"Three, you do the bottle round. Four and I will tidy the beds and do the back round. There are only ten that need doing."

Oh no, not more beds. I didn't think that my muscles would stand it.

"Come along, I'll introduce you to the patients as we go round. I'll take the trolley and you bring the billy."

A billy is a dirty linen trolley, similar to those used in supermarkets. Great when they are new, but impossible to steer when they are worn. It and I went down the ward in slightly different directions. Seeing my somewhat erratic progress, Staff smiled, and said,

"The best way with that is to put your foot on the centre bar, and scoot. Only be careful, if you scoot too hard the whole lot goes over."

She was right, it was much easier. She was also right about it falling over. However, it only did that when it was full of soiled sheets and the ward full of visitors.

"After dinner, we go round and tidy up the beds. All patients that are in bed have their pressure areas rubbed and their draw sheets changed. I expect that you were taught to use cream on pressure areas. However, Sister prefers hers done with soap, water and surgical spirit."

Did she really mean that, or did she mean that Sister wanted her method used on the patients! If Sister had ever had *her* backside rubbed with spirit, she would have jolly soon agreed that Zinc and Castor oil cream was the better treatment.

As I approached my first real patient, I tried hard to look as if I had been nursing for weeks, instead of hours.

"Hello, Mr. Porter," said Staff, "how are we this afternoon? Just roll over towards nurse, and we'll give your bottom a rub. This is our new Nurse Four. We have to be nice to her today, as it's her first day on the wards."

So much for trying to look experienced. Mr. Porter looked far too agile to need his pressure areas rubbed. However, his rear end was subjected to a brisk rub, then his draw sheet was changed. One done, nine to go. The next patient was fast asleep.

"Come on Mr. James, we want to do your bed."

Mr. James was not impressed. He opened one eye, glared at Staff, and simply said,

"Sod off."

Despite his reluctance, Staff pulled back his bedclothes and deftly rolled him over towards me. Before I could hold him, he rolled back to his original position. The next time he came towards me, I took a firm hold and hung on. He was not very happy.

"Bloody nurses, shame you haven't got anything better to do. Mind what you are doing with your hands woman, they're like bloody sandpaper."

Staff tut-tutted at him.

"Mr. James, Nurse Four is new today. We must try not to upset her. She isn't used to such bad language."

Without stopping to think, I said,

"It's okay, Staff. I grew up on a farm. I know all the words."

Mr. James looked up at me and winked. My first real contact with a patient. Mr. James was made comfortable, and we continued down the line of bed bound patients. They were all subjected to the same treatment, like it or not, need it or not, and as far as I could tell, they did neither.

"You can clear these things away, Nurse, and then go and help Three."

Off I shuffled with the linen trolley. Pushing the trolley through the ward made me feel very important. I didn't feel quite so grand when it came to pushing the billy. It showed a distinct desire to fall over.

I found Page in the sluice. We cleaned the bottles, scoured the sinks, mopped the floor, then polished the brass taps on the sinks. When the sluice was spotless, Page announced that it was time to butter the bread ready for the patients' teas.

As we walked up to the kitchen Page said,

"Whatever you do, keep on the right side of Milly. She can make life hell if she doesn't like you."

Milly, the maid, was even more Irish than Sister, and I found it hard to understand her speech. As we went into the kitchen, Milly held out a tray for me to take.

"Herself is waiting for her tea."

Dare I ask who "herself" was. I was saved by Page taking the tray from me.

As Page left the kitchen with the tray, Milly asked if I took sugar in my tea. I must have looked surprised, because she said,

"It's alright. Herself won't budge till she's had her tea."

I stood and drank my tea, then settled down to butter mountains of bread. I had just finished when Milly came into the kitchen with Sister's tray.

"Herself wants you."

Oh no! My first day not yet over and Sister wanted me. What could I possibly have done wrong?

When I reached the office, Sister beckoned me in.

"Have you enjoyed your first day, Nurse?"

"Yes, Sister." Another lie on my conscience.

"Good. Now take yourself along to the linen room, and tell them that I said they are to make your aprons and belts fit properly. I will not have my nurses held together with pins. When they have done that, you can go off-duty. The first day on a ward is always too long."

I agreed, oh how I agreed.

CHAPTER FOUR

I woke up the next morning to the smell of carbolic. Despite a long soak in a very scented bath, I still stank of the stuff. I felt fine until I tried to get out of bed. My shoulders ached, my legs ached, my feet ached, and I had muscles that I didn't know existed. It was an anatomy lesson that I could have well done without.

Going on duty held none of the fears of the day before. All the students left the dining room together, and the Ward One group entered the ward to report for duty as a body. The rest of the day was a repeat of the previous one. I made beds and cleaned, then made more beds, and did some more cleaning. I could have got a job as a chamber maid, and made more money. The hours would have been better too.

Wednesday and Thursday passed in much the same way as the first two, the only difference being that I had split duties on both days. That meant going on duty at 7:30 A.M., coming off at 1:00 P.M., then going back from 5:00 P.M. until the night staff came on at 8:30 P.M. The work was no different, and as Page had the same off-duty, all the cleaning and menial jobs were left for us. Having done their stint of the grotty jobs in their first year of training, the other two students were not going to do any of our work, nor leave any of the good jobs for us.

I had spent all week longing for Friday, a whole day to do as I liked. When it arrived I was too tired to do anything but sleep, and Saturday morning came round very quickly.

I was looking forward to working over the weekend. I no longer ached all over. I knew the names of most of the patients, and best of all, Sister was off-duty for both days.

The ward felt different as soon as we went on duty, somehow brighter. There was more activity, more conversation between patients, and one or two of them even said good morning.

After we had made the beds, Staff called us into the office for the report. "Sit down, girls."

Sit down. I was so surprised I nearly fell down. The others were obviously used to the change of management and had sat. I had never sat down in a starched apron before. It is not something that one does lightly. The sides have to be brought to the middle and overlapped, then the hem folded up towards the belt, making a thick pad on one's lap. It felt strange, and very clumsy.

Staff went through the patients one by one as Sister had done, but instead of issuing orders for the day's work, she explained what was wrong with them, and how they were being treated.

Then came the second shock of the day. Staff said,

"Four, you and I are both off this afternoon, and there is only us on this evening. I think it would be a good idea if we worked together this morning, don't you? That way we'll both know what to expect this evening."

Did that mean that I was going to have her help me do the cleaning? The mind boggled.

It did not. It meant that someone else had to do my chores, while I did all the running about that Staff usually did for Sister.

I spent a wonderful morning. I took pills to patients, ran errands all over the hospital, and was very proud of the fact that I did them without getting lost. I even helped Staff to give the patients their lunches, supervised, of course, by Milly.

My afternoon off was spent going over my notes on taking temperatures. With luck I might be trusted with a thermometer.

The afternoon seemed to drag. I was really looking forward to working as a nurse for the evening, and I was back on the ward well before five o'clock.

As soon as Staff had received a report from the afternoon girls, she let them go off duty. It was only just gone five o'clock! Roll on the day she became a Sister.

"There isn't anything to do until we give out the suppers," said Staff, "so we'll sit and talk about the patients. You can tell me what you know about each of them."

How was I going to make that last for an hour? What I knew about the whole lot put together could be told in five minutes. While I was getting my brain into gear, the phone rang. It was Casualty, and they were sending us a patient. Staff did not look very pleased.

"That is all we need. A perforated D.U. We'll put him in the bed by the office door, he is going to Theatre as soon as we have him ready."

We? I didn't know where to start.

The bed covers were ripped off the bed and flung onto the nearest chair, and a theatre canvas put on the bed. This was a long stiff piece of canvas with places at the side to take wooden poles, thus turning the canvas into a stretcher. The canvas was covered with a sheet, in an attempt to make it comfortable. We had just finished when the porters wheeled in the patient. He looked awful. With a bit of help from us, he struggled off the trolley and onto the bed.

"Run and tell Milly I need her."

Great, the first bit of trouble and I'm less use than the maid. Still, it didn't seem the time to argue. I was saved the bother. Milly just appeared.

Staff smiled at the new Patient.

"Hello dear, felling rough, are we? Don't worry, we'll soon have you sorted out. Milly will stay with you while Nurse and I go and get you something for the pain. Then we'll take you over to the Theatre. Only a few minutes, and when you come back you'll be as right as rain."

She was so convincing, even I believed her. As I followed her into the office, she said,

"Get Mr. Porter for me please."

Not content with using the maid as a nurse, she was going to get the patients at it now.

"Oh Jim, be a darling and fetch Milly a bucket. You'll find one under the sink in the sluice."

Sister would have a fit if she'd heard that.

"Right, Nurse, bring me that tray by the window, and then watch everything I do. When I've done it, you are going to have to sign as witness, and if it's wrong, we both go to court for manslaughter."

I watched her like a hawk. First she unlocked the drug cupboard. Then the cupboard inside that was unlocked, and a small box removed. When it came to entering the man's name in the D.D.A. ledger, we had to read it from the green card that had come with him. Neither of us knew his name! The card also stated what drugs the patient was to have, and I was told to read out what it said.

"I'm sorry Staff, I can't read what it says." It looked like an epileptic spider had fallen out of an inkwell onto the paper in the middle of a fit.

"Don't worry, we'll do it the other way round. I'll be the witness." Fine by me. I could read the writing on the box. It was printed. We checked that the dosage of the box of Omnopon and Scopolamine was the same as that written on the green treatment sheet, then removed one tube from the box. We then counted what was left and entered the number in the ledger.

"Now, we fit the cartridge into the holder, and fit a needle on the end, like this. Now we'll go and give it to him. You'll have to do it and I'm the witness." Now she tells me.

"Staff, I've never given an injection before." The mere thought had haunted me ever since we had been made to practise on those oranges.

"Don't tell the patient *that* for goodness sake, he's got enough to worry about."

There I was, about to stick a needle into a patient for the first time, and all she could think about was the patient. What about me? The way me knees felt, they could well give way, and then where would she be?

"Come on child, you've done it in practice. Just get on with it."

Anger took over, child indeed. I stomped up to the patient, injection tray in one hand, treatment card in the other. Staff was right behind me.

"Mr. Evans." I said, "Could you tell me your name please?"

It sounded stupid to me. Why ask the man to tell me his name when I already knew it. Still, the thought of a manslaughter charge loomed large. I was going to do this by the book of rules.

"My name is David Evans, Nurse."

"Fine, Mr. Evans, I am going to give you an injection in the top of your leg. First I'm going to wipe your leg with spirit, then give you the injection. It won't take long."

Ever the optimist.

I dipped a piece of cotton wool in the pot of spirit, and went to wipe his leg. I'd seen more meat on the bones my father gave to his dogs. I selected a spot that looked as if the bone was at least covered with a thin layer of flesh and went to work. As soon as the spirit touched him, he rolled over towards Milly, and was sick. Her reactions were fantastic. The stream of vomit was caught in the bucket, and not a drop went on the floor.

Staff looked towards me and said,

"While he's over on his side, stick it in his buttock. Stay where you are, Mr. Evans."

This time I moved quicker. He wasn't going to get away from me again. It was surprisingly easy. Much easier than injecting an orange. Much to my surprise, he didn't even flinch. The poor soul was too busy trying to fill Milly's bucket.

We returned to the office and I signed the D.D.A. book for the very first time. I felt very important. Then I disposed of the drug cartridge into the Dispensary basket and put the needle in the "sharp" box. The cartridge holder was put back on the tray ready for the next time it was needed.

The use of those wonderful cartridges has long since ceased. I often wonder why. They were easy and quick to use, and did away with any danger of cross infection from a dirty syringe. Perhaps they were too expensive. At least they would have saved the N.H.S. the vast expense of issuing drug addicts with disposable syringes.

Staff wrote out a label with the patient's name, ward and the reason he was going to Theatre, then fastened it to his right wrist.

"Nurse, we have to get his consent to the operation. Really we should have done that before we gave him any sedation, but there wasn't time."

Staff sat down on the edge of the bed, well out range of the bucket.

"Mr. Evans," said Staff, "we need your consent to the operation. You have to have it done or you will die. You have a duodenal ulcer, and it has burst. If is isn't closed up soon, you will bleed to death."

Dear God, woman, I thought. You told me not to worry the man, but you seem to be doing your best to send him into a state of shock.

Mr. Evans signed the form. The way it was put, he didn't have much choice.

The consent form was clipped to the treatment sheet, and he was ready to go. Staff phoned Theatre to see if they were ready, and asked for the porters to wheel him over. When they arrived, Staff said,

"You will have to take him over. All you do is enter his name in the book, and the time he was delivered. Then come straight back. The porters will look after you. Just tell the Theatre Staff that he has not been shaved."

Why bother about shaving the man, I thought, he wasn't going out on the town? By the look of him, he'd be lucky if he ever went out again.

The porters arrived. They looked to me rather like milkmen, dressed in their white overalls. They even wore white wellington boots. Mr. Evans was rolled to one side, and a pole pushed up the side of the canvas. Then he was rolled over, and the other pole inserted. The head of the bed was lifted off, the trolley moved beside the bed, and with the minimum of fuss, there he was on his way to the Theatre. I found myself running along beside the trolley, clutching what passed for his notes, and a receiver in case he vomited. It would not have done to have taken the bucket, however useful it might have been.

The porters had obviously been in the situation before, because one of them said,

"If he vomits, don't try to catch it. That thing won't be any good."

My sentiments exactly.

My injection must have done some good, because Mr. Evans was asleep. Either that or comatose, and I preferred to ignore that possibility. As we entered Theatre, a bell jangled. It was like going into a shop.

A green coated figure appeared, and I passed on the information that Mr. Evans had not been shaved. The figure said "Thank you, Nurse," and wheeled my patient away. I had expected that I would at least have been asked his name. It was like a science fiction horror movie. No wonder we had to label everyone! One of the porters showed me where to write the patient's details. That done, I fled back to the ward.

Staff had two of the patients helping Milly to give out the suppers, and another one helping her to give out the pills. I must have shown my surprise, as she smiled at me and said,

"It's called occupational therapy. As long as Sister doesn't find out, we're alright."

I didn't much like the sound of the "We."

In my innocence, I forgot all about Mr. Evans, and continued with the evening work, making sure all was clean and tidy, and the bed wheels straight. My calm was shattered abruptly. The phone rang, and Staff called out "Four, Mr. Evans is ready for collection. You'll have to go, as I can't leave the ward. The porters will look after you. All you need to do is to carry this over with you, and walk back beside the patient."

"This" was a receiver containing a collection of medieval looking instruments. The porters would probably have managed just as well without me, but appearances had to be maintained, so off I trotted to Theatre. Mr. Evans was waiting for me. Festooned with tubes, he looked like a Christmas tree. The green clothed figure nodded, handed me a sheaf of notes and walked away.

Great! Me and the porters alone with an unconscious man. I did as ordered, and walked along beside the trolley. It seemed to take hours to get him back to the ward, but luck was on my side, or his, because we arrived without incident. While I was putting the notes away, he was put to bed.

Staff drew the screens, and pushed a chair up to the head of the bed. Mr. Evans was laying on his side. He had blood going into one arm, and fluid into the other. There was a tube coming out of his nose.

"Now, Nurse, I want you to sit here and watch him. If he moves, call and I will be straight here, so don't worry. Keep an eye on the rate of the drips. They have to run through at thirty-three drips per minute."

Worry, not me. Panic perhaps, but I had passed the point of worrying. Until today I had spent all my time as the ward drudge. Now I was expected to nurse. I sat with my eyes glued to the infusions. I counted each one alternately. Neither were going at thirty-three drips, but since I had no idea what to do, I did nothing.

When Staff reappeared, I passed on the information that both the drips were wrong. She also did nothing. The night staff had appeared and we could go. The patient was no longer our responsibility.

I spent a very restless night, thinking of all the things that might have happened. I was amazed to see that Mr. Evans was still alive the next morning.

Once again, Staff had the patients doing most of my work. If they could do it at the weekend, why couldn't they do it all week? I would have been the last to complain. One of them even spent the day keeping the bed wheels straight.

I reported on duty, then wished I hadn't. I was detailed to look after Mr. Evans. The tube coming out of his nose had to have a syringe applied to it every quarter of an hour, and whatever was in it pulled out. It was apparently called a Ryle's tube, and went into his stomach. Anything coming out had to be measured. Yuk!

Both drips had to be watched, and every half hour his blood pressure had to be taken. Every hour he was to have his pressure areas rubbed. I was to have help doing that. Any urine was to be measured. Staff made it seem like an honour, so who was I to refuse?

"Mr. Evans is still very ill, and it will be better for him to have someone he knows looking after him. Someone strange might bother him."

Not as much as if he knew how green I was, I thought.

"I'll come with you and show you what to do, then you can manage on your own. Call if you want help." It all looked so easy when done by an expert. The drips fell at the required rate, and fluid came out of his stomach as if to order, and he had some blood pressure.

Taking the blood pressure of a healthy student nurse in a schoolroom was no preparation for trying to find the weak beat of a very ill patient. Getting the cuff round his arm was a work of art. I was surprised that so skinny an arm would weigh so much. Any movement caused the drip rate to alter. Thank goodness he was asleep and couldn't see my efforts.

Having got the cuff on, I did the unforgivable, and left it there. After all, Sister P.T.S. had the weekends off, so I was safe! Just in case she wasn't off duty, I had my defence ready. I was afraid of moving the drip needle. Terrified would have been more to the point. I had visions of the wrath of the doctors descending on my head if they were called out to put back a drip because I had pulled it out.

All went well for a while, and then I became too clever. Nothing had come out of the Ryle's tube, but I still kept on trying. I took out the plug at the end, connected the syringe and pulled. The plunger of the syringe shot back, straight out of the barrel and my hand, and on to the floor. Being glass, it did not bounce. I was left holding a syringe barrel from which dribbled a revolting green smelly liquid. Mr. Evans chose that moment to open his eyes, and the Doctor to come and see his patient.

My first contact with one of God's chosen race, and there I was looking a complete idiot.

"Everything alright, Nurse?"

"Yes, Doctor." Was he being kind, or was he just plain stupid. I was right on both counts. He *was* a very kind man, but he was also incredibly stupid. The records of my work were studied at great length. He then announced that ne needed to examine Mr. Evans, and would I sit him up. Who did he think I was, Tarzan?

"I'm sorry Doctor," I said, "I'll have to ask for help. I can't manage to lift him on my own."

I went to find Staff and told her that I needed help to sit Mr. Evans up, so that he could be examined. She was not amused, and said to the Houseman.

"Doctor, if you really need to examine this man, you will have to do it with him where he is. I am not moving him, and nor are any of my staff."

Well said! Why couldn't I have said that? I waited for the explosion, but none came. Out came the stethoscope, and a big show was made of listening to the patient's chest.

"Yes, fine. The blood can come down when you are ready, Nurse." and off he went.

When I passed on this information to Staff, she replied,

"There are three more pints of blood in the 'fridge ready for that man. We'll take the drip down when he has had them all, and not before."

Was that what the Doctor meant when he said, 'when we were ready?' And I had thought that the doctors were in charge. Yet another myth shattered.

I returned to my long suffering patient, and cleaned up the mess I'd made. I had been having trouble getting all the tasks done in time while he was asleep, but with him awake, they took twice as long. He watched every move I made. I hoped that he had never been in a hospital before, or he would have known how new I was!

When Staff next came round to check, she decided that Mr. Evans could have something to ease his pain. To my relief she asked one of the other nurses to act as witness for her. I was shattered. I would not have believed that looking after one man could be such hard work.

I went off-duty somewhat reluctantly, and rather later than I should have done. I was not convinced that anyone else could look after *my* patient properly. I have never become used to handing over the care of an ill patient to someone else. I would rather stay with them until I feel it is safe to leave, even if it takes days.

Such things don't happen now. The patient goes to the Intensive Care Unit, and is wired up to a machine that does all the observations. One nurse can sit and watch a bank of machines and thus look after several patients at once. The patient merely sits. I wonder whether Flo would have considered ICU's as progress?

Somehow I think not.

CHAPTER FIVE

Monday morning saw the return of Sister to the ward, and me to the sluice. Page had been promoted to higher things, like temperatures and urine testing. I was left in sole charge of the sluice and the bottle rounds.

I learnt a great deal about cleaning in those weeks. I discovered that hydrogen peroxide is marvellous for cleaning dirty sinks, and that liquid paraffin is great for putting a shine on metal.

My hands were in and out of water all day, and it wasn't long before they were red and sore. Milly came to the rescue. I was busy scrubbing the sluice sinks one day, and Milly was propping up the doorway, chatting, when she noticed my hands.

"Your hands are bad, Nurse. You should show them to Herself."

I did not for one moment, imagine that Sister would be in the least interested in my hands, and said so.

Milly thought otherwise, "You malign the woman. She's very caring really. I'll go and tell her that something must be done."

I couldn't think what, unless I would be allowed to use rubber gloves. Since it had been stressed in P.T.S. that one could not work properly in gloves, I thought that unlikely.

Within minutes Milly was back, bringing Sister with her. I exhibited my hands, and Sister agreed that they were in a bad state. I returned to my cleaning while they discussed various methods of hand care. At last a decision was reached and I was ordered to report to the kitchen before going off duty. Milly would look after my hands.

I was given a bag of sugar, a bottle of cooking oil, several pairs of thin plastic disposable gloves, and some thick elastic bands. I was to cover my hands in a paste of sugar and oil, put the gloves on and anchor them at the wrists, then sleep in them. It was difficult, and it was messy, but within a week of Milly's treatment, my hands, if not soft, were at least softer, and much less red.

In a strange way I was enjoying my work. I took a pride in my sluice, and when Sister had her weekends off, Staff let me do some real nursing.

Sister Ward One was one of the few Sisters that I have worked for that ever bothered to give praise or say thank you. I had spent all one Sunday afternoon polishing an old copper tea urn that stood in the ward. It was used to store cotton wool balls left over from dressing trays. By the time I had finished, it shone, and I was very proud of it.

As I went off duty that evening, I noticed a finger mark on it. I went back to the sluice, found a rag and polished off the mark. On my way back past the office, Sister called out, "Thank you, Nurse."

From then on, the urn became my responsibility. Sister warned every one, doctors included, that if they left dirty finger marks on the urn, they would have me to answer to.

I had been on the ward for six weeks, when Page was moved, and her place as Three was taken by a girl called Wright. Sister took an instant dislike to her, and after she had given us the daily report, Sister said,

"Four, you are to spend two days showing Three your jobs. Then she can take them over. You can come out into the ward and take over the jobs that the last Three was doing."

I must have looked worried, because she added, "Don't worry, you can still polish the urn!"

I *was* worried, I had heard all about Wright from Page. Even though they were in the same set she hadn't thought much of her. Wright had the reputation for being lazy, and even worse, being out to find a husband. Rumour said that she had started her training with the thought that she would persuade a doctor to fall for her. As soon as she had realised that the doctors were unlikely to even notice her, she changed tactics and went to work on the male patients.

Sister must have heard of her reputation, because in the month the Wright spent on the ward, Sister kept her as far away from the men as was possible.

Today, I look back on my first six weeks with nostalgia. It was the only time during my career that I was free from pressure.

Almost overnight, I changed from the ward skivvy to a junior nurse. Once Sister was satisfied that Wright knew what was expected of her, she called me into her office and outlined my new responsibilities.

I was to admit the routine patients, take the temperatures, help with serving meals, do the "backs," help with treatments and dressings, write out the dispensary list and then check and put away the medicines. Most important of all, I was to look after the fish!

The ward had a large tank of tropical fish, and they were Sister's pride and joy. I was to be responsible for checking the water temperature daily, and preparing their food.

Feeding the fish was a daily ritual. Their food was removed from the lotion cupboard, put on a tray, and the tray left on Sister's desk. At five o'clock, whatever else might be happening, Sister collected the tray and fed the fish. The whole process fascinated me. As Sister approached the tank, the fish all swam to the front, almost as if they recognised her.

Luckily, there were only fifteen patients for the first few days, so I had time to settle down gradually to my new routine. By the time the ward became busy, I knew what was expected of me.

The senior nurses did most of the actual nursing. I did the foolproof bits, but since most of the others in my set were still confined to their sluices, I was very happy.

As I became familiar with my tasks, they began to take less time, and Sister allowed me to help more and more with the real nursing. She was a very good teacher, and had a very definite pattern of instruction. First, I had to watch her, then she watched me. The third time, I was on my own, but she would position herself outside the screens, so that if I needed help, she was close by. From then on, I was expected to manage alone.

Looking through my Schedule, I am staggered by the amount of basic nursing procedures that have her signature beside them.

I no longer worried about giving injections. Most of the patients had a least one injection a day, and it soon became as routine as giving an enema. Sister had started nursing before the discovery of antibiotics, and to her, they were still a wonder drug. She insisted that any patient undergoing surgery have a post-operative course of penicillin.

Penicillin was dispensed in multi-dose bottles. One stuck the needle of the syringe into the bottle through the rubber cap and drew into the syringe the amount required plus one cubic centimetre. Then one removed the needle from the bottle, held the syringe up level with one's eyes, so that the marks could be seen, and expelled any air and the extra liquid.

Having given the injection, the syringe was taken apart. The two pieces were rinsed under the tap and then dropped into a bowl of Lysol. I know now that it is easy to become sensitised to penicillin through skin contact and inhalation. I wish I had known then. I would have taken a great deal more care.

Sister was also a great believer in "bowels." If the patient's bowels were moving, then he was, in her opinion, on the road to recovery. All routine admissions were given a bath, put to bed, then given an enema. "Just to make sure." Sure of what, was not made clear. Two pints of hot soapy water were run through a tube into the patient's rectum. The man was left on his bed for ten minutes, then allowed to walk down the ward to the loo.

As soon as patients had recovered sufficiently from their operations to eat, they were given nightly doses of liquid paraffin.

Sister was proud of the fact that none of her patients ever complained of constipation!

One weekend, a road accident victim was admitted. He had severe head injuries, and Sister was sitting with him in the side ward. "One" and I were left to get on with the ward work, with Milly as an extra pair of hands. Milly expressed the opinion that the new admission was "poorly."

Nurses, I have found, have a dislike of using the terms "Dangerously" or "Critically" ill. They leave that to the relatives. Thus a patient described as poorly is often very ill indeed. This man, in Milly's opinion, was for "The Lift."

I have never discovered why dying was referred to as "Taking the Lift."

During my first two months on the ward, there had been two deaths, both occurring when I was off duty. So far, I had been spared the experience of being present at a death. It was beginning to worry me. I knew that I would have to face it one day, but I was afraid. I confessed to Milly that I was worried about seeing death, or even a body. She told me not to worry.

"Sister," she said, "would take care of the matter."

Milly must have told Sister, because when the man died, Sister decided that I should help her perform the last offices. I was not told the man was dead. Sister just asked me to help her to move her patient.

It wasn't until we had laid him flat, that I realised that he was not breathing. He just looked as if he was in a very deep sleep. In a whisper, Sister explained what we were doing, and why. I don't know what I had expected, or why I had been afraid, but her attitude helped me to overcome any phobias I might have had.

At the end of the hour, we performed the last offices. We had special sheet marked with a purple cross that we used for bodies. The sheet was placed underneath the body, and then the sides were folded over the top, making it easy to uncover the face and hands.

Sister joined the man's hands over his heart, and placed in them a white flower. Then she somehow managed to form the top end of the sheet into a hood that folded down. By the time she had finished, he looked like a sleeping monk. I have had numerous attempts at making such a hood. I have not yet discovered how she did it. I bitterly regret that I did not take more notice at the time.

To me, Sister was perfect. I had heard all about her legendary temper, but had somehow managed to avoid being on the receiving end. She had her off days, like all of us, but most of the time she was fine. She worked as hard as the rest of us, and often harder. All she asked was that the patients were happy and well cared for.

Her methods, even compared to the rest of the hospital, were old fashioned, but she set a very high standard of nursing.

I thought that I might manage to leave the ward without upsetting her. I had one week left on the ward. Then I was going to Ward Eight, the Radiotherapy Ward, on night duty.

It was during that last week on the ward that I found myself on the receiving end of her temper. It was an experience that haunts me still.

We had admitted a young man that had been hit by a car. The mascot on the front of the car had caught the side of his face, just above his eye. It hadn't looked too bad when we settled him into bed, but as the day wore on, a large bruise developed and his eyelid became swollen.

Sister and I were on alone in the evening, and as soon as she saw his eye, she went into a paddy. The pressure of the blood inside the bruise had forced the eye right down into the socket, and the side of his face was still swelling.

Staff Nurse was just walking past the patient's bed on her way off duty, and, being nearest, received the full impact of the blast from Sister. I thought that I had best find something to do in the sluice. I didn't fancy getting my head blown off!

I was half way down the ward when I heard her bellow, "Four!"

I hurried back to the office, and was told, "Go and find one of the doctors. Switchboard tells me that none of them are answering their bleeps. I want one of them back here within ten minutes. I don't care which one. If you can't find one of ours, then get hold of one of the others. As long as he is a doctor, he'll do. If you have any trouble, then tell him, whoever he is, that I said that if Mr. Andrews loses his eye, I will hold him personally responsible."

I didn't even know where to start. If they were not answering their bleeps, they were either off duty or in theatre. I decided that the best people to ask would be the porters. They always knew exactly what was going on, and where.

I was right. They had seen Dr. Patel, one of the surgical registrars, walking out towards the car park. I hurried out, hoping to catch him before he reached his car. What they hadn't told me was that he had a girlfriend with him.

At first, he refused to even consider going back to the ward. He was, after all, off duty. When I told him that Sister was in a temper, he agreed to pop in and see what was wrong.

By the time we reached the ward, Sister had the side ward empty, ready to take the patient. Dr. Patel was told to sit in the office and read the patient's notes while Sister and I moved the bed. Moving a bed required a fair amount of skill. The top of the bed had a wheel at each side, built into the legs, but the bottom had only a central wheel that one could raise and lower by means of a handle.

It was important to lower the central wheel just enough to raise the foot of the bed clear of the floor. Too high and the bed rolled from side to side as it moved. In her anger, Sister had wound the handle too far, and the bed was impossible to steer.

Sister marched off towards the door, pulling the head of the bed after her. (Patients always left the ward head first, never feet first.) I was left to try and steer the foot of the bed after her. I was abused roundly for my incompetence. It did not occur to her that it was her fault. Whatever else she might have been, she was *never* wrong.

We managed to get the bed into the side ward, taking with us a fair amount of paint from the ward doors. I was sent to fetch the doctor from the office, and told to stay in the room in case he should need anything.

I had never seen Sister with a doctor before. I was astonished. I could still clearly remember the words of the Nightingale Pledge. It said that we would loyally aid the physician. Sister expressed her opinion of doctors in general, and Dr. Patel, in particular.

She *did* have right on her side, because Mr. Andrews had been admitted by Dr. Patel. Having seen the patient in Casualty, Doctor had arranged his admission, and left the rest to the Houseman.

Having poked and prodded the bruising, Dr. Patel announced that he agreed with Sister. If something was not done soon, the eye would be permanently damaged. We must prepare the patient for theatre. They would drain the eye socket.

Sister nearly exploded. I was glad the patient was unconscious, as the battle was being fought right over his head. Sister, it appeared, had expected the bruising to increase, and had made her own plans. She had arranged for the delivery of some leeches.

I couldn't believe my ears. Leeches were used in the dark ages. However, Dr. Patel knew when he was beaten, so he agreed to let Sister use her leeches. As Sister went off to get them. Dr. Patel turned to me and asked,

"Have you ever seen them before?"

When I said no, he grinned and said,

"I thought she might keep them in the fish tank!"

That had not occurred to me, but having been presented with the thought, it would not go away. From then on I gave the fish a wide berth.

Sister returned with a tray covered in a white cloth. She put the tray down and said,

"There you are, Doctor."

Dr. Patel looked horrified; I felt very sorry for him, as he obviously had no more idea of what to do than I had. Sister was enjoying his discomfort.

"I think Sister, since you are the expert on leeches, yours should be the honour. If they have not made any difference by the time you go off duty, I'm taking the patient to Theatre."

Listening to them arguing across the bed, was like watching a tennis match. My head swivelling from one side of the bed to the other.

Sister turned the patient's head to one side, and slipped a sterile towel under it. She then took a bowl from the tray and put in her hand, pulling out a small black thing that looked like a slug. This she stuck on the bruise. She then repeated the exercise five more time.

I was beginning to feel sick. The patient had a row of these revolting things all round his eye, and as I watched, they began to swell. Dr. Patel walked out.

Sister announced that the patient would do, meaning that he would recover, and out we went. I thought the woman had gone crazy, and I'm sure Dr. Patel did too. He spent the rest of the evening sitting in the office. He said he was catching up on his paper work. He seemed to have forgotten all about his evening off, and his girlfriend.

I was emptying bottles in the sluice, when Sister walked in and announced that she would be leaving the ward for a few minutes, and that I was to keep an eye on Mr. Andrews.

I finished the bottles, then went and looked into the side ward. I could see only five leeches. One had escaped. I crept as near the bed as I dared, and counted again. Still only five. I crept a bit nearer, and carefully searched the bedclothes. There was no sign of the missing leech.

I set off in search of Sister. Dr. Patel was still in the office, and suggested that I look in the kitchen for Sister. He had last seen her disappearing in that direction.

I had opened the kitchen door and managed to get one foot inside the room before Sister saw me.

"Out!" she yelled, and to make sure I got the message, she threw a plate at me. I ducked the plate, but not the scrambled eggs that came with it.

Somewhat shaken, I left the kitchen and went to the sluice to clean up. Doctor followed me and watched as I tried to remove the egg from my cap. Between us we removed the worst of it, and as we worked, he said, "She doesn't like being disturbed when she's in the kitchen. She goes in there for a crafty fag."

He might think it funny, but I didn't and said so. He had the grace to apologise. We were still in the sluice, laughing about the eggs, when Sister came looking for me. I was subjected to a five minute blast, during which I gathered that I was never again to enter the kitchen while Sister was in there.

Having dealt with me, it was Patel's turn. It was interesting to watch a senior member of the medical team being torn to shreds. His sin appeared to be that he had been found with me in the sluice. As soon as Sister stopped for breath, he explained that he was looking for a specimen bottle.

I was dispatched to find one, and when I returned Sister asked me how Mr. Andrews was. In the uproar, I had forgotten about the lost leech.

I told Sister that I had only been able to see five leeches. She looked as if she was about to explode again when Dr. Patel intervened, and offered to come and help in the search, saying,

"I enjoy hunting game."

Sister was not amused.

We searched in all manner of unlikely places, but there was no sign of it. It had disappeared.

Strangely, so had the bruising. There were five very large black blobs on the side of the patient's face, and his eye lid was almost back to its normal size.

Sister was triumphant. Dr. Patel was amused and I was amazed.

I spent my last two days on the ward expecting to find the thing stuck to my back, and I was relieved when I left the ward for the last time. I had liked the ward, but the thought of that leech did nothing for me at all.

As I went off duty, I was thinking about all that had happened during the last three months. Uppermost in my mind was the lost leech. It was then that I remembered the specimen bottle.

I suddenly realised what had happened to the missing leech.

Patel had pinched it.

CHAPTER SIX

The change from day to night duty was reasonably painless. As the whole set was going onto nights, we were allowed to stay in No. 9. Had only a few of us changed duty, we would have had to move home again.

As it was, No. 9 became a Night Home, and the rules were changed accordingly. We were allowed out until 1:00 P.M., then locked in until 7:00 P.M.

I found it impossible to sleep that first afternoon. Despite the thick blinds on the windows, I was aware that it was light outside, and my body was not programmed for sleep during the daylight hours.

Neither was my digestive system used to a breakfast of sausage and chips followed by rice pudding.

The Night Staff had for breakfast, what the Day Staff had for supper. We also had for supper, what they had for breakfast. Thus, having worked hard for twelve hours, we went to bed following a meal of cornflakes and a boiled egg. No wonder we were all so slim.

Although pleased to be away from Ward One, I was a bit apprehensive about night duty. How on earth was I going to stay awake all night? I could count on the fingers of one hand the times that I had been awake after midnight. Now I would have to stay awake until the morning. In my innocence, I couldn't imagine what there would be to do all night!

Before going on duty, we had to go over to the Assistant Matron's office and sign the Night Book. My senior was waiting for me at the door.

"I thought I'd wait for you. It's horrid going into a new ward on your own, isn't it?"

Bless the girl. I thought it was only me that felt nervous about new wards.

Her name was Johns, and although only just starting her third year of training, she could have put many a trained nurse to shame. Typically, although the patients loved her, she was very unpopular with the senior staff. It was probably because she had the idea that nurses were there to serve the patients.

Sister Ward Eight was waiting for us outside her office.

"All's quiet. No changes since this morning. See you tomorrow," and handing Johns the keys, she left.

As hand over reports go, it was certainly brief.

Johns grinned at me.

"I hope she's right. I could do with a quiet night. I'll come with you to do the drinks, then you can help me to give out the drugs. That way you will get to know the patients. They are a super bunch."

I failed to see how people under sentence of death could be anything but depressing. Still, who was I to disagree?

She was right. They were a really happy bunch, and I found it hard to believe that most of them would not be alive in a year's time.

The ward was very new. It had only been open for two years, and was divided up into seven four-bedded and two single rooms. The other major difference to other wards was the Station, a mini office area in the corridor between the rooms. Now, of course, all wards have them. Then, it was a great innovation.

From the Station, one could see all the patients and the ward door. It does not matter so much during the day, but at night, it is useful to be able to see the ward door opening. It is far better to be able to see someone approach, than to merely hear footsteps.

Our first task was to give the patients a bedtime drink. The Day Staff had left a large aluminum jug full of milk on the gas ring, and it looked unappestising to say the least. Having been simmering for an hour or so, it had a skin on the top like the hide of a rhinoceros. Even when this was skimmed off, the milk still looked awful.

The patients must have become used to the taste of burnt milk, because they did not complain, although many of them chose to drink the freshly made tea.

Giving patients tea at night was frowned on, as it was supposed to keep them awake. Coffee was strictly forbidden. Johns worked on the theory that most of them drank tea at home, so why try to alter the habit of a lifetime. They had enough to worry about without having to drink burnt milk.

As we went round the ward, Johns introduced me to the patients. gone was the title of "Four". I was now being called by my name. It was left to the patients to introduce themselves to me. Johns told them it was no good her reeling off their names, but if they told me who they were, I would get to know them by the morning.

She was right. By the time I went off duty, I could remember all the names, and put faces to them.

Having disposed of the drinks, we went round with the drugs trolley and gave out vast amounts of sleeping pills.

Then we made the beds, putting down back rests, and arranging pillows. It seemed to me that each patient had their pillows arranged in a different manner, none of them in the way that we had been taught. No wonder Johns was popular with the patients. She must have been the only nurse that saw them as people rather than bed occupiers.

There was none of the rush that I had become accustomed to on Ward One. We spent at least five, and sometimes ten, minutes with each patient. By the time we had finished, it was half past ten, the time the main ward lights were turned out. The patients were allowed to keep the lights on over their beds until eleven, but most of them settled down straight away.

I followed Johns into the kitchen, and she made us both a cup of coffee.

"Night Sister won't be round until after eleven, so we are safe. I always leave the kettle on, so that we can make a cup of tea for any one that wakes up. A cuppa and a chat soon settles them down again. When we have had our coffee, I'll show you round, and then we'll get on with the work. You have your meal at midnight, and I'll go at one for mine."

How on earth my stomach would cope with dinner at midnight I dreaded to think. It was still complaining about the sausages it had received for breakfast.

I couldn't imagine what work we would find to do, but, in fact, there was plenty. For a start, there were all the syringes to be cleaned and packed, and then the dressing drums to load.

I had never considered how the syringes transferred themselves from the dirty bowl to the box of sterilised tubes, nor what happened to all the unused dressings. Now I was to find out.

The syringes had to be washed, a fairly easy task if they had been taken apart before being put in the Lysol, but a rotten job if not. Once clean, they had to be oiled and then put back together.

Theoretically, an easy and mindless task. Practice was different. If the plunger was dipped too far into the liquid paraffin, it became too slippery, and fell straight out again. If not dipped in far enough, it stuck. I never really got the hang of the job, and was always being moaned at by the Day Staff.

Once reassembled, the syringes were put into aluminum tubes, and a foil cap put over the ends. The tube, foil end first, was pushed into a rubber gadget on the wall, which sealed it. That was great fun.

By the time I had finished the pile of syringes, it was time to go for my break.

The hospital yard was very still. There was none of the usual daytime bustle. Dim lights shone out of the ward windows. All it needed was a covering of snow and it would have looked like a Christmas card. Since it was the middle of summer, I had to use my imagination.

The dining room brought me back to earth. It was very hot in there, and smelt of cabbage! It was traditional for the junior nurses to go to first dinner, so we all sat and compared notes. I had been lucky, both with the ward and the senior nurse. Some of the others were having a grim time. Still, after Ward One I reckoned I deserved an easy time.

Eating a meal at midnight was not easy, but some of the food went down, and the hour went by very quickly. Then it was back to the ward, so that Johns could go for her break.

I was rather concerned about being left on my own, but having the keys made up for it. Not that I could have done anything with them, but at least I was in charge.

I spent the long hour that Johns was away going round the rooms, wishing that one of the patients would wake up so that I would have something to do. A darkened ward full of sleeping patients is a very lonely place, full of unrecognisable sounds.

Johns eventually returned, and then it was back to packing dressing drums. Some had to be packed with folded gauze squares and cotton wool balls, some with folded dressing towels and rubber sheets. I could not imagine how the Day Staff had managed to empty so many drums in one day, especially on a non surgical ward.

The next job on my list was to empty out the sterilisers, clean out the debris and refill them. It never failed to amaze me that so much junk could find its way into the large sterilisers in the course of a day. Cotton wool, gauze swabs, even needles settled on the bottom and had to be hauled out. If only people had checked things before committing them to the deep, that could have been a weekly job instead of a daily one.

Mind you, if tasks had to be done every day, they were done. Weekly tasks had a habit of being forgotten. Once cleaned, the sterilisers had to be filled with water. The small one only took a few minutes, but the large one took nearly half an hour. Many is the time that the clinical rooms had their floors washed in the middle of the night because the taps had been left on.

I soon developed a method, and did the sterilisers before I started on the drums. That way, I was in the room when the flood started. The sadist that set out the work list for night staff specified that the sterilisers were not to be emptied until after midnight. The reason being, that an emergency admission might need a dressing. I couldn't see what difference it made what time the job was done, as patients came in at any time on some wards. If one had waited for a quiet patch, the sterilisers would never have been cleaned.

When I eventually emerged, Johns had made a cup of tea, and we sat and drank it while we went through the patient's notes. It was a grim task.

They were of all ages, the oldest being only fifty-seven. They all had varying forms of cancer.

In the sixties, the only method of treating cancer was surgery, where possible, and large doses of radium. Even after treatment, life expectancy was very short.

To me, the treatment appeared to me to be far worse than the disease. As I got to know the patients, I marvelled at their strength and courage.

I spent three weeks on Ward Eight, and in that time, I never heard a patient complain about the treatment. Sure, they complained; about the food, about the uncomfortable beds, but always about trivial things. They were always ready with a joke, and prepared to help in a crisis.

At half past five, we cleared away the notes, and feeling rather depressed, I made the early morning tea. Once I started waking the patients, my depression lifted. It was hard not to laugh with them.

By the time we had them all awake, washed and tidied, it was time for the day staff to arrive. I was surprised to see Sister come on duty at seven-thirty with the rest of the staff. I was used to Sister Ward One coming on duty at eight. Sister took the report from us and sent us off early. As we left the ward, Johns told me that Sister Ward Eight always came on duty with the rest of her staff. No one knew why, she just did.

I had eaten my supper and had a bath by the time the rest of the set came off duty, and by ten o'clock I was in bed and asleep. Despite having an easy night, I was exhausted, and nothing woke me until the corridor alarm went off at 7:00 P.M. That was loud enough to wake the dead.

I met Johns walking over to the ward, and Sister was again waiting for us as we entered. Tonight there was to be no rapid report, as some of the patients had been for Radium Treatment. Johns had spent some time on the ward on day duty, so she knew what to expect, and what to do. I was still very new, and Sister took time to explain to me what had been done to each of the cases, what could go wrong, and what I was to do if it did. Sister handed me a blue plastic badge-like thing.

"Wear this all the while that you are in duty. It monitors the amount of radiation that you have been exposed to. If the level gets too high, you will have to be taken off the ward. You get a new one every Tuesday."

"Fine," I thought, "what happens if I get my overdose on a Tuesday night. By the time anyone does anything about it, my hair will have fallen out."

"Wear it in your pocket so that the patients don't see it." She continued, "It doesn't do them any good to think that the treatment they are getting might do other people harm."

Not to mention the fact that they might question what it was doing to them, I thought, or maybe I was just being cynical.

Johns and I did the drinks round together. It took much longer than the night before, because we had to hear all about what had been happening during the day. The patient's account was a lot more entertaining than that given by Sister.

The night progressed much the same as the previous one. As Johns went off to her break she said,

"Keep an eye on Mrs. Parkes. She has been up and down to the loo all the time you have been away. Perhaps she would like a cuppa. Oh, and Night Sister has not been over yet."

I made Mrs. Parkes a cup of tea, and she sat at the Station to drink it. She was a woman in her middle forties, and had come in the day before to have radiation treatment to the scar left following the removal of her left breast.

No wonder she was in and out of the loo, she must have been frightened.

When Night Sister came in, we were still sitting there chatting. I was a bit worried. Should I jump up and look busy, or stay put with the patient? I was not quick enough to hide my cup, and it was spotted.

"Is that tea or coffee, Nurse?"

"Tea, Sister."

"Would you get me a cup while I go round the ward. Then we can all have a chat. I haven't seen Mrs. Parkes since she came in yesterday."

When I got to the kitchen, I had to lean on the table, as my legs were still shaking. I had imagined a major rocket, for I had committed three sins in one go. I was sitting down; I was talking to a patient that should have been asleep, and I was drinking tea.

I tried to find a tray, but before I could, Sister came in to the kitchen.

"Do you smoke, Nurse?"

"No, sister."

"Then pop down to the Porters' Lodge and ask one of them to lend you a packet of cigarettes. Poor Mrs. Parkes has been trying to give up smoking. I think that's the reason she can't sleep. Tell them I sent you. I'll stay here until you get back."

Was there no end to the shocks I would receive. Things were very different at night. The porters dug out a packet of cigarettes, sending me back to the ward with a rather rude message for Sister.

I found her sitting in the kitchen with Mrs. Parkes, like a couple of old friends. I handed over the packet, without the message, and Sister smiled.

"Was there a message, Nurse?"

"Yes, Sister, but I don't think they really meant me to give it to you."

"I'll go and see them on my way out in the morning. they must get a bit cross with me, as I'm always borrowing things off them."

She opened the packet, offered one to Mrs. Parkes, and then took one herself.

I left them to it. I was going to have trouble enough ridding the kitchen of smoke, it would be even worse if I smelt of it as well.

My puritanical soul was shaken to the core. Patients were not allowed to smoke, and if nurses smoked, they did not do so when in uniform. Yet there was Sister in the kitchen, having a cup of tea and a smoke with one of the patients.

I told Johns what was happening as soon as she came back.

"Don't worry, I'll tell Sister when she comes on in the morning, but I don't suppose she'll say anything. The hospital rules don't count for much on this ward. It's the only ward in the whole place where the patient comes first. You'll get used to it in the end."

I never did.

After Night Sister left, Mrs. Parkes went back to bed, and slept for the rest of the night.

When Johns told Sister Ward Eight what had happened, she said,

"Next time that happens, there is a packet of cigarettes at the back of the top drawer in my office desk."

So much for rules.

I had the next two nights off, and I was faced with a problem. Did I go to bed for a few hours, get up, and go back in the evening, or stay awake until the afternoon and then sleep right round? I stayed awake until mid day, but was so tired that I went to bed. I stayed there until the next morning, surfacing briefly when the alarm went off.

Despite years of night duty, I have never managed to solve this problem.

Going on duty after my nights off, the ward felt different. The patients all looked the same, but something was not right.

Sister was again on duty, and even she looked strange.

"Good evening girls, Sit Down."

Now what had happened? I felt relieved that whatever it was, I was innocent. I'd been off for the last two nights.

"Simon is back, and not, I'm afraid for long. His mother is with him now, but when she goes home, one of you must sit with him. Under no circumstances must he be left alone. Can you manage Johns, or would you rather be moved?"

Johns looked pale and unhappy,

"I'll try Sister, but I think it would be better is Nurse sat with him. I expect Night Sister will take a turn as well."

"Fine, come on Nurse. I'll take you to meet him. What is your Christian name?"

"Mary," I told her, somewhat puzzled.

So started one of the most traumatic periods of my life.

I followed Sister into one of the single rooms, and met Simon. He was the most beautiful boy I had ever seen, or for that matter, have seen since.

"Simon, this is Mary. She is the new junior on nights, and it will be her job to look after you."

Simon did not look pleased.

"I know you would rather have Hazel to sit with you, but Mary does not have the experience to run the ward. We are not going to reorganise the hospital just to please you, young man, so you will just have to put up with her.

"If you come with me Nurse, I'll show you where all his medicines are kept, and what he has and when."

Sister took me into her office and shut the door.

"Simon has been admitted to us, because he is dying. He does not know, or at least, has not been told. He has sarcoma, (bone cancer) and it is spreading rapidly. At most he has a month. I want him kept free of pain, and happy. If ever you feel that you can no longer cope with his care, please say so.

"Night sister will put out the drugs that he needs. It is up to you to see that he takes them. Try to avoid asking Johns for help, as she and Simon were at school together. She is very upset."

As I came out of the office, Night Sister came in to the ward, and Johns told her that I had agreed to "Special" Simon.

Night Sister asked me,

"Do you know what to expect."

"Not really, Sister. I only know what is wrong with him, and how long he has."

"In that case I'll come round later and explain it all to you. In the meantime, just keep him entertained, and happy."

As we did the evening work, I tried to find out something about Simon from Johns, but all she would tell me was that he had been in and out many times in the last few months, and that he was a lovely boy.

Night Sister had left a glass of medicine for Simon. It smelt strongly of whisky. As I took it to him, his mother was just leaving. I made his bed comfortable for him, and then sat down. It could be a long night, with nothing to do except sit.

We talked for a while, then Simon fell asleep.

I could hear Johns bustling about outside, and I felt guilty that she was busy and I was just sitting. At least she had something to do. I was bored stiff already.

I heard Night Sister come into the ward, and at last, she came in to see me.

"Do you knit, Nurse?"

"Yes Sister."

"Then pop over to your room and fetch your knitting. It will give you something to do. It's nearly midnight, so go for your meal at the same time. I'll sit here until you return."

At dinner, everyone knew about Simon, and they all thought I was lucky to be looking after him. I was not so sure.

Simon slept a lot that first night. I spent the night knitting, and thinking about what Night Sister had told me.

The medicine that Simon was taking was called "Brompton Cocktail," a mixture first used at the Brompton Hospital, and was Cocaine and Morphine flavoured with whisky. Without this he would have been in a lot of pain, and when he could no longer swallow, he would be given the cocaine and morphia by injection. It was a race between the cancer and the drugs. One or the other would kill him.

As Simon became used to the drugs, he slept less, and we spent the nights talking about our hopes and dreams. Simon wanted to play Rugby for England, and I started knitting him a Rugby scarf.

We became very close during those long nights. I knew that he was dying, and I think he did too, but neither of us admitted it.

Night Sister suggested that I give up my nights off, taking them as a holiday "later." I agreed. I would not have slept anyway. I was having trouble sleeping during the day. Had I been asked, I would gladly have sat with Simon twenty-four hours a day.

During the ninth night, Simon went into a coma, and on the eighteenth night he died.

He was two weeks away from his nineteenth birthday.

His unfinished rugby scarf was buried with him.

CHAPTER SEVEN

I never *did* get the four nights off that they owed me. I asked if I could have a night off to attend Simon's funeral, but Matron refused. She said that there was no need for me to go. The hospital would be sending a wreath. My feelings did not matter. Night Sister was waiting for Johns and me as we went to sign the Duty Book the night after Simon's death.

"I have moved you both. I thought it would be best."

I was being sent to Casualty. It meant that my off-duty rota was changed, and instead of working two more nights, I had four more to go before I was due a night off. I worked twenty-two nights without a break.

Before I had time to think about it, I was in the Casualty department. Once there, I didn't have time to think.

Staffing a Casualty Department must be a nightmare. The situation can change in seconds from boredom to panic. Casualty was the only department to have its own permanent trained staff on duty at night. There was a Night Sister, and three Staff Nurses. Student nurses were moved to help in Casualty as and when they were needed, but there were always two of us there all night.

I walked into a waiting room that was full. I was greeted by one of the Staff Nurses. She gave me a pile of forms and said,

"Put down the names, date of birth, address and G.P.'s, if they know them. Mostly they don't. Then find out if they have been a patient here before, either in Cas. or as an in-patient. When you have filled in as much as you can, put the forms in that box. For goodness sake keep them in order."

It sounded easy, but it wasn't. Everyone thought that their case was an emergency, and that they were far worse than the person in front of them in the queue. It took a great deal of tact, something I don't have a lot of, to get some semblance of order out of the chaos, and it was well past ten o'clock before the Waiting Room cleared.

I don't know why, but people will suffer a pain all day. Then come to Casualty in the evening. The opening line hasn't changed over the years.

"I didn't like to bother my doctor."

Roughly translated, that means that they rang the surgery, and the receptionist told them that the doctor was too busy to see them and they could have an appointment in a week's time.

I had seen aching stomachs, painful feet, splinters in fingers and headaches, but nothing that could really be defined as a casualty.

Staff came back with a pile of Casualty notes.

"This lot have all been in-patients. If you come with me, I'll show you how to find the old notes."

We went up three flights of stairs, and into an office full of filing cabinets. First we rummaged around in the cabinets until we found a card that matched the name and date of birth with those on the forms that I had filled in. It was a bonus if the address was the same! The card had a patient number on it, and we went into a vast room full of old, and very often dusty notes, and searched for the ones that we wanted.

We managed to find most of them, but two sets could not be found.

"Its a waste of time looking too hard. Patients' notes get left in the most odd places. As long as you can find some of them, it shows that you have at least tried."

In the six weeks that I spent in Cas, I never managed to find all the notes that I was looking for. The Records Room fascinated me. There were notes in there for patients that had died ten years before. What earthly use they could be, I could not imagine, except to fill a space, and perhaps to make the records staff look busy.

I spent hours fantasising over the prospect of a glorious bonfire.

Having found our notes, we went back down the stairs to find that in our absence, the pubs had closed, and the Waiting Room was full again, only this time with real casualties.

In the sixties no one worried about drinking and driving. Cars were not required to be fitted with seat belts and motorcyclists did not have to wear helmets. Every night was the same. Once the pubs closed, there was a stream of road accidents.

It was back to filling in forms, only this time the task was more difficult. A person is somewhat hesitant about giving his name and address, having just hit a keep left sign that he was too drunk to see. They also showed a total lack of imagination.

"Could I have your name please?"

"John Smith."

"Address?"

"I'm from Manchester."

Sometimes it was Liverpool, or even Newcastle.

John Smith must be on the wanted list of every Police Station in the country. Had they said they were Albert Green, I might have believed them, and a false local address would have been more credible given the distinctiveness of the local accent.

It was well past midnight by the time the room was clear. Staff came in and sent me for my dinner.

"Tell the kitchen it's busy down here will you, and say we might be needing sandwiches. Come back as soon as you have had your meal so one of the others can go."

Having passed on the message, I ate my meal and went back to work. The Waiting Room was empty, except for Sister sitting at the desk.

"I'm sorry I have not said hello to you before now, nurse, but I have been busy. Would you like to go into Room One and tell the nurse there to go to dinner. Then you can stay with her patient."

Help! A patient. What if there was blood?

Strangely, I never had a problem with blood in Casualty, although there was often a lot of it about. The need to rush about and do things helped, and there was no time to faint.

The patient in Room One had a broken leg; even I could see that, and was waiting to have it plastered. She had been taking her dog for a walk when a car had mounted the pavement and hit her. Needless to say, the driver did not stop.

While she was telling me what had happened, a policeman came into the room.

"We've got your dog, Miss Grey. What shall we do with him?"

The matter was discussed at great length. It was finally decided that he should be taken to the Police Station, and Miss Grey would arrange for him to be collected in the morning.

Those were the days of the caring Policeman.

Luckily Miss Grey had not eaten since she had her tea at five o'clock, so there was no problem about her having an anaesthetic. All we had to wait for was the Plaster Room to empty. As they worked on a first-come first served basis, we had a long wait. I heard all about her dog, her elderly mother, and the problems that having a broken leg would cause. Since I knew nothing about the treatment of fractures, I was not able to offer any real advice. All I could do was to reassure her that she would soon be able to walk again. That was said more from a desire to say the right thing than from knowledge.

In her place, I'm sure I would have been more worried about whether or not the police had been able to find the car driver that had knocked me over.

At last it was our turn for the Plaster Room, and in we went. It was a large room with an enormous old white sink, piles of metal buckets, and hose pipes running all over the place. It looked just like the dairy at home. It had the distinct Plaster Room smell, a hint of disinfectant and a hint of anaesthetic together with the smell of wet plaster.

There were two men in the room, both in white overalls, green rubber aprons and wellington boots. Neither would have been out of place in the cowshed. One of them asked me for the patient's notes, and as I handed them over said,

"You're new. Find yourself a pair of boots."

I wondered what were they going to do.

"Now Miss Grey, I am going to put you to sleep for a few minutes while we get your leg in a straight line. By the time you wake up it will have been set, although we will probably not have finished with the plastering. You will only be asleep for the painful bit."

He had never broken any of his bones, that was for sure. The whole process is painful.

As soon as Miss Grey was asleep, the fun began.

In seconds her bent leg was straightened, covered in a thin string stocking and padded with layers of cotton wool. They had both done the job before, and by the look of it, more than once.

Then I found out the reason for the boots. The plaster of Paris used to splint limbs comes as a white dusty bandage. The cover is taken off, and the bandage is put in a bucket of water until it is "wet enough." How wet that is, depends entirely on the person applying the plaster. The wet plaster is then taken out of the bucket, and the limb bandaged.

As the plaster sets fairly quickly, the whole process has to be done rapidly. There is no time for artistry, it's out of the bucket and onto the limb. Water goes all over the place. So does the plaster.

Two small boys let loose in the Plaster Room could not have had more fun than those two. Mind you, I enjoyed it as well. Once the leg was immobilised, the Plaster Technician gave me a lesson in applying plaster. It wasn't as easy as it looked.

I thought the best bit was the washing-down afterwards. The hoses were turned on and the floor cleaned, in much the same way as in the cowshed!

The only difference that I could see was that when the drains got bunged up, it was with plaster of Paris.

By the time we had finished the cleaning, Miss Grey was awake, and I went with the porters to take her to the ward. Having handed her over, it was back to the fray.

It was half past two by this time, and all was quiet, not a patient in sight. The next hour was spent in clearing up after the rush. There were trolleys piled high with rubbish all over the place.

Every one helped with the clearing up. Even Sister came in and cleaned syringes. The jobs were handed out on the basis that the person nearest to the task did it. There were no jobs for the lowly, or the elite, there were merely jobs.

We were still clearing up when the doors opened, and two Ambulance men wheeled in a stretcher.

"Overdose. Pills, quantity unknown."

Sister swore.

"Whose turn is it then? Don't all rush at once.

"On second thoughts, I'll show Wallinger what to do."

I didn't much like the sound of it. I liked the doing of it even less.

The patient was a young girl, deeply unconscious. She had taken her mother's sleeping pills then 'phoned her boyfriend and told him what she had done. By the time he had managed to wake the girl's parents, she was out cold.

It was back to the wellington boots and rubber aprons. Sister passed a large rubber tube down the girl's throat into her stomach, then fitted a funnel onto the end of the tube. She then poured a pint of water into the funnel. As soon as it had gone, she lowered the funnel into a bucket, and out the water syphoned, bringing with it some of the contents of the girl's stomach.

This went on until all that came out was clear water. It took ages, and I was to and fro to the sink like a yo yo, getting more water and emptying the buckets. As I emptied the buckets, I had to strain out the stomach contents, so that we could find out what tablets she had taken, and how many. It was not a pleasant task.

All the while she was working, Sister kept up a running commentary, telling me what she was doing, interspersed with her opinion of people that took overdoses.

I don't know why, but we had at least one overdose every night that I was on Cas, and they usually came in between 2:00 A.M. and 4:00 A.M. On one memorable night we had seven. Mind you, that was the night following an Election, and they started coming in as the results were published. It rather jaundiced my opinion of the party that came to power.

When Sister had finished the wash-out, the Duty Casualty Officer set up a drip, and the girl was sent up to the Women's Medical. There was a great deal of discussion as to whether or not she should have been admitted to the Children's Ward, as she was only fourteen. Sister thought that she would have been better on the Gynae Ward, being convinced that the girl was pregnant. We learnt the next day that Sister was right. The girl was pregnant.

I was left to clear up the wash-out room. It was back to the mop and bucket, nothing in there as sophisticated as a hose pipe. I just filled the buckets with water, then threw them on the floor and swished the water about until it went down the drain.

The rest of the night passed without any more excitement. By the time the day staff appeared, we had the place all clean, tidy, and smelling nicely of carbolic.

I was well pleased with myself. I had managed to pass my first night on Casualty without disgracing myself. It had seemed a very short night.

Night followed night, the pattern was the same. Early evening rush, slight pause, road accidents and damaged drinkers. Then the nasty ones.

The only light relief was on a Friday. At the time there was a television programme called "Emergency Ward Ten!" It was broadcast at seven-thirty on Friday evenings.

We all got up early so that we could watch it before we went on duty. It gave us an idea of what to expect in the coming hours. If it was a surgical case, the nurses on the medical wards would have an easy night. Either way, they all came through Casualty, so it was nice to know what sort of equipment to have ready.

One evening, the emergency was a case of appendicitis. During that night we had eleven cases of suspected appendicitis, all of which were examined and admitted for observation. They all went home the next day.

Every Friday it was the same. We had a rush of suspected diabetics, gastric ulcers, brain tumours, even women convinced that they were about to have a miscarriage. Some of them weren't even pregnant.

I, for one, was relieved when the programme went off the air. It was not just our hospital that suffered. The same thing was happening all over the country, and thousands of pounds must have been spent doing tests on healthy, if somewhat hysterical people.

After we had dealt with the "Ward 10" cases on a Friday, we had to prepare for the car crashes and the fights. The Great British Public likes a drink at the weekend, and then, as now, many of them keep drinking until they are legless.

Now at least they think before driving home. Not, it seems, because they are afraid they might cause an accident, but because they are afraid they might be stopped by the police and have to blow into a bag.

It is a shame that people involved in fights cannot be breathalysed and prosecuted for being drunk if they are over the limit.

It is no fun, at the age of eighteen, having to cope with an aggressive drunk. In recent years the problem has become so acute in some areas, that security firms are brought in to protect the nurses at night.

Yet alcohol remains a socially acceptable drug. The money it brings the government in taxes must be more than offset by the cost of treating the results of its overdosage.

I went to work in Casualty as a young girl without any fixed opinions. At the end of my six weeks, I was a lot older, and had formed opinions that have not changed over the years.

I wanted to see any one driving a car when drunk locked up for a long while, and any man convicted of rape, castrated.

Nothing has happened since to change my mind, and I would like anyone that disagrees with me to spend a month in the Casualty Department of any large hospital.

I would advise anyone of a squeamish disposition to skip the remaining pages of this chapter, as I am going to explain why I feel like this.

One Saturday evening, four young people were brought in. Two of them had just become engaged to be married, and they had all been out to celebrate.

They had walked down to a local night club, and just after midnight had set out to walk home. They were hit by a speeding car as they walked across a zebra crossing.

The driver of the car was only slightly hurt, but had to be carried in to the department, as he was too drunk to stand on his own.

Of the four youngsters, only one went out of Casualty alive, and he was transferred to a unit dealing in spinal injuries where he died a few days later. One of the girls had to be identified by her engagement ring. Sister would not let the parents see the body. The impact of the crash had thrown her head-first into a lamp post at the side of the crossing.

Her fiance had tyre marks across his abdomen, and the other girl had the imprint of the car's radiator on her chest.

Four young lives ended by a drunk.

The driver of the car went home with some sticky plaster on his cheek covering a couple stitches.

I put those stitches in, and I did it without an anaesthetic. I was not particularly gentle either. Given the same circumstances, I would do the same thing again.

If you look in the dictionary, rape is defined as intercourse with a woman without her legal consent. Put like that, it does not sound too bad an offence.

Rape is, to my mind, the most evil of crimes that can be committed against a person, male or female, and I have seen the results of both.

I had been in Cas for nearly a month when I saw my first case of rape. It was not the last, unfortunately, but it was the worst.

A girl of fifteen had accepted a lift home after a dance from a friend of her family. He raped her. When he had finished with her, he took her home and sat her on her parents' doorstep. Her brother found her there when he came home from the same dance. She was unconscious, and in a pool of blood.

Ambulance men are generally a pretty hard bunch. They have to be, because they see the worst of any accident, but the two bringing Sarah were both very pale.

We had heard the Ambulance bell as it came up the road, so were prepared for something nasty. Only in dire cases did they ring the bell late at night.

As I was the only nurse that was not with a patient at the time, I went with them as they took her into a room. One look at her face, and I rushed off to find Sister.

Sister sent for the Doctor, he sent for the Gynaecological Houseman, who sent for his Registrar, who in turn sent for the Consultant.

Sarah's injuries were awful. Her face and neck were scratched so deeply that they had to be stitched. Her body was going green with bruising. She had lost so much blood, that the doctors had trouble finding enough blood to send a sample for cross matching.

Her vagina was torn, as was her uterus, and we could do nothing to stop the bleeding. Sarah's parents agreed to her going to the Operating Theatre. On the consent form they signed, it stated that they gave consent, "For whatever is necessary to save her life."

At the age of fifteen, Sarah had an emergency hysterectomy. Nothing could be done to save her uterus.

Her face and body would be scarred for the rest of her life. What effect it would have on her mentally, we could only imagine.

The man responsible went to prison for a few years, having been convicted of illegal intercourse with a minor.

I rest my case.

CHAPTER EIGHT

I was enjoying life in Cas. Sister treated all her staff the same. From doctors to porters, we were all members of her team, and as well as working together, we spent some of our time off together. On duty we were all very correct and professional. Off duty was a very different matter.

Sister was a great tennis player, and organised a game nearly every morning. I learnt from those games that one of the easiest ways of relaxing and removing tension is to hit out at a tennis ball.

One of the nicest things about the department was that no one was allowed to pick jobs. We took patients as they came in, and stayed with them until they left, wherever they went, be it home, the ward, or the mortuary. If it was a case that the student was unable to manage alone, then Sister sent a trained nurse to help, but the student stayed.

During the time that I spent in Cas, I was very lucky to get two "Jollys." These were patients that had to be moved to other hospitals.

The first happened when I had only been there for a few days, and I was terrified. A young man came in complaining of stiffness in his joints. He didn't look too bad, so he joined the queue in the Waiting Room.

When I picked up his notes and called his name, nothing happened, so I went to see what was wrong. He was so stiff that he could hardly move. I helped him into a treatment room and onto a bed. Sister walked past the door as I was taking a history from him (a brief outline of the illness) and she came in and listened. When I had asked all the routine questions, Sister asked one of her own, "Have you cut or scratched yourself in the last few days?"

He admitted that he had fallen off his bike the week before and grazed his knee.

Sister nodded, then left. She was back in seconds with the Doctor. Within five minutes both the Surgical Houseman and the Registrar appeared. The patient had tetanus.

There was very little that we could do for him. We did not have the equipment that is now so taken for granted. All we could do was to sedate him and move him to a specialist hospital as fast as possible. That meant a trip of at least fifty miles to London.

Half an hour after I had first picked up his notes, the patient, Dr. Sands (one of the Surgical Housemen,) and I, were in the back of an ambulance on our way.

The ambulance driver had been asked to go as fast and as smoothly and quietly as possible. Any sudden noise or movement might cause the patient to go into a spasm. That was the danger period, as the strain on the heart could sometimes be so great that it stopped.

It was a long and harrowing journey. We could see the patient getting worse. His muscles were getting tighter and tighter, and his breathing becoming more and more shallow.

Even Dr. Sands gave a sigh of relief as the ambulance stopped and the back doors were opened to reveal a team of doctors waiting to take our man. The drama occurred as they lifted the stretcher to move him onto a trolley.

Completely without warning, the patient went rigid. His back arched so much that his body was forming an arc, supported only by his heels, and the back of his head. His face went blue and the sheet underneath him was soaked in sweat. He was out of the ambulance and away before the fit had passed.

We had managed to deliver our patient alive. Just.

The ride back home was faster, and a lot more fun.

The second "Jolly" was even more traumatic, at least for me. It was an accident case that needed to be moved to a spinal unit. As he was my patient, I was allowed to go, again with Dr. Sands, but because the patient might need Morphia, one of the Staff Nurses came with us.

It wasn't until the porters wheeled the patient out through the front door that I realised that we were not going by ambulance. There was a helicopter on the front lawn! All I can remember of that trip was the difficulty we had loading and unloading the patient. Of the actual journey, I remember only the overwhelming feeling of fear.

The return journey was by police car. That was marginally less traumatic.

Life in Casualty wasn't all blood, sweat and tears. There were lots of laughs as well. Nurses have the most appalling sense of humour, and can find the most bizarre situations funny.

I was unfortunate enough to miss out on one of the best laughs that the department had for years. I was with a patient in the Plaster Room at the time it happened.

Having disposed of my patient to the ward, I went to report back to Sister. I found her in her office with the tears rolling down her cheeks. Getting no sense out of her, I went to find one of the Staff Nurses. Finding her in a similar state, I gave up and started to clear up the pile of patients' notes left on the desk.

The reason for the hysteria was then revealed. A gentleman had been asked by his doctor to provide an early morning specimen of urine. He woke up in early hours of the morning, and decided that he would collect the specimen then, rather than when he got up to go to work.

The only container that he cold find was a milk bottle, and as his hands were rather shaky, he stuck his penis in the top of the bottle. Stuck being the word; he was admitted complete with bottle.

The only person that was not at all amused was the duty doctor.

For a long while after that, the mention of urine samples sent Sister into fits of laughter. We took to putting the milk in a jug as well.

One amusing event that I did not miss was the birth of a baby. A rather flustered man came in one night and asked for a wheelchair. He said that he had his wife in the car, and she was unable to walk.

One of the porters took a chair out for him, pushed the woman into the Waiting Room, and left her there. That was the procedure for a patient that was conscious and not in any apparent need of urgent attention.

We were rushed off our feet that night, and it was some time before she was moved into a room to be examined and treated.

As I helped her onto the bed, I asked her what was wrong, and she said,

"Oh, nothing is wrong. I'm just having a baby."

We did not have a Midwifery Unit, that was in the Annex down the road. About six miles in fact. The rule being, if in doubt, ask, I went and found Sister.

"Sister, the woman I have just taken in to Room Three is going to have a baby."

"Not in here she isn't," was the immediate response, and off she went to evict the woman.

There followed one of the funniest scenes I have ever had the pleasure of witnessing. Sister was busy trying to convince the poor woman that there was no way that the baby could be born in a Casualty treatment room. The woman just got on with the job in hand, firmly insisting that she did not have time to go anywhere else.

None of Sister's arguments had any effect, and she tried them all, from:

"We don't have babies in here," to

"I refuse to allow you to have your baby here."

The point was reached when Sister had to admit defeat, and get on and deliver the child.

The sudden yell of a newborn baby caused a lot of raised eyebrows in the Waiting Room. We were then faced with the problem of what to do with mother and baby.

It was out of the question to move her to the Maternity Unit, as it was too far for them to travel. The Gynaecological Ward wouldn't take her because there was no one on duty with any midwifery experience.

The only ward with a midwife on duty that night was Ward One, so mother and baby were moved into their side ward. I would have given anything to have seen Sister Ward One's face when she came on the next morning. I bet the nurses up there had one hell of a day!

By the time my spell on Casualty ended, I was able to deal with any situation without panic. I was even getting used to dealing with drunks.

I discovered that there are two kinds of drunk: The amorous, and the aggressive. Of the two, I preferred the aggressive. Being in a room alone with a lecherous drunk can be rather difficult, whereas even the most aggressive of them seem to preserve some sense of chivalry.

The exception always proves the rule, and one night we had a party of football fans brought in. They had been in the pub over the road from the hospital, to continue celebrating their team's success.

By closing time they were as high as kites, and refused to leave when the landlord called time. When the police arrived, they had broken most of the glasses and had started on the bottles behind the bar.

The average bobby is no better with blood than I am, so the revellers were brought over for us to patch up, before being taken down to the local nick.

Unfortunately, one of them still had a broken bottle in his hand, and was using it as a foil to keep everyone away. Putting on my fiercest face, I went up to him and asked him to give me the bottle. He did, and I still have the scar on my arm.

That was the night that I found out that I was allergic to penicillin. When the carnage cleared, I showed Sister my arm, and she thought that it would be best if the Duty Doctor saw it.

It was not deep enough to need stitching, but he thought that it would be best to give me penicillin and anti-tetanus, in case the bottle was dirty.

My protests that the arm had been bathed in neat gin went unheard, and in went the jabs. I went out like a light. The only comment I got was from Sister.

"It was a good job we were not busy, you caused quite a panic."

I have yet to meet a sympathetic nurse! Neither did I get any thanks from Matron the next morning when I went to report my injury.

"We don't need any heroics here, Nurse. Nor do we need histrionics. You can't go off sick, we are too short of staff."

You would have thought that I deliberately made myself sensitive to the stuff so that I could have a night off. Had I received proper training in the administration of antibiotics, it would never have happened. All I got was a change of sticky plaster each night until the wound healed.

That scar served me well while I was in Cas. Whenever we had to deal with a really nasty drunk, I would show him my arm, and tell him that I had been attacked by a drunk with a bottle. That usually had the effect of sobering him up enough to allow us to treat him.

Casualty was L-shaped, with the main door and the waiting room at the corner of the L. The treatment rooms ran off to the right, down to the back door. The ambulance cases came in through the back door. One, because it was easier for them to park, and two, to save taking the messy cases past the patients in the Waiting Room. The Mortuary was opposite to the back door as well. That meant that DOA (dead on arrival) cases, and our failures, could be taken out of the back door. It is not a good idea to parade the Mortuary trolley for all to see. It hardly inspires confidence.

I had never been to the Mortuary before I went to work in Casualty, but by the time I left, I was an old hand at the procedure. Whatever Matron's faults, she had a great respect for the dead. A body was never taken straight to the Mortuary. It had to be left in the Mortuary Chapel until it had been formally identified. That made a grim task a little easier for relatives I'm sure. I wish more hospitals would do the same.

We took a pride in laying out a body, and always placed the crossed palms over the heart, placing a white flower in the hands. Finding a flower was not a problem on the wards, but there were never any flowers in Cas!

Our constant forays into the wards were greeted with cutting remarks, and I became so embarrassed that I made an arrangement with a local florist. At the end of the day, he used to put any fading blooms in a box beside his dustbin, and one of us used to go every night to collect them.

Apart from saving the reputation of the department, it had the added advantage of providing displays of flowers for the Waiting Room. There were usually enough left over for us to take some back to our rooms.

Years after I left the hospital, I went back on a visit, and the same florist was still supplying Cas with flowers!

One night there was not time to collect the flowers until very late. It was almost 4:00 A.M. before I had a chance to slip out, and then, only because we needed the flowers. As I walked back, I passed a bakers' shop, and the van was there delivering cakes and bread.

Always on the lookout for food, I stopped for a chat with the van driver. I found that all the stale cakes were put in the bin! From then on there were cakes to collect as well as flowers. Five o'clock tea in Cas rapidly became an institution, with invitations handed out to the privileged.

Only a dire emergency, such as Matron being around, would prevent these taking place. Had Matron made a habit of working at night, I'm sure a way would have been found to get round the problem. Since it only happened once a year, it was not worth the bother.

From the main door there was a slight slope up to the swing doors leading into the hospital. Between the front door and the swing doors were the sluice, linen cupboards and Clinical Room. The slope was a godsend. There was just enough fall on it to allow the water from the overflowing sterilizer to run out into the street. All we had to do was sweep the water out of the Clinical Room and off it went. It was such a common occurrence that a broom was kept by the door.

The trolleys used to move patients around were kept at the top of the slope, and we had endless fun having trolley races. Two trolleys were lined up, side by side and used as scooters. Had anyone come in through the main door, there would have been a nasty accident. Well aware of the dangers, we used to make up headlines for the local paper, such as;

"Man mowed down by speeding trolley."

"I never saw him, says nurse accused of dangerous trolley pushing."

"Runaway trolley causes accident on by-pass."

Another source of fun was watching the doctors going up to their rooms. The entrance to "The Hall," a grand name for a series of poky rooms, was half way along the slope. Doctors, like us, had to live in, and were not allowed to entertain after 10:30 P.M.

As there was a fire escape that served only "The Hall," this did not bother them a great deal. The fire escape passed across the outside of one of the treatment room windows. A young man would come in through the main door and go upstairs. We would rush to the window overlooking the fire escape, often to see a pair of mini-skirted legs disappearing upwards.

We would then let half an hour pass before phoning the switchboard. We would ask them to tell that particular young man that he was wanted urgently on his ward. He had to go, no matter what he was doing. We could hear the 'phone ringing upstairs from the corridor between the treatment room, and we used to time how long it took him to get downstairs.

The doctors must have hated us, although if we called them to see a patient, they were always very pleasant. Perhaps they hoped to win us round. No chance. We had to live like nuns, so why should they get away with it?

All this was rather childish I suppose, but it helped to ease the tension and relieve the boredom. The strain was terrific, and we were all so young.

The oldest person on the unit at night was the Doctor, and he was only twenty-six.

Sister had few rules, but such was our respect for her that they were never broken. As rules go, they were very fair. There was no picking and choosing over jobs. There was a book kept for the rotten jobs, like stomach washouts, and when you had done one, you put your name in the book. That way everyone had a turn.

We all had our favourite jobs, and given half a chance, I opted for the Plaster Room. I liked the challenge that the plaster bandages presented and enjoyed seeing my finished work, all smooth and clean. I liked playing with the hose pipes as well!

My pet hate was motorcycle accidents. Very few motorcyclists wore helmets in those days, and those that did wore helmets and goggles, rather than the full face helmets that are popular today. The open face helmets left a large area of facial skin to scrape along the ground when rider and machine parted company. Sitting pulling bits of grit out of a chin with a pair of toothed forceps was not my idea of fun at all. One of the Staff Nurses always volunteered for the job. She said she found it relaxing!

Sister liked dealing with the squashed nails, and she was an expert at the job. The first one I saw was enough for me, although I had to admit that the treatment was dramatic.

A taxi driver walked in one evening. The poor man was in agony. He had shut his hand in the door of his taxi, and his finger nails were black. Sister grinned at him,

"No problem. Ten minutes and you'll be back at work. Nurse, bring the patient into the kitchen." I could not see why we had to go to the kitchen when there were treatment rooms empty. When the patient and I reached the kitchen, there was Sister holding a paper clip over the gas flame.

"Sit the patient down with his hand on the table, then put a towel under his hand, and have another towel ready, just in case."

In case of what, I thought.

I soon knew. Before the patient knew what was happening, Sister had put the point of the white hot paper clip onto his finger nail and pushed. The heat from the clip burnt a hole in the nail, and the blood gushed out in a fountain. Hence the second towel. That was put on top of the nail to mop up. Five minutes, and all three damaged nails were done. One very happy patient. One very sick feeling nurse.

And Sister enjoyed doing it. There are some very funny people around!

There was a book in the department, labelled "Linen Cupboard." If anyone ever asked, it was a rota for tidying. Most ward linen cupboards are in fact small rooms with wide floor-to-ceiling shelves. The linen is arranged so that the most often needed things are nearest to hand. As pillows are not often changed, they tend to be kept on the top shelf.

Carefully arranged, they make a marvellous mattress, and in quiet times, Sister would send one of us to the linen cupboard for a sleep.

Of the linen cupboards I have since slept in, that one in Cas was the best. It did not have any hot pipes running through it, and so one did not overheat!

I had only been on Casualty for five weeks when the change list announced that I was to move to Women's Medical. I had hoped to spend the rest of my spell of nights on Cas, although I knew that it was unlikely.

I enjoyed the work. I enjoyed the friendly atmosphere, and most of all, I enjoyed the practical teaching.

When my final morning came, I asked Sister for my Schedule. I was surprised at just how much I had learnt in those six weeks.

I would have liked to have had a photocopy of the report that Sister wrote, if only to show to my parents. Never again was I called "a reliable and hard working member of the team."

I went off duty glowing. Sister's last words had been,

"If I am short of staff whilst you are still on nights, I will ask for you. I shall also ask Matron if you can return here for your fourth year."

My head was so swollen with the praise, that it must have shown. As I reached the swing doors, one of the porters held both of them open.

CHAPTER NINE

It did not take me long to discover that I did not like nursing women. Nothing that has happened in the following years has changed my mind. I still avoid all female wards, except geriatric, like the plague.

A woman that is slightly ill moans and groans as if she is dying. A really ill woman puts on a brave face and says she is fine. One needs to be psychic to find out how they really feel.

Ward Four was directly above Ward One. The ward layout was the same. There the similarity ended.

It was what is known as a "Heavy" ward, meaning that it was busy. I had been used to being busy in Casualty, but this was totally different.

The women seemed to think that we were there as servants, and would not lift a finger to help themselves, or for that matter, to help us.

Medicine can best be described as any treatment not involving surgery. All the unspecified conditions needing observation were admitted to the medical wards.

There were thirty patients, ranging from the dying to the malingerers. As I went round the ward saying Good Evening to the patients, I found it hard to tell which was which.

I soon found how to tell the difference. The really ill patients complained less than the others, and the malingerers always brightened up when the doctors were about!

My first task was to remove the flowers from the ward and stand them out on the flat. Sister Ward Four believed that, as flowers remove oxygen from the air at night, they were a danger to the patients. Therefore, every single vase had to be moved, which took ages. It was even worse in the mornings. I was supposed to find the time to remove any dead flowers, then change the water in the vases.

I managed to avoid the task. As I took the flowers out of the ward, I threw any that looked a bit sick into a bucket. Then, before I took the flowers back in the mornings, I used to run round with a jug and top up the water.

Having dealt with the flowers, the next job was to give out the "milky drinks." Just giving out the drinks took a long while. Nearly every one of the women wanted Horlicks, and that used to take ages to mix. The milk had to be put in a special mixing jug, the powder put on top, and the whole lot jiggled up and down with a special whisk. Even then, it was apt to have lumps in it. Someone at Horlicks must have heard our prayers, as it is now as easily made as instant coffee.

By a masterly stroke of bad planning, both of us on duty were new to the ward. The senior nurse was a Persian girl, Nurse Sashan. Her English was pure BBC, but she was slightly darker skinned that the rest of us pale mortals. The racial prejudice that she suffered from those women would have tried the patience of a saint.

After the drinks round came the bedpan round. They all wanted bedpans. None of them admitted to being allowed out of bed.

It was easier to give in than to keep checking the Kardex. By the time we had given out and collected the bed pans and wash bowls, made the beds, and rubbed pressure areas, it was getting late.

I went to my meal leaving a pile of unwashed and unemptied bedpans in the sluice. Had I been a really conscientious nurse, I would have returned from my meal and gone to work on the pans. However, I wasn't.

As Sashan left the ward, Dr. Sands came in to check on his patients before he went to bed. Since our last "Jolly" together, we had become friends. The one and only good thing about Ward Four for me was that Robert Sands had changed from Surgical to Medical Houseman.

If we hadn't seen each other on duty, we would never have seen each other at all. I had two nights off a week. He had one evening a week, and every other weekend off, if he could be spared. He was still working on the ward when Sashan returned from her dinner, so I left them to continue the round, and returned to the sluice.

As soon as I put a pan in the washer, a patient would call out wanting to spend a penny. The pile of pans waiting to be washed never decreased. In the end I became desperate, and just gave them a rinse under the hot tap. It was either that, or they would not have been washed at all.

We calculated that we would need to start the morning jobs at 4:00 A.M. Any later and we would still be washing faces when the day staff arrived. The situation called for drastic action. We went through the Kardex and wrote each patient's name on the back of a temperature chart. Then we checked the treatment notes, added notes such as "Up." "Up to toilet." "Bed." These were clipped to the chart board on the end of each bed.

When we woke them up in the morning, we had an easy reference system. They were not amused. The atmosphere was so thick you could feel it. They had been beaten by two new girls, and one of them coloured at that!

The only conversation in the ward that morning was between Sashan and myself. It was a relief to leave when the day staff arrived.

Sashan could at least look forward to two nights off. I had three more to go before my break.

The relief senior was a part-time staff nurse. She only worked two nights a week. In her hands the ward was very different. She was a very tall woman, I suppose about six feet, and in her forties. There was a distinct air of authority about her. No one tried to pull the wool over her eyes.

As I prepared to give out the drinks, she came in to the kitchen.

"Leave those. There is a patient on the way up."

Walking back into the ward, she announced to the patients,

"The drinks are in the kitchen. If you want one you will have to get it. Those of you that are not allowed out of bed can either go without, or get someone else to get it for you."

It worked. They all had a drink, although no one made any effort to clear the cups.

The new patient was an elderly, frail-looking soul. She had been having chest pains for a couple of weeks, and only saw the doctor because she collapsed outside his surgery.

She was for total bed rest, and if she made it as far as the morning, would have tests to determine whether or not she had suffered a heart attack.

The fact that she had been admitted to hospital was bothering her more than the pains in her chest. To her generation, only the dying went to hospital. Nothing either of us said made any difference.

She was right. She died in the early hours of the morning. By the time we went off duty, her bed had been filled by a large lady that had taken an overdose. I felt sorry for the nurse that had to wash out her stomach.

So many patients died at night, the worst time being between 2:00 A.M. and 4:00 A.M.. If one had an ill patient, that was the danger time. If they were still alive at four, there was a good chance that they would last out the day. At the time we accepted it as one of life's inconveniences. Now, I wonder just how many of those deaths could have been prevented, or at least delayed.

In 1965, a patient admitted with a suspected Coronary Thrombosis (Heart Attack) was given emergency treatment in Casualty, then sent up to the ward and put to bed.

We propped them up against a stack of pillows and watched them, if we had the time. We took their blood pressure every fifteen minutes, and if there was any change, we sent for the doctor. A lot can happen in fifteen minutes.

How different things are today. The ambulance staff are trained to give emergency treatment. The patient is often taken straight to the Coronary Care Unit, by-passing Casualty, put on a Cardiac Monitor, and constantly watched. The nurse knows even before the patient that another attack is imminent. Should the worst happen, and the heart stop beating, it is given an electric shock, and started again.

Such things are now regarded as normal. To us then, they were as unlikely as man walking on the Moon. Many of the things we did would cause a lot of raised eyebrows amongst today's young nurses.

If a patient needed oxygen, we had to get a porter to bring a bottle up from the store. Bottle being a loose term, they were, in fact, heavy metal cylinders about four feet tall and eighteen inches round. There was a bottle kept on the ward, but as it was for emergency use only, as soon as it was in use, another had to be brought in to replace it.

A porter crashing about with one of those in the middle of the night was guaranteed to wake up most of the ward.

A few of the more enlightened Sisters allowed the use of disposable oxygen masks, made of thin plastic, and called Polymasks. One simply fitted a mask to the tube from the oxygen bottle and put it over the patient's mouth and nose. It was then kept in place by a thin piece of elastic that hooked over the ears. Being disposable, they cut down the risk of cross infection.

Unfortunately, the majority of Sisters still preferred the oxygen tent. A metal frame was placed over the top half of the bed, and covered with a sheet of transparent plastic. Oxygen was then fed into the tent through a tube. The patient sat up in bed surrounded by oxygen. The amount of oxygen those tents consumed was horrendous. The porters were up and down with bottles all night.

There was one Sister that still insisted on the use of Tudor Edward Spectacles. They were a pair of hollow metal spectacles designed to conduct oxygen straight into the patient's nostrils.

The most barbaric treatment was used for the relief of oedema, the leaking of serous fluid into the tissues. Patients with heart failure were admitted with grossly swollen ankles and these were drained. The patient was nursed in a sitting position and a series of hollow tubes were put into the tissues of the ankle to allow the excess water to escape. Today, the same job is done far more effectively with an injection of a diuretic.

While we were using methods such as this, in South Africa Christiian Barnard was planning his first heart transplant.

Every Wednesday, both consultant Physicians did a ward round, and Sister would produce a list of patients that she thought were ready for discharge. It was known as "Sister's weekly clear out."

I loved working Wednesday nights! The ward was often half empty; only the really ill remained. By Friday it was usually full again.

By the time Sashan came back from her nights off, I knew all about the patients. Adopting Staff Nurse's approach, I had them giving out the drinks and even, on occasions, clearing away the cups. My efforts to get them to wash up the cups met with complete failure. The nearest I managed was to get them to put the empty cups in the sink to soak.

Every night was busy, and hardly a night went by without an admission. Usually it was an overdose sleeping off her pills, but sometimes we had something more interesting.

The trouble was, they all tended to come at once, and very often in threes. One admission a night we accepted, but if there was a second, then there was nearly always as third. Instead of being able to learn about the patient's diagnosis and treatment, it was just a rush to get her settled, then on to the next one.

Sashan was "fey." She had the ability to predict trouble. If she said it was going to be a busy night, then it was.

I was washing up one night when she came in and said,

"I think we should have some beds ready. We could have some admissions tonight."

Having made the beds, I jokingly asked her what sort of treatment trolleys I should lay up.

"One for a lumbar puncture, a drip, and just in case, the Last Offices Box."

That night we admitted a diabetic in a coma. She needed a drip. A suspected meningitis, she needed a lumbar puncture, and an overdose that had been found too late. She needed the box.

From then on I treated Sashan's predictions with a great deal more respect. That she had some sort of "gift" was without question. Not many students like working with her. They thought her "spooky." I thought her a great asset on the ward. I liked advance warning of trouble, and I liked her attitude to her work.

The only time I saw her ruffled was when Mrs. Penn, the mother of one of the surgical housemen, died. Mrs. Penn had been taken ill while visiting her son, and was admitted to the side ward. That she was dying was obvious, and Sashan sent for Dr. Penn. She was told that he was in Theatre, so, she rang Theatre. They told her that they would give him the message as soon as was convenient!

To say Sashan was annoyed would be putting it mildly. She continued to 'phone every five minutes, until it was too late.

Mrs. Penn died in the same hospital in which her son was a doctor, but he could not be spared to sit with her for her final few moments. What made it worse, was that she was conscious until the end. She died looking towards the door.

We were sitting having a coffee one night when Sashan jumped up and rushed down the ward. I followed and found her pulling the screens round a bed. Without even looking at the patient she said,

"Phone Dr. Sands and tell him Mrs. Evans has died. Then tell Night Sister."

She was right. How she knew defeated me.

I don't remember learning very much about nursing during the time I spent on Ward Four, but I learnt a lot about people.

It never occurred to me that illness could be self-induced. Psychosomatic was a word I had never heard, until I went to Ward Four. I also thought faith healing was a joke.

One evening Casualty rang to tell us that they were sending a patient up to us. She was in her early twenties, and was to be admitted to the side ward. She duly arrived, accompanied by an elderly Religious Sister. The Nun told me that the girl's name was Heather, and that she was a member of a very strict religious order.

I was also told that the nurses were to keep their contact with Heather as brief as possible, and that we should not try to make conversation. Should there be a question that needed an answer, then we were to address her, and not Heather.

My first thought was "Balls." I was nursing the girl, not the old trout that had come with her. I repeated the conversation to Sashan, and although her comment was in Persian, it sounded similar to mine.

The fun really started when the doctors came up to examine Heather. Robert appeared, together with his Registrar. He said he needed some moral support! Before they arrived, Sashan and I had tossed for the pleasure of being in the room during the examination. I won, but Sashan announced her intention to stand with her ear glued to the keyhole.

I went into the room first, and told the Trout, (I never knew her name, but we all referred to her as the Trout) that the doctors were coming to examine Heather, and would she please sit outside for a few minutes. She refused to move, saying,

"I must not leave my sister alone."

I gave in. I was glad I did. It would not have been half as much fun without her there.

Her first problem was that the doctors were both male. She refused to even acknowledge their presence.

"Is it not possible," she asked me. "to find a lady doctor?"

As the nearest we had to a female on the medical staff was a very butch anaesthetist, I explained that there were no "lady" doctors.

Once that had sunk in, she agreed that the doctors could look at Heather, but they were not to touch her. I had to avoid looking at either of the men. I was having enough trouble keeping a straight face as it was.

It was the most ridiculous examination ever. Robert asked Heather the questions, the Trout answered, and I did the "touching."

We were told that Heather had fainted during her evening prayers, and when she recovered from the faint, she could not move. In fact she could neither move nor feel. I stuck a pin in her foot, at the suggestion of the doctors, and she didn't even flinch.

Having seen as much of their patient as they were allowed, the doctors left the room. I followed. I was no longer amused. I was angry. The whole examination had been a farce. There was no way we could treat the girl with that woman sitting there.

The doctors decided that the only way that they were going to be able to find out what was wrong with Heather was to get a priest to come and remove the Trout.

It was a brilliant idea, although, as Robert later admitted, it was not original. They had met the same problem before. The Priest simply gave his permission for a full examination, and that was that. In the following days, Heather had every test imaginable, but no cause could be found for her paralysis.

As a last resort, the psychiatrist was called in. He went into the room, evicted the Trout and shut the door. Three hours later he walked out with Heather beside him. All that he had written on the notes, was that it was a trauma-induced paralysis.

By the time we went on duty that evening, we had heard all about the miracle cure on the hospital "Bush Telegraph," but even having been warned, it was a surprise to see the girl walking about.

I questioned Robert about it, and he said that they had decided that Heather could not cope with the strict rules of the order, and her brain had simply shut down. I felt so sorry for her. It seemed such a waste of a life, to spend day after day in silence, shut away from the world behind a high wall.

The only light relief on Ward Four was Mrs. Day. She was an elderly diabetic, and all attempts to stabilise her diabetes met with failure. For some reason, she became hyperglycaemic every morning, usually as we started the early bedpan round. No reason could be found, and attempts to rectify it sent her hypoglycemic.

I could never remember whether hyperglycaemia was too much or too little sugar. I knew that the opposite was hypoglycaemia, but not which was which. Confessing my ignorance to Dr. Sands one night, he solved the problem for all time. I never confused the two words after that.

"If you can remember that a po goes under the bed, you can remember that in hypo, the sugar levels are below the norm."

Normally a very quiet and gentle person, the extra sugar in her blood made Mrs. Day act as if she were drunk. As she was a staunch member of the Salvation Army, I don't imagine she had ever been in that state through the use of alcohol.

The sound of bedpans rattling seemed to be the catalyst. Perhaps it reminded her of the sound of the band. As soon as the trolley came into the ward, she would sit up in bed and sing.

"Onward Christian Soldiers,
Marching as to war."

There was never any more, just the two lines constantly repeated. Years of following the band had given her a very powerful voice, and I would find myself marching round with bedpans in time to the beat of her voice.

The ward was not the same after she died. As I came out of the sluice the morning after her death, I found myself humming *her* hymn, and marching along in time with the music.

Many, many bedpan rounds later, I am still doing the same. I only have to come out of a sluice with a bedpan in my hand and I'm off;

On-ward Chris-tian Sol-diers, Mar-ching as to war.

One day I'll learn the rest of the hymn.

CHAPTER TEN

I was very glad to see my name on the change list, especially as I had been given two weeks holiday. It made the last week on Ward Four a bit more tolerable. I packed my case before going on duty for my last night. I was all ready to go as soon as I came off duty. I couldn't wait. Two whole weeks of freedom. No alarm bells in the corridor. Home cooking. My own room. Bath water as deep as I liked; I might even be able to stay out later than ten-thirty at night.

I had to wait for two hours after I came off duty before seeing Matron to collect my holiday pass. The pass allowed me to leave the hospital for thirteen nights. I was to report back by 8:00 P.M. on the Sunday, ready for duty the next day.

I thanked her for her kindness and fled. Nurses had been known to have holidays cancelled, even after getting their pass. If she wanted me back, first she would have to find me!

I spent the first few days trying to get rid of the smell of carbolic and catching up on my sleep.

I didn't bother to 'phone to find out which ward I would be on when I got back. Just as well, or I would probably have stayed at home.

I reported back to Matron, thanked her for allowing me a holiday, and went to look at the Change List. Not only was I moving ward, but hospital as well. I was in for a spell at the Annex.

Home Sister gave me the choice of staying in town, and going up each day on the hospital bus, or moving into the Annex Home. I chose the latter. I would rather lose my social life than my sleep. It was bad enough getting up at 7:00 A.M. I would never have managed 6:30.

I was rapidly coming to the conclusion that having a doctor as a boy-friend was a total waste of time. Our evenings out were limited to one a week, unless we went for a drink in the local pub and took the bleep with us. That was definitely not my idea of fun.

Life in the Annex Home was reported to be easier. There were less rules up there. We didn't have to be in until eleven o'clock at night. The Home Sister up there was said to be very open-minded.

The only disadvantage was that I was going to the Eye Department. Sister Eyes had the reputation for being rather odd.

Once again, I packed up my rapidly growing collection of treasures and moved on. The move was complicated in that it all had to be done in one go, and my suitcase would only hold a fraction of my things. Home Sister, anxious I felt to see the back of me, found a tea chest. I was loaded onto the hospital bus, together with my suitcase, two boxes and a tea chest, and off I went.

Sister Eyes had given me Monday off to allow me to unpack, but I was to be on duty at 7:30 A.M. on Tuesday.

The Annex had enjoyed a chequered career. Originally it had been built as a workhouse. Later an isolation hospital had been added in the grounds. The main building was a tall grim-looking place. Nothing could be done to disguise the fact that it was an old workhouse, and was still known locally as "The Union."

When no longer needed to house the destitute, the workhouse was converted to a hospital. From then until the birth of the NHS, it served as a general hospital. In 1947, it was decided that two hospitals within six miles of each other was not a very efficient concept, so they were amalgamated to form one large general hospital. As the number of diphtheria and smallpox cases had fallen dramatically in the years between the wars, all but one of the isolation wards were converted into general wards.

Polio and tuberculosis were still rife in the late forties, but by the time I was there, the Isolation Ward was mostly used as an extension of the Children's Ward. It took children that had reacted badly to the common childhood illnesses.

The old workhouse building now contained the administrative offices for the two hospitals, along with the Maternity Block and the Geriatric Wards. The old isolation wards now housed the Eye, Orthopaedic, Children's and Minor Surgery Wards.

The old isolation wards were long single story buildings. They were all built facing the sun, with long wide verandas on the sunny side. Attached to each building was a small operating theatre, and these were still in use in theory, for minor surgery.

The whole complex was built on the side of a hill, with the workhouse perched on the top, and surrounded by a tall brick wall. From the road, it looked more like a prison than a hospital.

The Nurse's Home was comparatively new, having been built just before the war. After living in three Victorian homes, it was heaven. The rooms were large, light, and single. As well as a bed, there was an armchair, and a wash basin. There was also a fitted wardrobe and a dressing table with a mirror. It was better than my room at home.

Each floor of the Home had a kitchen, with a proper cooker and a 'fridge. There was also a laundry with a washing machine and an iron. On the ground floor was a large recreation room, dominated by a table-tennis table. The only disadvantage was that it took fifteen minutes to walk from the Home to the Eye Ward.

As I strolled along on my first morning, the birds were singing and the sun was shining. It was a fine September morning, but there was a distinct autumnal nip in the air. I wondered what it would be like in the middle of November with the wind blowing and the rain coming down in buckets.

I was on the ward well before seven-thirty, so I hung up my cloak, and waited for the rest of the day staff.

When they arrived, I was told to wait in the office until Sister came on duty at eight. She did not allow "strange nurses" into the ward until she had seen them. It felt like a long wait. I had heard some very odd things about Sister Eyes, and I was not looking forward to meeting her. I had hoped to just be absorbed into the ward routine without her noticing me!

The office was cluttered. There was hardly a flat surface that was not piled high with notes, papers, photographs and old magazines. How on earth she ever managed to find anything I could not imagine.

I had never seen her before, and I had rather a shock when she came in. She was tall and thin, with wispy grey hair that stuck out all over the place, and she was wearing a pair of vintage NHS spectacles with very thick lenses. Her uniform looked as if she had slept in it, and she had so many keys pinned to her belt that she rattled as she walked.

"Good morning, Nurse. Do you think you are going to like working here?"

I could hardly tell her that I thought not, as the bit I had seen so far was not very promising. I settled for a compromise and said I hoped so.

"You have a lot to learn. We had better make a start. I'll warn you now, my teaching methods are not popular with the tutors, but I can guarantee that the lessons you learn on my ward you will not forget."

She was right on both counts. The tutors did not like her, and I never forgot anything she taught me.

"If you don't like the way I do things, you can go to Matron and asked to be moved. I have been on this ward since 1928 and I am not going to change things to please anyone, even Matron."

Her office certainly looked as if she had been there for thirty-seven years! I wondered which pile had been the first to arrive. There were probably some 1928 newspapers in there somewhere.

"Have you ever been in hospital as a patient?"

When I told her that I had, she wanted to know where, why and when. I scored a point for having been a patient in her old training hospital, but lost it again because she considered the treatment I had received as being "newfangled."

"You will never be a nurse unless you know how it feels to be a patient. I insist on all my staff experiencing life as a patient on this ward. It either makes good nurses of them or they go. I will not tolerate half measures. Now run along to your room and get your night clothes and your washing things. By the time you get back, I will have a bed ready for you."

No wonder she was thought odd, I thought. Crazy would have been a better description. Still, a day in bed couldn't be all bad. It would beat work, that was for sure.

As I picked my way round the junk on the floor she said,

"You had better take the bike. You'll be all day otherwise. You will find it by the front door."

Sister's bike had obviously been on the ward as long as she had, if not longer. Provided one did not try to make it work too hard, it was fine. Any attempt at speed, and it threw off its chain. Both wheels had suffered over the years, one being slightly oval, and the other out of alignment. Still, it was quicker than walking. Just.

It says a lot for hospital discipline that I did as I was told. I wonder what reaction I would get, if I said the same to one of the modern breed of student nurses?

I didn't have much chance to think about what might happen when I returned to the ward. On the way to the Home, I was too busy trying to master the vagaries of the bike. Returning to the ward I had the added problem of carrying my bag.

As I went into the ward, Sister was waiting for me. Taking my bag, she led me to a bed in the corner of the ward.

"Now girl, we are going to pretend that you have had an accident and have damaged both eyes. I am going to bandage both eyes now, but after lunch I will uncover one of them."

Before I could protest, my cap was off, and both of my eyes were padded and bandaged.

"Now, I'm going to take you along to the bathroom so that you can get ready for bed."

I was pulled to my feet. I felt totally disoriented. I was not even sure where the floor was. Sister took hold of my elbow, and I was pushed along the ward and through a doorway. I knew it was a doorway, because I hit my free arm on it as I went through.

I heard Sister put my bag down, and then the door shut. I had no idea whether she was in the room or not.

I felt utterly isolated. I put up a hand to raise a corner of one of the pads. I had to see what was happening. As my hand went up Sister spoke.

"What did you learn from that exercise?"

"I don't think I learnt anything, Sister. All I felt was panic. I didn't know where I was or who was with me."

"Good. That is just how a patient would feel. Your things are on the chair. I will leave you to get changed. Promise me you won't cheat."

I promised, and I heard the door close. It took me ages to find the chair. Then the bag tipped up, and my things spilled all over the floor. I was down on my hands and knees trying to find them, when Sister returned and took pity on me. With her help, it only took a couple of minutes to get out of my uniform and into my nightdress.

The journey back to the bed was a lot easier. Sister tucked my hand under her elbow, and led me. As we went, she gave me a running commentary.

"Four steps, and we will be at the door. Then we are going to turn sharp left. Ten steps will take us along the corridor to the ward door. Now we are going to take seven steps to your bed. If you put out your hand, you will feel the bed."

It seemed as if I had walked a mile. My feet felt as if they were a long way from my body.

I climbed into bed. It was like climbing Mount Everest. I put out my hands and held onto the sides of the mattress. The bed felt as if it was miles up in the air. I was too terrified to move in case I fell out.

"I'm going to leave you for a while. Think about what we have just done, and see what lessons you have learnt."

I heard her walk off down the ward. Clink. Clink. Clink. I heard all sorts of strange sounds. People were moving about, doors were banging, and I could hear a tap dripping. After a while, each drip sounded like a drum beat, and the sound seemed to get louder and louder. In the end, all I could hear was the tap.

A sudden noise close by made me jump. I could smell, lavender. I didn't associate the noise with the smell. A voice said,

"I said, do you have sugar in your coffee."

So that was the noise. I hadn't realised it was a voice. The smell of lavender belonged to the voice.

"I'd rather not have coffee, thank you." I said. I could not think how to get it from the table to my mouth.

"Sister says you must. Here you are."

I put out my hands, and a cup was placed in them. I sat and held it for a while, then tried to find my mouth. I was rather pleased. I only spilt a few drops.

I couldn't find anywhere to put the empty cup, so I held onto it. After an age, a smell of violets, came and took the cup away.

Time dragged. I tried to sleep, but there was so much noise. But at least the tap had stopped dripping. I could hear people laughing, people walking about, and sometimes a car went by on the road outside.

Suddenly I heard a sound I recognised. Clink. Clink. Clink. Sister! As she came nearer, I could smell food. The overwhelming smell of hospital cabbage.

Oh no! I was going to have to try and eat. I could feel the tears behind my bandages.

"Your ordeal is nearly over, girl. I am going to feed you a forkful of each thing on the plate. Then you are going to have a wash and clean your teeth. After that I will take off one pad. It won't be so bad after that."

As each forkful came towards me, Sister just said,

"Open your mouth."

I opened my mouth somewhat reluctantly. I would have liked to know what it was I was eating. Once it was in my mouth, I was none the wiser. It all tasted the same.

"There. That was beastly wasn't it? I'll just take away this plate and get you your washing things."

Soap is very elusive when you can't see it. In the end I gave up. Putting toothpaste onto a toothbrush is not easy either. I felt very proud that I was able to get the brush in my mouth. Even if I *had* needed Sister to tell me where my mouth was. I did not do so well with the mouthwash!

"Right. I'll clear away these things, and then I'll come back and uncover one eye."

Off she went, clinking at every step. After what seemed like a long while, she clinked her way back. I felt her hands on the side of my face, and then there was a blinding light in my eye. It took a while before I adjusted to the brightness.

For the first time in my life, I realised how wonderful it is to be able to see. One eye was better than none, but far from easy. I was allowed to walk around the ward, as long as I kept well away from the beds. I found that I could not judge distances, and walked into things. Sounds coming from my "blind side" made me jump. I had to concentrate to see anything clearly.

Sister had said that she would take off my bandage at two o'clock. I looked at the clock every five minutes. The time went by very slowly. At five minutes to two she came back, and took off the remaining pad.

"Now go and get your uniform dress on. Don't bother with your apron. When you have collected your things together, come along to my office."

That did not sound very promising. I jumped into my clothes, and went along to find Sister.

"You have done well, girl. Not many can take it. I'll show you round the ward, then you can have the rest of the day off."

The ward was basically a cruciform shape. The Women's ward was on one arm of the cross, and the Men's on the opposite arm. Each ward had sixteen beds. Between them was the six-bedded Children's ward, and opposite that the Operating Theatre.

The kitchen, office, treatment and storage rooms were in the middle.

Having completed a lightning tour, Sister said,

"Go off duty now, and take a nice long walk. Think about all that you have learned today, and thank God for His Blessing of sight. When you come on duty in the morning, make sure you wear some perfume. If you don't have any, then use perfumed talcum powder. It helps the patients if they can identify the nurses, even if it is only by smell."

Six hours as a patient. It had seemed like years. She was right. I have never forgotten my first day on Eyes. It was weeks before I stopped having nightmares about it.

CHAPTER ELEVEN

Looking back, I find it incredible that we put up with such treatment from the Ward Sisters. There were some that were almost human, but not many. Most of them lived in the Sisters' Home, and the only life they had was their wards. No wonder they were such tyrants. They must have regarded the student nurses as a threat to their supremacy. One day they would have to retire and hand over their kingdom. It would probably be one of their past students that inherited the crown.

In the outside world, changes were taking place. Hem lines were going up. Wages were going up. Women were becoming liberated. The world was entering an age of enlightenment, or so the newspapers told us.

The changes passed us by. We still had our hems two inches below our knees. We were still being paid a pittance, and we did what we were told without question. We were not encouraged to think. I lost count of the times I was told,

"You are not here to think, Nurse. Just do as you are told."

Even the junior doctors were ruled by the sisters. Fresh from Medical School, they were full of bright ideas and wanted to use the new drugs and treatments that they had learnt about during their training. Within a couple of weeks, they were doing just as the Sisters ordered, using the old tried and tested drugs and treatments.

I asked one of the doctors why, if they considered the drugs out-dated, they prescribed them. Why not insist on prescribing what they wanted? They were, after all, the doctors, and nurses were supposed to carry out the doctor's orders, not issue them. His reply saddened me. He said that he had tried to change things when he first arrived on Ward One. Sister had made his life hell, until he gave in and did as he was told.

Sister Eyes was a prime example. Any drug or treatment that was less than ten years old was just dismissed as "newfangled."

The ward was efficiently run and the patients well cared for, but if she had only accepted the inevitability of change, instead of spending most of her time opposing it, everyone would have been a lot happier.

Her attitude towards patients' relatives had to be seen to be believed. Nearly every new patient came up to the ward with a friend or relative. The patient was met, fussed over, and taken into the ward. The relative was left standing by the door, her only acknowledgement of their presence being,

"Wait there. I will send out the suitcase for you to take home."

Telephone enquiries were discouraged, as Sister said that the 'phone bell disturbed the patients. Only the very brave, or very worried, rang more than once. Information was given only to the next of kin, and they were told,

"Your relative is comfortable. There is no need to you to make further enquiries. Should you be needed, you will be summoned."

Visiting times she thought an unnecessary disruption to ward routine. Despite pressure from all sides, she limited visiting to an hour on Wednesday and Sunday afternoons. She justified her decision by saying,

"It does the patient no good at all to have visitors. They only get upset when the visitors go."

Of course they got upset. Most of them had both eyes bandaged, and had all day in which to lie in bed and think about whether or not their operation had been successful. It was only natural for them to look forward to the twice weekly visits, and since the visits were so short and so far apart, they must have felt abandoned when their families left.

Children were not allowed visitors at all. The poor child was taken from its mother at the ward door, and did not see her again until she came to take it home.

Sister genuinely thought that her way of running the ward was best. Nothing would convince her that perhaps there was a better way, or that modern drugs and treatments might be an improvement on the ones she had learnt to use during her training.

The Consultant in charge of the Eye department had died earlier in the summer, and a series of locums had kept the place going until a new one could be appointed. Sister was furious that she had not been asked to sit on the selection panel. The new Consultant, Dr. Majors, was doomed before he ever came to the ward. Without even having met him, she described him as,

"A young upstart, full of newfangled ideas."

He started work after I had been on the ward for a week. I felt so sorry for him. Every indirect insult possible was handed out.

Nothing was ready for him when he came to the ward to do his first Ward Round. Sister had shut herself in the bathroom with a patient, and he had to sit in her office and wait until she chose to emerge. He was not even offered a cup of coffee while he waited.

His request to be shown round the ward was rejected. Sister said that she had no time to waste on conducted tours. If he wanted to look round, then he might do so, but he would have to go alone.

Dr. Majors came out of the office looking angry. I was the nearest person to the office door. We'd all been standing in the corridor straining our ears to hear what was going on. I hadn't moved fast enough to get out of the way when we heard him get up.

"You. Come and show me round and tell me about the patients."

I was the last person to choose. I didn't even know all the patients' names, let alone what was wrong with them. I had spent most of the last week counting how many footsteps it took to get from one place to another. I explained that I was new to the ward, and didn't know the patients.

"Never mind. You must know more than I do."

I doubted it. I don't think he was very impressed!

When we reached the Operating Theatre, I thought he was going to explode. All the windows were wide open.

"What the Hell are they doing open?"

I could answer that question. I'd opened them.

"Sister told me to open them, Sir. She said the room smelt stale and needed airing."

He turned round and walked out. Nothing was seen of him for the rest of the day.

The following day, a patient was sent up from the Out-Patients Department. The letter she brought with her informed Sister that her name was Mrs. Barrett, and that she was to be ready for surgery at 9:00 A.M. the following day.

The letter also said that Dr. Majors himself would be up in the evening to see her, and to give her any medication he thought necessary. The bandage covering her left eye was not, under any circumstances, to be removed. He would prepare the Operating Theatre himself. All he needed was two competent nurses.

War had been declared. Sister had a patient she knew nothing about. She was furious, and she clinked about the ward in a frenzy.

Her anger had not diminished overnight. She sent me, still only a first year nurse, and a nurse just out of P.T.S. to the Theatre to help him. Neither of us had ever seen an operation before, never mind prepared a theatre. There was no way either of us could have been described as competent. Incompetent would have been a polite description!

Dr. Majors arrived at eight-thirty, bringing with him Sister Wood, one of the sisters from the main hospital Operating Theatres. I'd have loved to have seen Sister Eyes' face when she saw them arrive. She had met her match at last.

Neither Dr. Majors nor Sister Wood seemed at all perturbed that the nurses sent to help were worse than useless. We were set to work. The whole theatre was scrubbed, and with something he had brought with him, not carbolic.

While we were scrubbing the floor and the walls, he and Sister Wood boiled up instruments and unloaded dressing and towel drums from his car. He had brought everything he was going to use with him, even the sterile gowns and gloves.

When everything was ready, I was sent to collect Mrs. Barrett.

"Sit her in a wheelchair, and bring it as far as the door. She can walk the rest of the way."

There was no sign of Sister Eyes. I collected the patient, wheeled her up to the Theatre door, and then walked her to the operating table. Luckily she was fairly agile. Getting her on to it would have been difficult otherwise.

Once her bandage was removed it was obvious what she was going to have done. Her left eye was opaque with a cataract.

It was also obvious that the whole operation was a set up. Never before, or I would think, since, has a cataract been removed as a semi-emergency operation.

I found it fascinating. A squirt of local anaesthetic, a snick with the scalpel, a push on the side of the eyeball, and there it was, a nasty thick lens sitting on a piece of gauze. Two stitches in the side of the eye, and the job was done. Not a drop of blood to be seen.

My fascination must have been apparent. Dr. Majors handed me the lens and said that, as it was my first cataract, I could have it as a souvenir.

I put it in a match box and kept it for ages. Then as I moved it one day, it just disintegrated.

Mrs. Barrett was lifted off the operating table and returned to her bed. Instructions as to her nursing care were printed in capital letters on a single sheet of paper, and handed to Staff Nurse. Sister had shut herself in the office.

That afternoon, seven patients were admitted for surgery the next day. The hospital messenger brought a letter for Sister. We were all agog to know what was in it. It was rather an anti-climax when she emerged from her office and pinned it on the notice board. It only said that Dr. Majors would be operating full time for the next two days. Nurses Wallinger and Arnold were to have their off-duty rearranged so that they could assist in Theatre.

Dr. Majors had won the first round.

For me, the next two days were bliss. In between the operations, we scrubbed walls and floors. The theatre had never been so clean.

Sister Eyes ignored us, and even went so far as to put a line through our names on the off duty list. As far as she was concerned, we no longer worked on her ward. That suited me fine.

I was a bit concerned about not having any off-duty though. Sister Wood promised that she would see Matron, and get something sorted out. Matron decided that it would be best for Arnold and myself to work a straight day, 7:30 A.M. to 5:30 P.M., Monday to Friday, then work a half a day on Saturday and have Sunday off. We were to work full time in the Eye Theatre.

It was at that point that I started to feel sorry for Sister Eyes. She had reigned supreme in her little kingdom for the last thirty seven years. It couldn't be long before she was due to retire. Why not let the old dear work the rest of her days in peace?

The sole topic of conversation in the Home was the "Eye War." Everyone took sides. Those that had worked on Eyes took Dr. Majors' side. Those that hadn't, took Sister's. Being stuck in the middle, I kept quiet, and for once in my life I tried to keep out of the controversy. I might just as well have joined in and had my say, because each side accused me of sympathising with the other.

I just wanted to be left alone to get on with the job, and that became more difficult as the week went on.

Sister was being as obstructive as only she knew how. Patients were not ready for us, and we spent hours standing around waiting. The crunch came on Thursday.

A patient had been admitted the day before with a detached retina. The retina is the "screen" at the back of the eye onto which light is focused. Very occasionally it becomes loose and the patient gradually goes blind. If caught in time it can be welded back in place.

Sister was of the opinion, having never seen it done, that such a thing was impossible. She lost no time in telling everyone it was a waste of time. She even told the patient, adding that he was being used as a guinea-pig.

Not unnaturally, he believed her, and refused to sign the form consenting to the operation.

Doctor spent half an hour with him, explaining that it was a new idea, and that he had performed several such operations, all of which had been successful. Eventually the patient agreed to the operation. By the time he was ready for surgery we were running two hours behind schedule.

Most of Dr. Majors' surgery was done under a local anaesthetic, but because of the length of time he expected to take over the retina, the patient was to be given a general anaesthetic. The anaesthetist was not happy at being kept waiting for two hours. Tempers became a little frayed.

We had been told that, once the operation started, we would be on our feet for four hours. That was fine for Arnold and myself as we would be able to move about, but Doctor and Sister would be standing still. I did not envy them their job. Dr. Majors had described to us what he was going to do. He likened it to gluing a cobweb onto the inside of a ping-pong ball with sewing needles as tweezers. He also warned us that he was likely to lose his temper if we made a mistake.

No sooner had he made the access hole in the eye ball, than the gardener started mowing the grass under the window with a motor mower. I am sure that sister had nothing to do with it. The man just thought that it was time the grass was cut, and cut it. The noise from the mower made life very difficult. Doctor had to shout to make himself heard every time he wanted something.

Calm prevailed in Theatre until the patient was returned to his bed. Then the storm broke. Matron was ordered to the ward. We couldn't help but overhear the telephone conversation. The 'phone was only just outside the theatre door, and by some strange chance, something had got stuck underneath the door wedging it open a crack!

We didn't have to resort to eavesdropping when she arrived. I reckon Dr. Majors could have been heard down by the main gates. Unfortunately, Matron didn't raise her voice. Only hearing one side of an argument is very unsatisfactory.

I thought that his demands were reasonable enough. He wanted a ward staff as competent as his theatre team. Arnold and I were very smug after that. We had been described as competent, and to Matron at that!

It took a while for the dust to settle. Then it was back to the cataract removals. Nothing went right for the rest of that day, and we got more and more behind. By the time we had cleared up, it was nearly eleven o'clock at night. The day staff were long gone by the time we emerged.

We heard the news at breakfast the next morning. Poor old Sister Eyes had heard every word Dr. Majors had said. Not waiting to see Matron, she had left the ward. There were several versions. Some said she had left in tears, some in a temper. All versions agreed she had ridden off into the night on her bike. The only person to mourn her passing was the ward maid.

Selfishly, my immediate concern was the loss of the bike.

When we reached the ward, we found it was true. Sister Eyes had left. Matron and the Hospital Secretary had spent all evening packing up the junk from Sister's office into boxes, and carted it away.

I found the whole incident very upsetting. For the first time in my life I had seen a battle for power. I could sympathise with both sides. I wanted them both to win. Arbitration was unheard of then. There were no compromises, only winners and losers.

The ward was not the same without her clinking about.

Staff Nurse ensconced herself in the office and started acting just like Sister! She even managed to clink as she walked. It was obvious that nothing was going to change.

Matron sent a message asking to see Staff Nurse, and off she went, confident that she would inherit the crown.

When we left the ward at five-thirty, she was still not back. No one knew what was happening, and we still hadn't heard by Sunday evening. Once again the Eye Ward was the centre of conversation at meal times. At least it made a change from the weather.

Monday morning, all was revealed. Arnold and I were a bit surprised when Sister Wood did not come on duty. We decided she had missed the bus and was coming up with Doctor, or maybe he'd changed his mind and was not going to operate today after all. Since no one ever thought to tell junior nurses anything, we didn't worry a lot.

A least we were insulated from the fracas out in the ward. No one from the ward was allowed past the outer room doors. A large sign had appeared saying, "Theatre Staff Only Beyond This Point."

Arnold and I saw that it was strictly adhered to. We didn't want anyone with germ ridden feet stomping about over our sterile floors.

There was definitely something going on, we could tell that by the change in the noise pattern coming from the corridor. By eight-thirty we would not wait any longer. We had to know what was happening. I changed my shoes and went along to the loo. The nurses were all busy in the ward. That in itself was strange. There was usually someone in the cloakroom.

Mindful of the fact that we might be having our first patient at nine, I went back to theatre, having learnt nothing. I was getting jolly bored with cataracts by that time, and we had a glaucoma on the operating list. Sister had also promised that I could "Scrub", (assist during the operation by handing the instruments to Doctor) so I was hoping that we were going to operate.

Sister Wood arrived at last, so we finished off the preparations for the morning's list.

Dr. Majors breezed in well before nine.

"Right girls, let's go!"

The first surprise came when a couple of porters brought in the first patient. They were even wearing theatre gowns, hats, masks and boots. The work load was suddenly halved. I was disappointed in the glaucoma. It was even more simple than the cataract operations, but at least I had acted as Scrub Nurse. By 11 o'clock we had finished.

Then came the second shock. One of the porters brought in a tray of coffee with four cups!

Feeling brave I asked,

"Doctor, do you know who is going to be appointed as Sister Eyes?"

The infuriating man just said "Yes. Ask Sister Wood. She'll tell you. She knows the new Sister well."

Sister Wood glared at him, and replied, "No one is supposed to know until Matron publishes the Change List. Until then, I am here in charge of the Theatre. If I have any free time, I will spend it on the ward."

Arnold, bless her, asked,

"What happens when the Change List goes up?"

"Then, I officially become Sister in Charge of the Eye Department. I warn you now, the first person to call me Sister Eyes, gets a kick in the backside. If either of you tell a soul, the first thing I do as Sister on this ward will be to have you moved."

The wind of change was beginning to blow. The change list was hardly up before the rumours started. Sister Wood was Dr. Majors' mistress/ wife/ sister. Every form of relationship except mother!

None of the senior staff nurses wanted to accept the fact that Matron had simply appointed the only nurse in the hospital with an Ophthalmic Certificate. To be fair, not many of them knew that Sister Wood had worked at Moorfields, the London eye hospital, and was a very experienced ophthalmic nurse.

All they could see was that she was young, and had trained *somewhere else*. How were standards to be maintained when just anyone could become a Ward Sister?

The last time a "foreigner" had been appointed as a Ward Sister was in the forties, and that was only because all the local nurses were fighting for their King and Country. (Or perhaps they had seen the war as a chance to escape from the confines of the hospital and find themselves a man!)

Sister Wood must have had a hard time. She was, rumour said, not yet thirty. She had only qualified in 1957, far too young and green to manage a busy ward. The youngest of the other ward sisters at the Annex had qualified in 1938!

It might have been said that they were too old and staid to run a ward.

Once the word got around that she refused to be called "Eyes" they had something else to worry about.

They were all convinced that the hospital was on a downhill path to ruin. Where would it all end? No discipline. No standards. What was the world coming to?

Arnold and I were in great demand. We were the only nurses at the Annex that had worked with her, and we had great fun telling the most appalling lies. Lies, I hasten to add, that had been suggested to us by Sister Wood.

Even with her sense of humour, Sister couldn't cope with living in the Sisters' Home. She did the only thing possible in the circumstances.

She got herself a flat and moved out.

CHAPTER TWELVE

Having Sister Wood in charge of Eyes meant that Arnold and I had to go back to the ward. The department was again run as a single unit. Our spell as full-time theatre nurses was over.

I was glad to be back with patients again. I'd liked working in the Ophthalmic Theatre, but a week of it was enough.

Once Sister Wood was officially in charge, things started to happen. Her first morning was spent ringing all the patients' next of kin and telling them that the visiting hours had changed. Visitors were to be allowed from 2 to 4 every afternoon, and from 7 to 8 in the evenings.

That met with the patients' approval, but strangely, not as much as the introduction of radios. Somehow, Sister managed to get hold of two wireless sets, one for each of the wards. The women chose the Light Programme, but the men opted for the Home service. (Now known as Radio One and Radio Four.) Apathy and boredom vanished, even among the staff.

After a few days a twice daily visiting, I could see why Sister Eyes had been so anti-visitor. For a start, three hours disappeared from our working day. All the treatments had to be done before the visitors arrived, as well as getting the patients and their beds tidy. That meant two more bed-making sessions each day.

On top of that, as teas were served to the patients during afternoon visiting, Sister thought it would be nice if we offered the visitors a cup of tea at the same time. It was a nice idea, and the visitors were very appreciative. Annie, the ward maid, threw a fit. Her basic complaint being that she had far too much to do already. In fact she did very little. It was a wonder the patients didn't all die of salmonella, as the ward kitchen was filthy.

The first afternoon that we offered the visitors cups of tea, I collected up the dirty cups and wheeled the trolley into the kitchen. Annie informed me that she was not going to do the washing up; as I had dirtied the cups I could wash them. My temper has always had a short fuse, and it had been a trying day. I was not going to be told what to do by Annie, and I said so. Annie walked out, and I was left to wash the cups. Having washed up, I spent half an hour cleaning the sink and scrubbing the draining board. I used a whole tub of Vim on the sink before I removed the layers of grease, and a bottle of peroxide on the draining board before the wood came clean. I was very pleased with myself. I thought I had managed to score a point over Annie.

Most of the maids had been on the same ward since they had first come to work at the hospital, and had become very insular. They were responsible for the cleaning of the floors in the ward and all the kitchen cleaning, we did all the rest of the ward.

The good ones were great, and most of them were good. They kept their wards spotlessly clean, acted as surrogate mothers to patients and nurses, and were not above reading the riot act to a sister if they thought she deserved it. The bad ones were awful – lazy, bad tempered, and apt to run to Matron threatening to leave if someone upset them.

As soon as Annie saw *her* sink, she went straight to Matron. I was given a lecture and told to watch my temper or I would be in very serious trouble. Wards, Matron said, could not be run without the maids.

Since the maids all had Sunday off each week, and we managed very well without them then, I couldn't see that as a valid argument. However, I had the sense to keep that observation to myself. Determined to get even with Annie, I declared my own private war on her and did all I could to make her life hell.

Apart from the battle of wits with Annie, life generally was not so different under the new management. The ward routine was unchanged; the patients had the same treatments as before; there was just a different person in charge.

I kept thinking of all the changes I would have made if I had been Sister. Luckily, Sister was not a thought-reader, and went on her own merry way. The reason nothing had changed was son obvious.

Sister wanted to bring the ward up to date and banish some of the more outdated equipment. Before she could do this, first Matron had to agree, then the tutors were consulted. All that took a month.

Gradually things changed. Mostly they were small things that made our life easier, but there were three major changes. The first did not really affect the nurses a great deal. The patients started to get daily visits from one of the housemen. Housemen had long ago been banished by "Eyes" as being totally incompetent. The only doctors she would allow on the ward were consultants.

Being seen every day by a doctor made a great deal of difference to the patients, even if he did come from the geriatric department. They were not bothered that he knew little about eyes. To the patients, he was a doctor, and that was enough.

The second change saved us a great deal of time. It was the introduction to the ward, and to the hospital, of urine testing tablets. Instead of boiling and mixing urine samples to test for sugar, all we had to do was put five drops of urine in a test tube, add ten drops of water, drop in a tablet, and wait for one minute. The test for acetone was even easier. All that needed was a few drops of urine onto a tablet.

Charts were supplied with the testing kits. You simply carried out the test, then held the test tube against the chart to compare colours. It was al so easy.

Now, even that seems totally old-fashioned. Today, one simply removes a plastic stick from a bottle, dips it in the sample, then reads the result from the side of the bottle.

I found that there was a slight problem at first with the test for sugar. As one dropped the tablet into the solution of water and urine, there was a violent chemical reaction, and the liquid tended to boil out all over the place. The test tube also became very hot. It didn't take me long to learn that it was easier, and less painful, to take the chart to the tube, than the tube to the chart.

The third of the changes caused the most controversy. We started to use disposable syringes. The case for was that they were more hygienic and saved time; the case against was that they were light, and it was difficult to expel the air that invariably entered the syringe.

I am now ashamed to admit, that I was firmly against the change. I could not get used to the feel of them. They were made of plastic, and compared to glass syringes weighed nothing. One had to put weight behind them to get the needle under the skin.

Expelling air from the glass syringes was easy, but the air stuck to the sides of the plastic ones, and still does for that matter.

I decided they were not worth the extra effort, and since the night staff had to do the cleaning and packing, I could not see that they saved me any time at all.

I continued to use the old one until Sister Wood lost patience with me and banned the use of glass syringes. Rather than give in, I simply avoided giving injections. I thought myself rather clever, until she asked me why I was being so stupid.

I was then forced to admit that I did not like the feel of the needle going into skin. It gave me goose pimples.

"Right. That's easily solved. I'll teach you how to give an injection." was her immediate reply.

I thought I already knew, but since she was in one of her very bad moods, I did not dare to argue.

To say the least, Sister Wood's technique was different form any I had seen before.

"First wipe the skin. Then hold the syringe with the needle pointing toward the injection site, like you would hold a dart."

Fine. I knew what a dart looked like, I'd even thrown one. I could see some of the more refined young ladies having trouble though!

"Then you give the skin a sharp slap, and throw the syringe. Just like you would a dart. Simple."

She stood over me whilst I did it, and she was right. I have used the same method ever since, except when taking exams. I reasoned that, as it was not the approved method, it would probably cause me to fail.

It has the added advantage that the patient is so surprised at the slap, that he relaxes the muscle. Before he has a chance to tense, the needle has found its mark. The difficult bit is knowing just how hard to slap!

Having converted us to using disposable syringes, Sister started on her next change. Instead of us all looking after all the patients, we were each given the total care of a few.

I was responsible for one side of the men's ward, eight beds in all. Each side of the ward was arranged so that we had a mixture of double-padded, single-padded, and sighted patients.

We looked after them from admission to discharge. If our patient had an operation, then we went to theatre and helped. Sister expected us to know everything about our patients, not just their diagnosis and treatment. We had to know their hobbies, likes, dislikes, even the names of their children.

Each ward had a relief nurse to cover the off-duty periods, and after a few teething troubles, the new system worked to everyone's advantage.

The "blind" patients gained most, as they knew who would come if they called, and that their nurse was always within calling distance.

It was such a simple system; I could not understand why no one else had thought of it. In 1982 I attended a conference on the "Introduction of the Nursing Process", only to find that it was a similar system to that which Sister Wood had introduced. Not bad. Seventeen years for it to become recognised, adopted, and given a fancy title.

"My" men were a mixed bunch. I had two cataract patients, two glaucomas and the detached retina that I had seen repaired. The rest of the beds were empty. Five patients do not sound many, but none of them were allowed out of bed. The two cataract patients were double-padded so had to be washed and fed. The others just had one eye padded, so were reasonably self-sufficient.

My main concern was to keep all five of them from moving. For the first week following eye surgery, patients were kept flat on their backs to enable the cut in the eye to heal. The second week they were propped up on pillows, but were not allowed out of bed until after the tenth day, when the stitches were removed.

I was glad that I had men to look after. They moaned a bit about having to keep still, but at least they did as they were told. They were allowed to lay on their sides to eat and drink, but that was all. The rest of the time they had to lay flat.

Once their stitches came out, life improved for them. Although the patients that had cataracts removed had to keep pads on their eyes for another week, they were at least allowed out of bed.

The lessons I had learned on my first morning were invaluable at this stage. I knew the best way to lead a patient round the ward. I knew exactly how many steps it took to get from place to place. Having lain in a bed double-padded, I was at least able to imagine roughly how they were feeling.

I was very proud of my men and had soon established a daily routine. There was no wasted effort at all, neither mine nor my patients'. I had plenty of spare time to talk to them, and to plot Annie's downfall. I devised a master plan. I was going to wash part of the kitchen floor, just to show how dirty it was.

The following Sunday, I swung into action. Just how I was going to find an excuse to wash the floor I hadn't considered, but fate stepped in and helped. Sister dropped the gravy container as she was giving out the dinners. The spillage rapidly congealed, as only hospital gravy can, forming a nasty gooey mess. Attempts to wipe it up resulted in an even nastier mess, so I volunteered to wash the floor.

Out came the scrubbing brush. It had taken me three days of searching to find out where it was hidden. The floor was covered in large cork tiles, and they had become black over the years. The few I scrubbed looked rather nice, but the difference was not marked enough to satisfy me, so I poured neat peroxide on them.

Hydrogen peroxide is marvellous stuff. I forget what we were supposed to use it for, but there were always bottles of it in the lotion cupboard. It disposed of the most difficult of stains, and the tiles I had treated were almost white. I was well pleased. Annie couldn't help but notice, as the clean bit was just inside the door. She would have to scrub the rest of the floor to match.

Not Annie, she went straight to Matron. I get into a terrific row, worsened by the fact that the peroxide had eaten holes in the hem of my apron. Annie banned me from the kitchen. That was fine by me, as I didn't have to do the washing up when she was off duty. However, it made getting drinks for my men difficult.

Sister solved the problem and moved me into the Children's Ward. Round one to Annie.

Most of the children had their mothers staying with them all day, so there was not a great deal to do except supervise the mothers and play with the children. The days seemed very long. The admission of a baby eighteen months gave me more than enough to do. He had spent his life in a children's home, and was to be adopted after his operation. Adoption could not be arranged earlier as he had been born blind. Both his eyes were clouded by congenital cataracts, a condition rarely, if ever seen today. It was caused by venereal disease in his mother.

Even though he was heavily sedated, I had a full time job keeping him still until his stitches came out. The problems started when the pads came off his eyes. Small amounts of light had been able to enter his eyes before the operation, so he had probably been able to distinguish between dark and light. Suddenly he could see things moving about. He was terrified.

The only way I could stop him crying was to carry him. I found that if I sat him astride one hip, he could bury his face under my arm. He had the comfort of human contact, and could hide away from the world at the same time. Very gradually he became used to the outside world, and began to explore, reaching out to touch things. Eventually, he became adventurous and started to crawl around the ward. Soon he was declared ready for discharge.

I was devastated when he went back to the Children's Home. I consoled myself with the thought that it would not be for long, as the home had already found prospective adoptive parents for him. Just before I left Eyes, he was re-admitted for a day to be fitted with spectacles. He came with his new parents, and did not need me at all. I felt very jealous.

As October gave way to November, there was a general clear out of the ward. Beds would be needed for November the fifth, bonfire night. Any patient that could be sent home was. The theatre was prepared ready to cope with any emergency, and we were taught the basic emergency treatments.

People with damaged eyes were generally brought straight to us rather than casualty, but we only had the occasional patient with scratched eyes or foreign bodies, nothing that washing out the eye and a pad and bandage couldn't put right.

The fifth of November was very different. The ambulances started to arrive soon after the children came out of school, eyes burnt by sparks, being the most common cause for admission. The children's ward soon filled, and the overflow went into the adult wards.

Just was we were going off duty at 8:30 P.M. we had the worst case of the day. A young lad of nineteen had been helping at a bonfire party. He had seen a group of boys put an un-opened tin of beans in the ashes to heat. Realising the danger, he tried to hook it out. As he did so, it exploded.

There were beans embedded in one of his eyes. Luckily, he had stood sideways onto the fire, and only one of his eyes had been hit. The pieces of the tin had also missed him. I saw the beginnings of the operation to remove his eye. I started to feel sick as the remains of his eye were scooped out, then the world went black! By the time I recovered from my faint, the lad was back in the ward.

I have never, since then, attended a bonfire party. My own son was eight before a family friend managed to sneak some fireworks into the garden for him to see. I was relieved that he was not at all impressed by them.

The walk to and fro to the Home had become a bind. Winter was rapidly approaching, and the days were getting shorter, colder and wetter. The fact that generations of nurses had put up with the trek did not console me at all. Apart from having to walk through the rain, and so get wet, we had only forty-five minutes for our dinner break. It took us fifteen minutes to walk to the dining room. Thus, we had only fifteen minutes in which to eat our meal before setting off on the return journey.

I used to enjoy meal times, as they were a chance to sit down for a while and relax. Not any more. Food had to be bolted or not eaten at all. I gradually became faster at eating, and by the time I had finished working at the Annex, I could even find time for a cup of coffee.

It took me a lot longer to re-learn the art of eating slowly. Years later, my husband used to refuse invitations to dinner parties, because I would have finished my soup before anyone else had picked up their spoon. I solved the problem by waiting until the other guests had nearly finished before I started.

Despite my constant complaints, nothing was done about the walk. We would arrive on duty like drowned rats, spend the morning drying out, only to get wet again at dinner time. In a fit of desperation, and as there were no unions locally, I wrote to the Royal College of Nursing. The R.C.N. suggested I join the Student Nurses Association, a body claiming to uphold the rights of the student nurse.

What rights, I asked myself? None the less I joined, and proudly pinned my S.N.A. badge to the collar of my cloak. It hadn't been there for a day, when I was summoned to Matron's office. You would have thought I had joined the Nazi Party. She went on and on. I couldn't see what had upset her so much. The Students in some hospitals all belonged to the S.N.A., which was after all a branch of the R.C.N. Even she had an R.C.N. badge on her cloak.

Had she ignored my stand against oppression, I'm sure I would soon have got bored, and forgot about it, but being told that I was not to renew my membership annoyed me.

I sent for a pile of application forms, and set about convincing other students that they should join. The Annex rapidly became a stronghold of the S.N.A.. I spent more and more time in Matron's Office. The interviews always followed the same pattern.

"Nurse, unless you desist from this disruptive behavior, I will be forced to consider disciplinary action."

I was merely trying to get enough students to join so that we could be a strong group, able to effect some changes. I didn't want to change the world. I was just fed up with being wet all day.

The day came when most of the Annex students were S.N.A. members. We held a meeting and wrote to Matron listing our complaints, asking that something be done. I had the sense to send a copy of the letter to the local R.C.N. representative, Sister Wood!

Within a week I received an answer. The Annex nurses were to have one hour for dinner, and they would be allowed to wear navy blue gaberdine raincoats or dark blue duffle coats when walking to and from the wards.

I declared the battle a draw. Whilst we had won an extra quarter of an hour for dinner, none of us could afford to buy a coat. We only just managed to afford to buy stockings. £7 does not go very far in a month when stocking are 5 shillings and 11 pence a pair. (30p) I calculated that it would take me about three years to save the money for a coat.

Home Sister came to the rescue, and started visiting jumble sales for us. Nearly every week she managed to find at least one coat. The most expensive one she found was 7 shillings and 6 pence. (37.5p) She even let us have them on hire purchase, paying her a shilling a month. (5p)

The difference the coats made was staggering. We arrived on duty dry. A coat also gives much better protection from the wind than a cloak, which flaps about in the wind. I was very proud of my second-hand duffle coat. It represented my first triumph over authority. I found it the other day when I was clearing out a cupboard. Twenty-four years has not improved it much, but I couldn't bring myself to throw it away.

Annie was not so easily beaten. She refused to have wet coats dripping all over her floors. Yet again I went to see Matron. This time I was determined to win. I had heard Annie complaining about the coats, and so I carefully prepared my argument. There was no difference, as far as I could see, between the water coming out of a coat, and the water coming out of a wet cloak.

Matron agreed. Round two to me.

I was beginning to lose interest in the war with Annie. I had more than enough to occupy me. The preliminary exams were getting frighteningly close. I knew that I had to get a good pass mark in the hospital exam, or I would get the sack. I had caused Matron a lot of bother in the last few weeks, and felt that she would not need too much of an excuse to get rid of me.

I had been on Eyes for nearly three months, and was due to be moved. I was a little concerned about where Matron would send me next. I had a feeling I would be sent to the geriatric wards. That was what usually happened to dissenters. A few weeks of wet beds and heavy patients had the effect of bringing most people to heel.

I was right. I was to move from Eyes to Female Geriatric at the end of November. I would be on the geriatric ward for Christmas. Two things kept me from resigning, one was the knowledge that it would only be for a few weeks. We were due to go back into school at the beginning of January, and Matron still owed me two weeks holiday. The second was that Matron wanted rid of me. I would stay to spite her.

CHAPTER THIRTEEN

It took me a couple of weeks to get used to nursing elderly people. The whole concept of geriatric nursing was so different from anything I had done before. These patients were never going home, either because they no longer had a home, or were beyond the care of their relatives.

Geriatric care is now a separate discipline, with a full medical team supported by day care units, physiotherapists, occupational and speech therapists. Money, a lot of money, is spent on improving the lives of our elderly. They are no longer herded into old workhouses to await the release of death. Geriatric units are now wards for the treatment of elderly patients, and I would think that the number treated in the course of a year is only slightly lower than that of a general medical ward.

How different it was then. The first thing that hit me as I went into the ward was the smell. Our cowshed smelt better. The place stank of urine. The ward housed twenty women, the youngest being seventy-eight.

None of them were able to walk unaided, few could feed themselves, and most of them were incontinent.

Yet, after the initial shock, I began to think that it wasn't such a bad ward after all. It was heavy, in the true sense of the word. Each one of the old dears had to be lifted out of bed every day and sat in a chair. They had to be lifted from the chair to the commode, lifted in and out of the bath, and lifted back into bed. The beds were not the modern type that one can raise and lower. These were fixed and high, and they all had cot sides attached to them.

The cot sides were fine when pulled up, but we had to lower them to attend to the patients. Then they were pain. My ankles kept colliding with the lower rail, and my stockings suffered as a result. Luckily it was winter, and woollen stockings were repairable.

The nearest thing we had to a hoist was a bent pole at the top of each bed. This hung forward over the bed, and had a thing like a parrot's perch dangling form it. In theory, the patient pulled herself up by holding on to the perch. In practice, the poles swung round, catching the unwary nurse on the side of the head.

It was easy to get a patient out of bed; we had gravity on our side. Getting them back in, gravity was against us. It could all have been sordid and undignified for the ladies, (Sister did not like them referred to as patients) yet somehow we managed to preserve some of their self-respect, often at the expense of our dignity.

We had one patient that had only the use of her right hand, and she was heavy, very heavy. To get her into bed, we lifted her, and sat her on the side of it. Then one nurse held on to her while the second ran round to the other side of the bed. Kneeling on the side of the bed, the second nurse lent forward, grasped her under the armpits and hauled her backwards, so that her bottom was in the middle of the bed. At the same time, the other nurse lifted the patient's legs, and swung them into the bed.

It was very difficult to do this without the patient overbalancing and falling backwards, trapping the unfortunate nurse underneath. There was no way one could remain dignified when squashed between the patient and the pillows, especially when the patients had wet herself with laughter.

The first week nearly killed me; I ached all over. I used to almost crawl up to my room each evening and collapse onto my bed.

Gradually I got used to the smell, and in the end didn't notice it at all. I knew that it was me getting used to it, rather than it going away. The other nurses never came near us "Geriatric Nurses" at meal time, they said our smell put them off their food!

Most of the staff on the ward were permanent. Student nurses were not required to work on the geriatric wards as part of their training, so it was unusual for there to be two students. Both of us were there because we had fallen foul of Matron.

Sister was the only S.R.N., the rest of the staff being Enrolled Nurses, only one of whom had done any training. The others had been Nursing Assistants during the war, and had been given State Enrolled Nurse status after the armistice.

Most of the staff, including Sister, had been on the ward sine it opened in 1950. A couple of the patients had been there that long as well.

Under those circumstances, and considering the work load, the place should have been depressing. However, it was one of the happiest wards I worked on during my training. The ladies tended to treat the nurses as their family. Most of them still had relatives living, but few had visitors. I commented on the lack of visitors one day. Sister's answer struck me as being rather cynical, but, as I found out later, was true.

"You wait until one of them dies. The relatives appear like wasps round a jam jar, weeping and wailing, just in case the old dears have left any money."

There was no rush. If the baths didn't get done one day, there was always the next, or the next. Most of them hated being bathed anyway, and we would spend longer in persuading them to come to the bathroom than it actually took to do the bath.

I didn't blame them in the least; I hated doing the baths myself. For a start, there was no heat in the bathroom. The ward was heated by two large coke burning stoves, one at each end, and whilst these kept the main ward warm, the heat never reached the bathroom. Then there was the trauma of the bath itself.

Having undressed the patient in the ward, we sat her in a wheeled chair, covered her with a blanket and pushed her into the bathroom. There were two methods of transferring the patient from the chair to the bath.

One: we stood her up. Then three of us, one at each end and one in the middle, lifted her and lowered (or, as frequently happened, dropped) her into the water.

Two: we stood her up and swung her round so that she was sitting on a plank placed across the bath. Then we launched her into the water.

By the time the poor old soul had been washed and then hauled back out, we were all exhausted. The nurses were often wetter than the patient.

There did not appear to be a great deal of routine either. The day just happened. One morning Sister would decide that it was time we did some baths, another that we should turn mattresses or clean out bedside lockers. The only things that happened at the same time each day were meals, and that was because Gladys, the ward maid, took charge of them.

It wasn't that Sister was vague; well, not entirely, but she tended to become involved in things, and the ward work was forgotten.

For some obscure reason, Sister had decided that for Christmas, the ward was going to be decorated as a tropical island. Sister suddenly realised that there were only three weeks to go, and the island was still at the planning stage. Panic set in and we were all set to work.

Yards of crepe paper were cut to resemble palm leaves. Two long cardboard tubes, from the inside of rolls of carpet, were covered in brown crepe paper to from the tree trunks. As these rolls were heavy, it was impossible for the patients to manage them. Yet another job for the nurses.

A shop in town had loaned one of its display dummies, and this was to be dressed in a grass skirt and a necklace of paper flowers.

What the ladies lacked in expertise, they made up for in enthusiasm, and paper flew in all directions.

Ten days before Christmas, the trees were finished and the dummy dressed. Now the Christmas decorations were complete, perhaps we might even be able to get on and do a few more baths.

No chance. Ten more days gave us time to create an even more elaborate island. Yards more paper, and a grass hut appeared. Then some idiot thought that it would be nice to have a few birds about.

"Peacocks." said Sister. "I know just the thing." She rushed off out, and was not seen for the rest of the day. The next morning, with eight days to go, we were presented with rolls of very second-hand small mesh wire, and yards and yards of brightly coloured net material, the sort that ballroom dancers wear as petticoats.

The wire had to be fashioned to resemble a peacock, then covered with the material. Sister must have been watching *Blue Peter*. Wire bending was beyond the patients, so, once again, it was up to the nurses. If you have ever tried to make rusty wire look like anything other than rusty wire, you will appreciate our difficulty. As soon as we had made a shape even vaguely resembling a bird, it was whisked away and given to the patients to cover. they threaded the net through the holes in the wire, and surprisingly, the effect was quite convincing. Between us, we managed ten colourful, if somewhat odd shaped, birds that were easily recognised as peacocks because of their large and gaudy tails.

Christmas Eve had been set aside for the building of the island. The hut was no problem; we had already assembled that in the storeroom. We stood the dummy outside the hut; it looked great. Then came the trees. Now, a cardboard tube will not stand up unless it is supported. However hard we tried, the damn things just fell over.

How we missed flattening any of the patients I'll never know. Advice flew in all directions, and so did the paper off the trees.

The ever-practical Gladys saved the day. She pointed out that all we needed to do was to tie the trees to the beds. Then they would stand up. Magic. There was our island, palm trees, peacocks, dusky maiden, and two old ladies; beds and all. Not for us Christmas trees and fairy lights.

The trees must have been fairly lifelike. Sister had a Pekinese dog, named Fang. He was so called because of his habit of sinking his teeth into nurses! Never patients, just nurses. Fang was allowed to wander around the ward, and he cocked his leg on the trees so often that the bases went soggy and they started to list.

I hated that dog, almost as much as he hated me. He was fat, pampered, smelly, and the ward pet. On nice sunny days, when I would have enjoyed taking him for a walk, he would curl up on one of the beds and sleep all day. As soon as it was wet, windy and cold, he would decide to break the habits of a lifetime and want to go out for a pee. It was always me, being the youngest, that had to take him out for walk. When I arrived back, cold and wet, I had to towel him dry in case he caught a cold.

I wouldn't have minded so much if he had been house-trained, but he was as incontinent as the patients. It was bad enough having to clear up after them; at least one knew which of the beds or chairs was likely to be wet. One only found where the dog had been by accident!

On the odd occasions that Matron came round, only twice in the five weeks I was there, Fang hid. He must have known that, had she seen him, Matron would have banned him. She must have known about him, if only because I always went past the offices when I took him for a walk. Perhaps she was afraid that if the dog went, Sister would go as well. It was hard to find staff willing to work on the geriatric wards.

Having decorated the ward, we hung a stocking at the end of each bed, ready for Father Christmas. In our spare time, mostly while off duty, we had made small gifts for the patients. There were twenty bags of peppermint creams, the only soft sweets we could think of that could be made in the ward kitchen.

Sister found us some old sheets, these we had cut up and made into lavender bags and handkerchiefs. The lavender had been picked from the hospital garden in the summer. Each hanky had an embroidered initial in one corner.

Long after we should have gone off duty, we were still on the ward, wrapping up parcels, then creeping back into the ward to put them in stockings.

When all the stockings were filled, I went back to my room to get ready for the carol singing. I think all hospitals have the same tradition; certainly all those I have worked in have. The nursing staff, usually led by the Matron, tour the wards late on Christmas Eve singing carols.

Matron was going to be at the Main Hospital, so our Home Sister deputised for her. We turned out cloaks inside out, so that we looked "Christmassy" and we carried an oil lantern. It was a very picturesque scene, all it needed was snow to make it perfect. We called at every ward and sang a carol.

Every ward, that is, except the geriatric wards. "Someone" in authority had decided that it was a waste of time going into the geriatric wards as the patients wouldn't have appreciated the carols.

It was the first time I had come across such an attitude, and it annoyed me that Sister just accepted it. I was still angry the next day, so I asked her why she did not insist on her ward being included in the round.

"I've long since given up being bothered by them." she said. "If they choose to see my patients as living dead, well that is their loss. I know what my ladies are really like. That is all that matters."

I didn't agree with her; I'd have fought for patient equality. I never was one for taking the line of least resistance.

There was no off-duty on Christmas day. We all worked from 7:30 A.M. until the night staff came on at 8:30 P.M. It would have been unfair for any one nurse to have the day off. It also meant that the workload was lightened because there were more of us there.

By 10 o'clock in the morning, all the ladies were sitting up in their chairs, and then the presents were opened. The pleasure they got from those few small gifts was most touching, and several times my eyes needed a surreptitious wipe!

One of the few regular visitors ran a television repair shop. He came twice a week to see his mother, and it the weather was nice, took her out for a drive on a Sunday afternoon. Sister had just happened to mention how nice it would be if the ladies could see the broadcast of the Queen's Speech.

On Christmas morning he appeared with a TV set as a present to the ward. It was far from new, but the excitement was terrific. The ward did not have a day room; each patient just say by her bed all day. In order to make a place for the television, with room to gather the patients round it, we spent the morning shifting beds closer together.

There had not been much room to start with, but by the time we had finished, we only had eighteen inches between each bed, just enough room for a bedside locker. We had achieved our object, we had a large clear area around one of the stoves at the end of the ward. It was just big enough to hold all the chairs and the television set, but it rather destroyed the effect created by the tropical island. There can't have been many grass huts with a TV set stood outside.

In case the set would not work when the time came for the Queen, we had a trial run. The set was ceremoniously switched on and warmed up. The plan had been to turn it straight off again, but there was a church service on. I stood and watched the ladies as they sat and took part in the service. They sang the carols and joined in the prayers as if their lives depended on it. I could not take it for very long. I found something to do in the sluice where I could vent my anger on the bedpans and have a good cry in peace.

These poor old souls had been left out of the carols on Christmas Eve, because "someone" had said they would not have appreciated them. Yet, there they were, singing their hearts out. I would dearly have liked to have had words with that "someone."

The same someone had decreed that the geriatric wards would receive their turkey ready-sliced. Not for us, the excitement of carving the bird. Nor were we to have Christmas pudding, goodness me no; it was far too rich for the poor thing's digestions. The kitchen had sent down jelly and ice cream. I ask you. Jelly and ice cream for Christmas dinner!

Gladys saved the day, bless her heart. She had made a pudding at home and brought it in. Sister raided the medicine cupboard, and the medicinal brandy was ceremoniously poured over the pudding and set alight.

As the afternoon wore on, the excitement increased. Royalists all, they were impatient to see their Queen. Somehow, Sister had found, begged, borrowed or stolen a bottle of sherry, and more surprising, some sherry glasses. By 3 o'clock each patient and each nurse had a drink with which to taste the Queen's health. We all sat and listened to what the Queen had to say, then, at the end of the broadcast came the National Anthem. The sight of those ladies sitting to attention and signing *God Save The Queen* was too much for me. I fled back to the sluice.

I had never given much thought to Christmas before. At home we always had lots of presents; we ate our traditional dinner, then dozed in front of the fire until it was time to feed the animals and do the evening milking. Then Dad and my brother would disappear outside for a couple of hours. I don't ever remember volunteering to help.

I was pretty useless on the farm anyway. They would probably have declined the offer. Yet we were a close family, and at sometime during the day, we would see my Grandfather and the aunts and uncles that lived close by.

I felt very homesick, but at the same time, would not have left the ward to go home, had I been given the chance. I felt very angry. Most of the ladies on the ward had at least one relative living, and yet only three had visitors on Christmas day, and only six had received presents from relatives.

Had they been forgotten, or could their families not be bothered? Was it too much effort to get up from in front of the fire and visit Gran? Did they not feel any duty to their aging relative? A few minutes out of their day would have made such a difference.

I was busy banging bedpans around, my favourite method of releasing tension, when Sister came in.

"It doesn't do to get angry you know. People are basically selfish. As long as you feel that you have done all that you can to make this a happy day for our ladies, then you must be content. You will never change relatives, no matter how hard you try. Now, go and take Fang for a walk; work your temper off on him. It's cheaper than denting the bedpans."

I didn't really feel any better after the walk, but at least I had been out in the fresh air. After a day in the ward, I certainly needed it.

When I arrived back, the patients were being put to bed, a task we had complicated by squashing the beds so close together. Somehow we managed; we made sure we did. It would have been too much of a disappointment if there had not been room for the television set.

I wonder if there are any wards today that do not have a day room attached?

By the time everyone had been settled in bed, it was time to go off duty. I was exhausted. As I went round the ward saying goodnight, one of the ladies called me over. My heart sank; she either wanted a bedpan or it was too late, and there would be a wet bed to change.

"Thank you dear. That was the nicest Christmas I have had since my husband was taken."

As I joined the other nurses outside the ward I was glad it was dark. They wouldn't be able to see the tears rolling down my cheeks.

CHAPTER FOURTEEN

After the festivities of Christmas Day, Boxing day was something of an anti-climax. When I went on duty in the morning, the first thing I noticed were raised voices coming from Sister's Office. Not an unusual occurrence, the S.E.N. on duty with me that morning was always complaining about the night staff, and took every opportunity she could, to point out their failings.

S.E.N. Roberts' voice carried well. Used to raising her voice to patients, most of whom were hard of hearing, she shouted at everybody. Roberts was refusing to take the keys. She would not accept responsibility for the ward and the night staff would have to wait until Sister arrived at 8 o'clock. It was obvious that they had done something of which Sister would not approve, and they were going to have to tell her themselves.

I didn't take a lot of notice; I was used to Roberts and her funny ways. There were only two nurses in the whole hospital that she trusted. One was Sister and the other herself.

The season of goodwill was obviously over.

I collected the breakfast trolley from the kitchen and pushed it into the ward. I wasn't expecting any help for a while; the argument sounded as if it would continue until Sister arrived.

Then I noticed something really unusual. Above the usual ward aroma was a strong sickly, revolting smell. The patients seemed odd as well. Instead of sitting up waiting for their breakfast, many of them were fast asleep. I decided that they were all tired after the previous day's excitement, and started giving out the porridge. I didn't have much success. Seven of the ladies I could not wake up. One woke up briefly, declined food and was asleep again before I had reached the next bed.

The remaining twelve ladies were as normal, though complaining that the ward had been noisy all night. As I took the trolley back to the kitchen, Sister came in through the ward door.

She just stood by the door and sniffed. Then she walked into the ward and looked at every one of the ladies. Having completed her round, she stormed off into her office.

I took the cup of tea Gladys had poured me, but that had a funny taste; it tasted of the smell in the ward. I put the cup in the sink, and said to Gladys,

"Sorry, Glad, I can't drink that. It tastes revolting."

I waited for the lecture that was bound to come. Gladys had but one fault. She could not bear to see anything wasted and was constantly telling us that, in India, millions were starving while we threw away food. This morning even she was different; she just said,

"Paraldehyde."

I hadn't a clue what she was talking about, so I asked her what she meant.

"Dope. Them good-for-nothing girls have doped the ladies with paraldehyde. That's what the smell is. Sister will soon give them what for. You wait and see."

Gladys was right about the smell, and about Sister's reaction. No wonder Roberts had made the night staff wait. If she hadn't, then *she* would have been on the receiving end of the blast.

Apparently the ladies had given the night staff a hard time. Tired out after the excitement of Christmas, they had all been fast asleep well before the night nurses could give them their sleeping pills. By midnight most of the ladies had slept enough, and were wide awake. The unaccustomed rich food had them calling for bedpans or else simply soiling their beds.

The night nurse in charge decided that enough was enough and sedated the more troublesome ladies, using paraldehyde.

Of all the unpleasant drugs that I have had to use over the years, paraldehyde is the worst. As it was a powerful hypnotic without any side effects, it was freely prescribed, especially for sedating elderly patients. Apart from the smell of the stuff itself, it "scented" the patients' urine and so the smell lingered for days. It was very difficult to administer; it tasted as bad as it smelt, and so was given by injection. It had the ability to dissolve plastic syringes. Luckily it went out of fashion in the early seventies.

Sister's anger at the night staff was not helped by a message from matron's office, suggesting that the patients all had a light diet for a day, to give their stomachs a chance to recover.

No change was made to the ladies food. Sister simply said,

"If they don't like dirty beds they can work somewhere else. They should be used to them by now."

Since most of the day was spent in wiping bottoms, they probably had a point, but as it was only for one day a year, why worry.

In between cleaning up the patients, we had to clear away the decorations. All signs of Christmas had to be gone by the next day.

Sister had a phobia about throwing things away, so everything except the dummy was put in the storeroom. That had to be returned to the shop.

Most sisters were the same. They would never put anything in the bin, however useless it might appear, in case it came in handy one day. Ward storerooms were like Aladdin's cave, full of outdated equipment, past years' Christmas decorations, and scores of old knitted blankets that had been laundered one too often and had become "felted."

Having found that there was no way the tree, hut, and peacocks were going to fit, I decided to spend my afternoon off having a grand clear out. I thought that it would be safe to throw out some of the junk, as Sister was off duty for the afternoon.

I put a pile of rubbish by the dustbin, only to find that Sister had seen it on her way back and had rescued most of it. What she was going to do with a perished rubber air-cushion I could not imagine!

At the end of the day, all that was left of Christmas was the television, the day area that we had created, and the overwhelming smell of paraldehyde.

Life was never the same on the ward. Instead of sitting the ladies beside their beds, we sat them at the end of the ward, gathered around the television set. The set was not turned on until after dinner, so they sat and chatted to each other. I loved to eavesdrop on their conversations. Since they had all spent their lives locally, most of them had someone or something in common, and to hear them reliving past experiences was often very amusing.

Mrs. French, one of the more active ladies, was going out for the day on the following Saturday. Her granddaughter was getting married and she was going to the wedding. Before the advent of the Day Area no one was in the least bit bothered. Now it was a source of interest to them all. Past weddings were discussed at length, and Mrs. French received a lot of advice as to what she should wear.

Mrs. French had been a patient for ten years and her son and his wife came regularly to see her. They would often bring their children with them, so the bride was known to everyone. By the time that Mrs. French's grandson arrived at 2 o'clock to drive her to the wedding, she had collected a pile of goodwill messages to give to the bride.

We waved her off, and forgot about her. She was not expected back until after we had gone off duty. The ladies nearest the windows thought that they might be able to see the wedding cars go past the hospital gates on their way from the church to the reception, and for once, they took an interest in the traffic.

Long after the cars were due to have passed, they were still watching. Suddenly there was a commotion at the window. Two cars decorated with white ribbons were coming up the drive. The bride and groom had decided to call in and thank the ladies for the messages they had sent. They had left the reception and all their guests, bringing with them the best man, the bridesmaids, and an uncut tier of wedding cake.

By the time the cake had been cut and the couple toasted with the sherry left over from Christmas, there was hardly a dry eye in the ward, mine included.

I wondered what the night staff would have to say about that excitement.

The next day was my last on the geriatric ward. All I heard about that day was the wedding. Mrs. French was obliged to recount, again and again, every moment of the day. By the time I went off duty I was sick of hearing about it, I was almost glad that I was leaving the ward.

When I gave Sister my Schedule to sign, the only procedure that she could sign off was "The care of the incontinent patient." Sister said she was sorry to see me leave the ward, and hoped that I had not found the work too trying.

I was able to assure her that I had not, and that, in fact, I had enjoyed the short time I had been there. I volunteered to return if ever she was short of staff, if I could be spared from where I was working.

I might not have learnt very much that would count towards my training, but I *had* learnt a lot that was to stay with me for the rest of my career. I knew when I left the geriatric ward where my future lay. I wanted to nurse the elderly.

I was due two weeks' holiday. Then, when I returned it would be to Block, two weeks in school with hospital prelims at the beginning and State Prelims at the end. As it was Matron's weekend off, I had to wait until Monday to get my pass.

I was to see Matron at 8:30 A.M. at the main hospital. That meant I would have to catch the 7:30 bus, get my pass, go back to the Annex, change out of my uniform, pick up my case, then catch the bus back to town to get the train home. I decided to shorten the proceedings. I put all I would need for the journey in my duffle coat pocket, tucked my P.T.S. folder under one arm and held my cap in my hand. When I got off the bus, I crept into the Main Home and left my coat and folder outside the dining room. Then I put on my cap and waited outside Matron's office. I hoped that my lack of a cloak would go unnoticed. Matron didn't notice, but I certainly did; standing around outside her office I nearly froze to death.

With my pass I was given a lecture. My exams were due in a month's time. She said that I would have to suppress my militant tendencies and concentrate on my work etc. She went on for ages. I was beginning to think she had decided that I should work through my holiday when she handed me my pass, and I made my escape.

I collected my things form outside the dining room, and as soon as I was alone, whipped off my cap and stuffed it into my pocket, put my coat on and jumped on the first bus that went past. I'd done it. I was at the train station at least four hours earlier than I should have been, having committed the cardinal sin of leaving the hospital in uniform.

Once at home I spent my time trying to get rid of the smell of the ward and reading all my P.T.S. notes that I should have been learning over the past year. I had been a nurse for one year and the Preliminary exams were looming. I might have learnt a lot in that year, but I doubted whether the examiners would be impressed by any of it. All the facts they were likely to want were well buried in my subconscious.

The whether forecasts threatened snow. The thought of having to explain to Matron that I was late because of the snow, worried me a little, so I returned from my holiday on Saturday. Life on a farm in the depths if winter is not much fun, so I wasn't that bothered.

As I packed my uniform, I tried to keep it as smooth as possible. The last thing I wanted was the laundry complaining about screwed up aprons and caps. Questions might have been asked as to how they came to be in such a state!

I had chosen to remain at the Annex Home for the two weeks of Block, going to and fro each day on the hospital bus. The food was better at the Annex, and as Home Sister had told me that she had "heard from a little bird" that I would be at the Annex for the next three months at least, I didn't see the point of moving home just for two weeks.

I was the only one of our set to be living in the Annex then, the other two that were working there had chosen to travel up each day. They must have spent more time on the bus than they did in their rooms when they had a split shift!

I was definitely not looking forward to the next two weeks. For one thing, we would be having Sister Tutor teaching us, and for another it was exam time. My total lack of studying would be apparent for all to see. Matron, I decided, would really enjoy telling me that I was to leave. She'd been looking for an excuse to get rid of me for the last three months.

Sister Tutor was an unknown quantity as far as I was concerned. She had assumed responsibility for our training at the end of our first ward. We saw nothing of her whilst on nights, and from then on, I'd been at the Annex. As she never set foot outside the hospital, it was left to the ward sisters up there to take over our tuition.

Sister Tutor was definitely one of Flo's nurses. A small round woman in her sixties, she lost no time in telling us that, as a small child, she had been taken to see Miss Nightingale. Although nearly ninety, Miss Nightingale had been very kind to her, and told her that she should be a nurse when she grew up. One of her proudest possessions was a letter with Flo's signature on it.

Sister Tutor knew all about us it seemed, and as others handed her their Schedules, she had some comment to make about their work over the last year. I wondered what comment I would get. She must have heard something of my doings over the last three months, even if I had been well out of her way.

She looked at me for a while then said,

"Poor lamb, he was such a nice boy. You can't have enjoyed your time on Ward Eight, such a shame. Never mind, you will just have to settle down now and work."

Perhaps she hadn't heard of my recent exploits, or perhaps she had just put it down to my having had a difficult time on Ward Eight.

The main object of this period in school was to get us through our exams. The first day was to be general revision. The next day we were to take our hospital written exams, and the day after we would be divided into pairs to take a practical exam. Great! Straight off the wards and into the exam room. Matron was going to love me when she saw my results; I was sure that I would be giving her the chance she had been waiting for.

All day, we were bombarded with long forgotten facts, but put in such a nice way that we were able to remember them. Sister Tutor would say,

"I'm sure you remember," or "As I am sure you are aware."

At the end of the day, I was a little more confident than I had been in the morning. Not a lot, but enough to convince me that I probable knew enough to get through.

There were to be two written papers. The morning one was to last two and a half hours, and contain questions on anatomy. The afternoon paper was only two hours and was going to be the difficult one. It was on the Nursing Theory. I could probably remember enough anatomy from school to get by, enough at least to get the 50% pass mark. That would give me time to swot up ready for the State exam. I would just have to rely on luck for the afternoon paper.

The Practical was another matter. I had no background knowledge to fall back on. All my experience had been gained in the last year, and as most of that knowledge was learnt after I had left P.T.S., I was going to have to be very careful. Even more so, as the examiners were to be Matron and Sister P.T.S.

First they had us make a bed. Then we had to prepare a bed for a patient coming from theatre following a below-knee amputation. So far so good. Then we had to spilt up and spend twenty minutes with each examiner.

They had our Schedules so that they could test us on things that we were supposed to know.

I had Matron first. At least it got the worst part over. I had to lay up trolleys for removal of stitches, preparation for surgery, last offices, and stomach washout.

I could manage that all right, although I had to think about it a bit, and decide whether the method used on the ward was the same as we had ben taught in school.

Having looked at the trolleys, she asked me to explain the use of each of the things I had put on them. Then I had to explain why I had omitted certain items. Of all things, I had forgotten to include a consent form on the preparation trolley.

By the time I left her to go to Sister P.T.S., I was convinced that she would fail me. The first think we were supposed to do when getting a patient ready for theatre was to get him to sign a consent form.

Sister P.T.S. had me demonstrate the procedures for which I had prepared the trolleys. A real patient had volunteered to have his stitches removed, and I achieved that without doing anything too awful. Then, as I was wondering which of the other three trolleys, I was to use next, Sister went over to the dummies. Thoughts of Mabel flooded back. Luckily Sister also remembered. She said,

"I don't think I need you to demonstrate Last Offices; we can do without heads rolling today."

There was, I found, a great deal of difference between doing a stomach washout in Casualty, and doing one in the classroom. For a start, here, there were no rubber aprons. Second, if I put too much water down the tube into the dummy's stomach, it flowed out of its mouth. The stupid thing had a stomach capacity of only half a pint. By the time I'd finished, the bed was soaking wet. Before I had time to clear away, the bell rang, signalling the end of the hour.

At last, it was over. All I could do was to wait until the papers were marked. Then I would know my fate. It was no use worrying. Convinced that I would fail on the practical, I went back to my room and read a novel. I didn't see the point of studying. My days were numbered now, so why not relax and enjoy life.

Sister Tutor came into the classroom the next morning with a sheet of paper in her hand.

"These, my lambs, are the results of your hospital examinations. I will read out your names and your pass marks. I will start with the lowest mark."

I was a bit surprised that the lowest mark was 60 percent, and even more surprised that it wasn't my name she called first. By the time she had reached 80 percent, I was convinced that I had failed. She had said that she would read out the pass marks; obviously I had not passed. When there were only two of us that had not been given a mark and 88 percent had been reached, I knew I'd failed.

Then I heard my name. 92 percent! Surely that couldn't be right. 29 percent I could have accepted; 92 percent never! Not only that, but I had come second, the top mark being 93 percent.

The rest of the day passed in a daze. Now I would *have* to study. Matron would have to allow me to take States, and I must pass. I listened intently each day to all that Sister Tutor had to say, then went back to my room and sat up half the night reading over the notes I had taken.

The day after we received our hospital results, we were each given our entrant's card for the State exam. It looked horribly official, and contained the shocking information that the first paper would not only be on Anatomy, but also Physiology and Personal and Communal Health. The second paper was to be on the Principles and Practice of Nursing, including Bacteriology and the Principles of Asepsis and First Aid.

The card also held the number 325, my candidate number to be used throughout the exams instead of my name. The exams were to start on Tuesday the first of February. I thought that if number 325 was going to have anything to write about that day, then Sister Tutor was going to have a very busy couple of weeks trying to teach me something!

By the time I sat down to write the State papers I was exhausted. At the end of the day when the others were holding the inevitable *Post Mortem* over the exam papers, I couldn't even remember which questions I had answered.

The Examiners for the Practical were Tutors from another hospital. Neither of them even looked at my Schedule; they were going to test us on what we ought to know, according to the rules of General Nursing Council. If we didn't know all we should, that was not their problem, but ours.

They must have run out of difficult things to ask. All I had to demonstrate, was a blanket bath. Then I had to prepare to admit a patient. Finally I had to prepare to give an injection of Morphia. When it came to the Morphia, my mind was a blank. The treatment card said the patient was to have half a grain, and I could not remember how many milligrams there were to a grain. I had seen enough Morphia on Ward Eight to know that the ampoules were no longer dispensed in grains. Guided by the Casualty maxim of, if in doubt, ask, I said,

"I'm sorry; I have forgotten how to work out the dosage."

The reply I received surprised me.

"I did not expect you to; that is the job of the trained nurse."

Saved by the bell, I left the room consoled by the thought that the G.N.C. had the same opinion of junior nurses as ward sisters.

To their minds, we were all totally stupid.

CHAPTER FIFTEEN

One of the nicest things about being in Block was that the set was together for the first time since leaving P.T.S., although we were somewhat diminished in numbers.

Three members of our set had given up the fight for survival and left in the last year, and we were now down to nine. They had not been able to cope with the rules, and rather than try to alter the system, they had just asked to be allowed to leave.

The remainder of us decided to celebrate the completion of Prelims and our first year by visiting a local coffee bar. Throwing caution to the winds, we each had two cups of coffee. A cup of coffee cost 6d. (2 1/2p) and the loss of 1 shilling out of our pay would cause problems by the end of the month, but we were in a reckless mood.

We were due a pay rise at the end of the month, another £2, as we were now second year students. I was a little better off than most, as my grandfather sent me a ten shilling (50p) postal order in the middle of each month. But even with the extra money, I had to watch every penny.

Thursday and Friday morning were to be spent in the classroom preparing us for the extra responsibilities we would be facing as second year nurses. On Friday afternoon, Matron would see us individually to give us our new belts, caps and aprons. Once we had our new uniforms, we would be free for the weekend.

How I wished that my name began with an "A." Being a "W," I was always near the bottom of the list, the last girl being named Young. We all sat about in the classroom trying to look as if we were studying. One by one, the others returned to display their new white belts, aprons without the cross over bands and caps without tails.

Our new aprons finished at the bib. As there were no straps to support them, they had to be pinned to our dresses. Although the back of the bib had tags, so that a safety pin could be used as an anchor, the left side was always held with a fob watch, and the right side with a tie pin. Trained staff used their badges as a pin, using either their G.N.C. or hospital badge.

Not having a tie pin, I decided to move my S.N.A. badge form my cloak to my apron. I didn't bother to tell Matron; I was going to let her find out for herself!

My interview with Matron was painful to say the least. I was lectured on my disruptive behavior, my inability to conform, and my lack of involvement with the hospital social scene. She said that now I was in my second year, I should be setting an example to the junior nurses. There was to be a stop to all the nonsense of the last year.

Not a word of congratulation on my exam results. I thought I had been setting an example, and not just to the juniors. I had been trying to encourage the students to stand up for themselves. Whilst I might have engineered a few changes, I couldn't see that I had caused any disruption. As for the hospital social scene, debating societies and group bible readings never had been of any interest to me. I failed to see that my presence would add anything to the proceedings. Perhaps she hoped that I might expend some of my aggression as hot air.

Our names had not been on the last change list, just in case we had failed our exams. It had been left for Matron to tell us where we were going. When she eventually stopped finding fault with me, I was handed my new belt, cap and apron, and given the information that I was to work on the Children's Ward.

I wasn't too sure how I would like working with sick children. I had several younger cousins and a baby brother, but looking after them was hardly preparation for nursing children.

I knew nothing about the Sister either, other than gossip, and there was plenty of that. Sister Kids was an enigma. Her idiosyncrasies were excused by the fact that she was not a "Proper Nurse," merely a Registered Sick Children's Nurse, and not S.R.N. It was rumoured that she had been appointed Sister during the war, when S.R.N.s were in short supply, and now they were stuck with her. Even the student nurses looked down on her as an inferior being.

The gossips had a grand time with her. Her had a son in his late twenties, and no one had ever heard her mention a husband. She lived in a large house about four miles from the Annex, and came to work each day on a moped. How she managed to maintain the house on her pay was a constant source of speculation.

I was to start work a 1 P.M. In Monday. That did not please me a great deal. I hated late starts, as there was not enough time in the morning to do anything, and it always seemed a very long shift.

The Children's Ward was one of the old Isolation huts and had been built into the side of the hill. The back of the ward was level with the road, and the front was a long way up in the air. The view from the balcony along the front was fantastic.

I was met at the ward door by Sister. Had she not introduced herself, I would not have known who she was. The sisters I had seen before had all worn dark blue dresses, caps and aprons. This one wore a large flowery overall, and looked more like an old fashioned farmer's wife than a Ward Sister. The similarity was further increased by the fact that she was rather short, and a little on the plump side.

I was taken into her office. I had never seen anything like it. There was a large roll-topped desk overflowing with bits of paper, and shelves lined all the walls. One wall of shelves was covered in photographs of children, and there were teddy bears and dolls of various ages and stages of repair in amongst the books on the others. It looked rather like a doll's hospital.

I gave Sister my Schedule, but she handed it back, saying,

"You keep it, Nurse. If I have it you will never see it again. Mark it as you do things, then when you leave I'll sign it."

Sister got up suddenly and left the office, telling me she would be back in a minute. When she came back she had brought with her a screaming toddler, and a child of about six years old riding around on a tricycle.

I found it hard to take the woman seriously. There she was, telling me what she expected of me over the coming months, and at the same time trying to stop the baby crying. The six year old kept riding in and out of the office. Every time it came in, it managed to push the door so that it swung back and crashed against the shelves. Having told me what to expect, she dispatched the tricycle rider to find Nurse Gale. Gale would show me the ward, and I would work with her for the rest of the day.

It was like a madhouse in the office, but the ward was even worse. Only the very ill children were kept in bed, the others being allowed to do just as they wanted. The ward was a warren of rooms, the smallest holding only a bed and a cot, the largest, four beds. One end of the ward was shut off from the rest by a pair of swing doors. That was the babies' end. It was really a self-contained unit. As well as incubators and small cots, there was a kitchen for preparing feeds and a small operating theatre.

Gale was nearing the end of her third year, and confided that she was hoping Sister would ask her to stay for her fourth. I couldn't imagine anything worse. By the time I had been shown all the nooks and crannies, I was very confused. I couldn't ever imagine being able to find my way around.

Having completed the tour of the ward, we gave the children their tea. Each child had a drink, bread and butter, and a piece of cake. Those that could, sat up to the tables in the rooms; the rest sat on or in their beds to eat, scattering crumbs everywhere.

Clearing away the tea things took longer than it would on any other ward, as we had to wipe hands and faces as well as table tops. The noise level was staggering. The children seemed to all talk at the same time. If no one took any notice, they just kept on raising their voices until some one was forced to listen.

I couldn't imagine that any of them were ill. They all seemed full of beans, and even the children sitting on their beds had clothes on, none of them were wearing pyjamas or nightdresses.

Once we had cleared away, there did not seem to be much to do. There were lots of mums about, and they appeared to be doing most of the work. I felt a bit bewildered. I had never been in the situation of having to look for work before.

I was amazed when Sister bustled in, this time with a small baby in her arms, and said,

"Nurse, the boys in the end room want to watch the television. Sit in there with them, will you?"

Whatever next! After a few minutes I understood the need for there to be someone supervising the boys while they watched the television. First we had to decide which channel they were going to watch. Given that there were four boys, all about ten or eleven years old, and only two channels to watch, one would have thought that a decision would be easily reached. Not so. In the end, I solved the problem and chose one myself, whereupon they all decided that they wanted the other one.

I was unmoved. If they couldn't decide for themselves, then they would have to accept my decision. From that time on, the boys decided I was an ogre. That was fine my me; at least it meant that they did as I told them. I was on the ward for fourteen weeks, and during that time, the population of the room changed several times, but my reputation remained. Passed down from boy to boy was the fact that Nurse Wallinger was a beast, and could get very cross.

Right in the middle of a jolly interesting programme, Gale came in and asked me to help her with the suppers. My reputation suffered another serious setback when I switched the set off before I left the room. I could just imagine what would have happened had I left it on. The channels would have been changed so often that the switch would have melted.

Giving out the suppers was even worse that the teas. There was soup, beans on toast, and finally, jelly and ice cream. Each child had a choice; they could have some of everything, or just one course. The only rule was that they had to have something to eat.

Once again, we cleared away the plates, then wiped up the mess from the surrounding furniture. After that, we started on the children, youngest group first. Once they were clean, they were dressed in their nightclothes and put to bed. When all the children in one room were in bed, the lights were lowered and a bedtime story read to them.

As I did not know the ward, I was left to read the story while Gale started on the next room. I have always hated reading aloud, and my time on Kids did nothing to alter it. In the end, I gave up trying to read and told them stories that I made up. The stories often became so complicated that I forgot the plot. The children never did, and they were always ready with a prompt. My stories became so popular that it was difficult for me to have an evening off.

If I wanted to go out for the evening, although not a very frequent occurrence, I had to go off duty, get changed, then go back for bedtime. Sister was always very fair; if I was going back to the ward for story time, she would send me off duty an hour early.

However, on this my first evening, the story-telling was confined to reading from a book.

At last the little horrors were all in bed, and if not actually asleep, then at lest they were quiet. We spent ten minutes putting away the toys that were scattered all over the ward, then there was nothing left to do.

Gale suggested a cup of tea, and as we went into the kitchen, I was surprised to see a group of mums in there eating. We collected our tea, then went and sat in Sister's Office.

Gale was anxious to infect me with her enthusiasm for the ward, and was keen to tell me all about the routine and what I could expect to learn while I was there. If a nurse was anxious to learn, she explained, then Sister would teach her all that she could. Any nurse that did not like the ward was tolerated for the minimum six weeks expected by the G.N.C., then rapidly moved.

Sister also organised her own night staff, moving nurses from day to night as she liked. Gale saw this as a wonderful system, as the patients did not wake up in the night and see a strange face. I was not so sure. I preferred doing my spell of nights in one lump rather than in sessions of a few nights at a time.

I wanted to know about the mums in the kitchen, so I asked Gale why they were eating supper on the ward whilst their children were asleep. Surely they should have gone home.

Gale said she would only tell me if I promised not to tell a soul. I was not even to tell Sister that I knew. I duly swore to keep anything told me to myself, and Gale recounted the most amazing story. It sounded so fantastic, that I felt that she should have started the story with "Once upon a time......"

Sister had a son called Henry. When Henry was four, he had polio and was admitted to the Isolation Ward. Never having been away from his mother before, he was terribly unhappy, and this was not helping him get better. As his mother was a nurse, she was allowed to break the "No visitors" rule, and visit him every afternoon for a short time. Gradually his condition worsened, and the ward staff warned Sister that if his condition deteriorated any more, they would have to put him in an iron lung.

This did not impress Sister at all. She knew her small boy better than the nurses looking after him, so she decided to stay and care for him herself. She went home and collected all she thought that she would need for a short stay, then returned to Henry's bedside and refused to move.

Day and night she sat there for two weeks, not nursing, just sitting beside Henry's bed. From the moment she started her vigil, Henry began to improve. At the end of two weeks, he was discharged home to his mother's care. The only effect the polio had on him was to leave him with a slight limp. The mortality rate amongst children with polio then was very high.

Once she had arrived home, Sister began to think about what had happened, and to compare Henry's case with children she had nursed. She came to the conclusion that Henry, and a lot of the children, had failed to respond to treatment because they were literally pining away. If the transfer from home to hospital could be de-traumatised, then the child would respond to treatment far better. The only way that could be achieved would be to admit the mother as well as the child.

Having made this discovery, she told one of her ex-colleagues about it. Although herself in charge of a children's ward, the woman declared the idea as preposterous. It was recognised fact that children were far better in hospital without their parents. At that time, the mid 1940's, very few children's wards encouraged visiting. Short-stay patients were not allowed visitors at all, and only the long term patients or the very ill had visits.

Bitterly disappointed, Sister gave up trying to change the way things were, but vowed, that if ever she had her own children's ward, then she would allow parents to stay with their children. Having been out of nursing since Henry was born, it seemed unlikely that this would ever happen.

In 1943, when Henry started school, Sister thought about returning to work. Her local hospital was pleading for trained nurses to return to work, most of their staff having joined the forces nursing services. Sister went back to work, fitting in duties around Henry's school hours. The fact that she was not an S.R.N. meant that she could only work with children, and she saw a chance to implement her ideas.

Sister soon found that, as a staff nurse, she had no say in the running of the ward, but convinced that she was right, contrived to get mothers into the ward when the Sister was off duty. In 1944, the Sister left, and our Sister was offered the job of "Sister in Charge" of the Children's block.

Knowing that as the only person in the hospital with children's training, she was in a very strong bargaining position, she laid down her terms:

Henry was to be allowed to come to work with her when he was not at school.

There was to be no outside interference from the Hospital Board of Governors.

She, and she alone would arrange the ward off-duty, day and night.

She would be able to refuse entry to the ward to anyone that she thought undesirable.

The Matron was desperate. She could not continue to admit children without a Sister on the ward. In fact, Sister was the only trained nurse on the ward. Matron agreed to all the demands. Sister was not content with a verbal agreement, and before she accepted the job, asked for her terms to be agreed in writing.

At this point Gale got up and handed me a framed letter. It was the original copy of the letter appointing Sister and agreeing to all her terms, preserved for all to see.

Once she was her own boss, Sister gradually began to change things. At first, mothers were allowed to stay all day, going home each night. Then the mothers of dangerously ill children were offered the chance to sleep in a bed in the same room as their child. If necessary, siblings slept on the ward as well.

The average length of each patient's stay dropped dramatically. This was fortunate, because the word spread rapidly that if a child was ill, the "union" was the place to take it, rather than the hospital up the road.

As was bound to happen, the Board of Governors heard about the mothers staying on the ward. Their immediate concern was how much extra it was costing to feed and house the parents. It would have to stop, they decided. Sister received a letter telling her that, as the hospital relied on charity to finance it, all unnecessary expenditure was to stop. The board added that they considered that the cost of boarding the parents of children unnecessary.

The latter was also framed. In the same frame was a copy of the reply Sister sent to the Board. It simply said that she had agreed to accept the post of Sister on condition that she was left to run the ward her way. If the Board did not like her methods, then they had better find someone else to run the ward.

The Chairman of the Board then decided to pay the ward a visit. He never even got inside the door. His admission to the ward was refused by Sister, she considered that his visit was likely to upset the children. She simply refused to let him in.

After that, Sister was left alone to do as she liked for twenty years. Then one of the national radio stations broadcast a programme about her and her nursing methods. By then, the old Board had been replaced by a Hospital Management Committee. Their reaction was much the same as that of the old Board. The letters were all framed, and were not much different from the previous letters, only this time there were more of them. There was also a scrap book, bulging with letters from parents, offering Sister all the support she might need to ensure that she was allowed to continue doing things her way.

Since then Sister had continued to do just as she pleased. Mothers, fathers, brothers, sisters, all were given the chance to stay with a very ill child. She even housed a pet mouse at one stage.

Sister expected the mother of any child admitted to be on the ward all day. If the child was under ten, then the mother was expected to sleep on the ward as well.

The parents of babies were allowed to visit as and when they liked. The ward was open to visitors twenty-four hours a day.

As Gale was telling me the story I became more and more amazed; not with the idea, although it was certainly radical, but that such a dumpy little Mother Hen character had taken on the might of the Board, and won.

Then I remembered that I had been sworn to secrecy. Why, if the whole world knew what was happening, was it to be kept a secret?

Gale explained. The last letter Sister had received from the Management Committee had simply said that, if she continued to disregard the hospital rules, she would be asked to resign.

From that moment on, the movement "went underground."

CHAPTER SIXTEEN

The care of sick children has come a long way since then. Mothers now take for granted the fact that they will be able to stay with their children, and children's wards are designed to accommodate parents. There is even an association, NAWCH, The National Association for the Welfare of Children in Hospital, that offers help and support for the parents of ill children.

It would be a brave sister that tried to ban visiting on a children's ward, or even to restrict it. Although many hospitals refuse to feed the mothers, sending them to the staff dining room to buy their own food, none would consider trying to save on the cost of providing sleeping accommodation. Even if they did, they would be no better off financially, as the wards would need a lot more staff to cope with the extra work load.

I would like to think that hospitals are allowing mothers to stay for humanitarian reasons, but being cynical, I wonder how much the increase in nurses' pay has contributed to the acceptance by the NHS of "live in" mothers. Their labour comes much cheaper than that of student nurses.

As I went round the ward before going off duty, I took more notice of the occupants of the beds. There were eighteen children, all fast asleep. Beside ten of the beds, small camp-beds had appeared. The mums were all in the kitchen. Some were sitting round the table; two were washing up, and one was setting a trolley with breakfast things ready for the morning.

When the night staff appeared I was surprised to see four of them. Gale explained that Sister always had at least four nurses on duty every night, one for the children, two for the babies, and one in case of an emergency. No wonder sister organised her own night staff.

The walk back to the Nurses' Home was very difficult. There had been a heavy fall of snow during the evening, and the slope was icy. It was so steep that we had trouble staying upright. If more snow fell during the night we might have problems getting back on duty in the morning. Then I remembered that Sister came to work on a Moped.

"Gale, what happens if it snows and Sister can't get in?"

"Oh," replied Gale "She'll get in if she has to get the snow ploughs out to clear the way."

She was right. It was still snowing the next day as I slid down the slope on my way to the ward, and there was a good two inches on the ground. As I peered through the curtain of swirling snow I saw Sister riding along. Both feet were hovering just above the ground, and she was travelling at a walking pace, but there she was. I arrived at the ward door just before she did, and held it open for her.

"Goodness me," she said, "I was beginning to think I would never get here; the roads were nearly blocked in places. That slope looks dangerous. I'll have to get the porters to clear it or I won't be able to get out tonight."

She bustled into her office and started to peel off layers of waterproof clothing. I left her to it and went to hang up my coat. I was half way along the corridor when she called me back.

"Yes, Sister?" I asked.

"I'm sorry Nurse; I didn't say good morning."

Amazed, I went along to the cloakroom and hung up my coat, then shook the snow off my shoes and cap. Gale and five others were already there, discussing how late "Mother" would be.

"Who is Mother?" I asked.

"That is what Sister liked to be called." was the reply. I should have known; she looked like a pantomime Mother Hubbard.

"She is here already. I've just seen her come in."

Gale grinned. "I told you she'd get here. I'll go and take over from the night staff. Please will one of you check and see that Sister has had her breakfast."

As we followed Gale out into the ward, I realised that there were only three of them senior to me. I was no longer part of the junior staff. Like it or not, I was soon going to have to accept some real responsibility.

As Gale and I were both due to have the afternoon off, Sister decided that we should work together so that I could learn the ward routine. Gale was a good teacher, and by the time we went to dinner, I knew all there was to know about the patients in the ward. I had not seen anything of the baby ward, apart from the look round the night before.

I was rather surprised, when we prepared a dressing trolley, to find that the gauze and cotton wool was no longer packed in drums. Instead, it came in sterilized, sealed paper bags. Gale explained that attempts were being made to change over to a Central Sterile Supply Department. Eventually, the dressing drums would be phased out, and everything would come from C.S.S.D.

By the time we went off duty for the afternoon, Sister had managed to get the porters to clear most of the snow from the road outside the ward, and the slope was slightly better to walk on than it had been in the morning. A handrail would have been a help, I thought. Perhaps I should campaign for one.

When we reached the dining room it was nearly empty. We had been late leaving the ward, and then picking our way up the side of the hill had made us even later. By the time we had collected our meal, the only other person in the room was Home Sister.

Tradition demanded that I sit on the table reserved for second year nurses, and Gale sit at the third year table. As we passed Home Sister, she indicated the empty chairs at the Sister's table.

"Sit here girls and keep me company. The maids won't mind. They will be able to clear up and get the other tables ready for tea."

I felt strange, almost guilty, to be sitting at the top of the room. The table was laid with a tablecloth and silver cutlery. The nurses had to eat off a plain table and use stainless steel knives and forks. Sister smiled at me.

"Relax, you are here as my guest. No one would dare to tell you to move."

I tried to relax, and I tried not to bolt my food. It wouldn't do to finish before Sister. We began talking about the weather, then Sister started telling us about some of the things that had happened to her in the past. The winter of 1947 was the worst that she could remember. The hospital was cut off for nearly a week before the road was opened.

"The funny thing was, it was three days before anyone realised that we *were* cut off. Of course nowadays they would notice straight away." Sister went on,

"Times are beginning to change. It won't be long before nurses are given more freedom. It might even happen in my time, but if not, then certainly in yours."

A maid appeared with three cups of coffee, all in the thin blue and white china reserved for Sisters. We *were* honoured.

Once Home Sister had started on her reminiscences, there was no stopping her. I found it fascinating. I thought that we had a hard time, but our life was easy compared to the things that she had to contend with in her training days. She had trained at the Nightingale School in the mid-twenties, and times were hard. Off-duty was very limited, and lectures had to be attended in the nurses' free time.

There were no antibiotics; blood transfusions were given direct from donor to patient, and patients frequently died of septicaemia. She described how one nurse had lost a finger because a small wound had become infected.

We heard how, after she qualified, she came to work at the Annex as a nurse, then a Sister. At the start of the war she chose to remain, rather than join the forces, and was eventually appointed Matron. When, with the birth of the NHS, the two hospitals amalgamated, rather than apply for the post of Group Matron, she decided to apply for that of Home Sister.

Gale asked if she did not find it difficult handing over her hospital to a stranger.

"Not really." was her reply. "My hospital no longer existed. It had become a dumping ground for the patients that no one wanted in town. The staff at the main hospital saw to it that all the acute wards, the theatres and casualty stayed with them. We had to have the geriatrics, the paediatrics, the isolation and the maternity wards; as they saw it, all the trouble.

We spent the afternoon sitting in the dining room listening to her stories, and it wasn't until people started to come in for tea at 4:30 that we realised how long we had been there. I just had time to change into a fresh apron before going back on duty. I arranged to wait for Gale at the Home door, so that we cold walk down the hill together.

It was much colder outside, and the slope had frozen over. I was tempted to give up the battle to stay on my feet and just slide down. However, I managed to get to the bottom without falling over.

Sister spent ten minutes telling us what had been happening during the afternoon, then prepared to leave. She donned layer upon layer of coats, then, once her helmet was on, she was ready for the journey home. At least she did not have to climb the hill, as there was a road that led straight from the ward to the main gate.

No sooner had she gone out the door then she reappeared.

"Could one of you come out and hold my moped while I get on? It keeps falling over."

I fetched my coat and went to help. The road was like an ice rink. I had trouble standing up. How Sister thought that she was going to get home, I could not imagine. I had to hold the bike for her while she climbed on it, then run along behind holding it upright while she pedalled to get it started.

By the time she was successfully launched on her way home, I was frozen solid. As I watched her wobble down the road I wondered if I would ever feel the same commitment to a ward that she did. I doubted it. I could not see myself riding a small motorbike to work in the snow and ice. I was not of the generation that put the hospital before home and family.

One of the mums had a cup of tea waiting for me when I went back into the ward, and I sat behind the door in the kitchen to drink it. I really don't know why we always sat behind the kitchen door to drink our illicit cups of tea. Perhaps we thought that we were hidden from sight. The senior members of staff must have done the same when they were students, and would know just where to find us.

The mums were having a very heated discussion about a child that had been admitted that afternoon. Sister had told us that a boy of two had been admitted with suspected Hirschsprung's Disease. It meant nothing to me, so I left the worrying to Gale. She obviously knew what Sister was talking about.

The women in the kitchen appeared to know all about it as well. There appeared to be some controversy over whether or not he should have an operation. Rather than admit my ignorance, I finished my tea and left to find some work. I walked round the ward and tidied up some toys, but there was nothing else to do. Not knowing the ward, I went to find Gale and ask her to find me a job.

She found me first.

"Doctor wants to examine Mark Bone, the new child in the blue single room. Can you go with him. Ask the parents to wait out in the corridor for a few minutes. Don't let them stay in the room while doctor is there. If they make a fuss, just tell them the room is too small for all of you to fit in."

They did make a fuss, or rather the father did. Mum just sat and held the child's hand. However nicely I explained that all we wanted to do was examine the child, it did not help. The man refused to move. The doctor eventually lost patience, and said,

"I am not going to examine this child while you are in here. Either you leave the room, or I do. If I leave, the child will not be examined until the morning. By then it could be too late to do anything to save him. The choice is yours."

The mother stood up and went out, and the father followed, protesting as he went that he did not trust people in white coats. I had never seen a child examined before. It was a very slow process, as Mark was too young to be able to tell us where he had a pain. He was a most unhappy child; he didn't cry, just sat and looked morose. Mark had very large dark blue eyes, and every move that we made was watched.

I found it rather disconcerting to be under such close scrutiny. One felt that he was storing up the information to use against us later. Apart from his eyes, the only difference between him and any other child, was his stomach. It was very hard and distended and, the skin was so tight that the wave-like movements of his gut could be seen.

Dr. Kerr chatted away to Mark, telling him what he was going to do, and that as soon as we had finished, his Mummy would come back and sit with him. Nothing seemed to register and I began to wonder if the child was deaf.

When the examination was over, Dr. Kerr asked me to tell the parents that they could come back into the room, and that he would like to see them in Sister's Office in a few minutes' time. First, he wanted to write down his findings in Mark's notes.

I passed the message on. Mark's mother went straight back to his room, but his father wanted to know what doctor had done and what was wrong with his son. He never, at least in my hearing, called the child by name. It was either "my son," or "the child."

All I could tell him was that the doctor had examined Mark. I had no idea what he thought was wrong. My initial dislike of the man was growing stronger every minute. As soon as I could, I made my escape and went along to the office to see what I should do next.

Dr. Kerr was sitting at the desk writing up the notes, and Gale was searching through a pile of papers, looking, as she told me, for a form. If she couldn't find it then "someone" was going to have to brave the elements and go up to Matron's Office and get another one. I had a good idea who that someone was going to be — me. I did not relish the thought of venturing out in the snow and ice, especially as I would be expected to wear a cloak. We were only allowed to wear coats going to and from the Nurses Home. If we made any journeys whilst we were on duty, we had to wear our cloaks.

Dr. Kerr put an end to my worries by saying that it was not desperate; the morning would do, adding,

"I think it would be better for the bosses to do it anyway."

Do what? I wondered. Should I ask or keep quiet. Before I had a chance to decide, I was sent to tell the parents that Dr. Kerr was ready to see them. Mark's mother was sitting beside the cot, holding her child's hand. His father was standing, looking out of the window. When I passed on the message, he turned to his wife and said,

"You stay where you are. I'll deal with this."

Then he pushed past me and went straight into the office. I felt very sorry for Mrs. Bone; she was obviously very worried about her son, and, by the look of it, was not getting a lot of support from her husband. I offered her a cup of tea, which she refused, saying she did not want to be any trouble.

I went to get her one anyway. From what I had seen, it was not her that was going to be trouble; it was her husband. The women in the kitchen were still arguing, and when I told them I wanted a cup of tea form Mrs. Bone, one of them offered to take it to her. I refused the offer. In view of the strength of feeling that Mark's admission had aroused, I thought it best if I took it myself. Mrs. Bone had enough problems coping with her husband; the last thing she needed at the moment was aggravation from strangers.

The mums must have read my thoughts, because one of them took the cup and said,

"I'll take it. I know Mrs. Bone well; we go to the same church."

Before I could protest she was gone.

"What do you think, Nurse?" one of the women asked.
"About what?" I replied.
"Them not letting Mark have an operation."
"Who said Mark was or wasn't going to have an operation?"

I had often seen the "Bush Telegraph" at work amongst the nurses. A patient would be admitted, and by the time they were settled in bed, the whole hospital knew all about them. This was the first time I had seen it at work amongst patients or relatives. There was no way I was going to be drawn into the argument, so I said,

"Dr. Kerr has only just examined Mark, and I was in the room al the time he was with the child. He said nothing to me about operating." Perhaps that would keep them quiet.

It didn't. They just directed their anger at me, saying that I was as bad as the rest. The poor child would be left to die, all because of his father, who, they had decided, was a pigheaded bigot. I agreed with their description of Mr. Bone, but kept that to myself. The mood *they* were in, one of them was quite capable of telling the man that Nurse Wallinger had said he was pigheaded.

I refused to be drawn into the argument. I could hardly voice an opinion when I had no idea of the facts. I excused myself, saying that I was going to get the children ready for bed. They took the hint and said they would all get their own children into bed, leaving me free to look after Mrs. Bone and Mark.

I went along to see how they both were, and found that Mr. Bone had returned to the room. His temper had not improved and as I went into the room, he pointed at the cup of tea.

"Take that away! I will not allow my wife to drink it. Who knows what it might contain?"

I took it. Had the cup of tea been prepared for him, he might have had reason to be suspicious. The strength of feeling against him was now so strong that the cup might well have contained cyanide! The thought of him being poisoned made me smile. Before he cold notice and comment, I took the cup out of his way.

Gale called out to me as I passed the office.

"Pop back here as soon as you are free, and I'll tell you all about Mark."

I put the cup in the now empty kitchen and went back to the office. Dr. Kerr was still sitting at the desk. He looked angry and Gale was rather flushed.

"What," she asked, "do you think of Mr. Bone?"

I paused before answering. Should I say what I really thought, or should I be diplomatic? Diplomacy won, so I said that I had found him rather difficult.

Dr. Kerr looked up at me and said,

"Difficult. He is the most objectionable sod I've met for months."

Gale looked as if she agreed. I certainly did.

Gale offered to go and make us a drink, while the doctor explained to me what was happening. I hoped that the women were still busy with their children. She looked upset enough already; she didn't need any more aggravation.

Dr. Kerr explained all about Mark. Although he was not sure, he thought that Mark had a condition known as Hirschsprung's disease, a congenital abnormality of the large intestine. A section of the gut did not work because of a faulty nerve supply. The only remedy was to operate and sever the offending nerves.

Because of his religious beliefs, Mr. Bone had refused to consent to any form of surgery had was threatening to take Mark home.

The women had been right after all.

"Can't you do *anything* to help Mark?" I asked.

"I have spoken to my boss, and he said to leave it to Sister. She will probably be able to sort things out in the morning. All we have to do is to make sure that they don't take Mark home before she gets here."

Gale looked at me, and said,

"Have you any idea of how we can persuade Mr. Bone to let Mark stay the night?"

I had plenty of ideas, ranging from putting him in a straight jacket, to a bang on the back of his head with a sandbag. Dr. Kerr did not appear to be bothered, he said,

"Don't worry; he won't take Mark away tonight."

I wasn't so sure. When I went along to see how Mark was, Mrs. Bone was alone with him; Mr. Bone had gone. I was convinced that he had gone to get his car ready to take Mark home.

When I told Dr. Kerr, he was still very calm. He was adamant that Mark would spend the night on the ward.

We were both right. Mr. Bone *had* gone to fetch his car, but it would not start. Mark stayed on the ward, and his parents walked home.

I wondered why the car would not start; was it an act of God, or was it an act of one of the porters? I would not have been in the lest surprised to have heard that someone had immobilised the car!

Either way, it gave Mark a chance. Sister would solve the problem.

CHAPTER SEVENTEEN

The weather worsened during the night, and as we walked down the ward, the snow came over the tops of our shoes. When we got to the ward door, there was Sister's moped. Somehow, she managed to get through the snow.

As we went through the door, she greeted us with the words,

"All of you take off you shoes and stockings. You'll be better off with bare feet than you will in wet things."

Since she insisted that the ward was kept very hot, she was probably right. We did as we were told and spent our first two hours on duty walking around in bare feet. Our stockings were hung over the radiators to dry, and we packed our shoes with newspaper and put them under the hot pipes in the corridor. By the time we had finished, the ward looked like a chinese laundry.

I was glad when Sister passed my stockings as dry and I could get partly dressed. My feet and legs were very cold. Being made of leather, my shoes took longer to dry, and it was half way through the morning before she let me put them on.

Sister told us that it had taken her nearly two hours to get to work, but she had expected it to be a difficult journey so had allowed plenty of time. She must have left home at about 5:30 A.M.

She had told the night staff to go as soon as she arrived. We were all on the ward well before 7:30 and it had taken us nearly fifteen minutes to walk down. As we hadn't passed them on the way, they must have left soon after 7:00 A.M.

Sister dispatched three nurses to the baby ward, then told the rest of us that she wanted us in her office for a chat. Once we were all settled, she began. It was more like a briefing session for a battle than a chat.

Mark was to be made a Ward Of Court. That meant that the courts became his legal guardians and would be able to consent to him undergoing surgery. She expected Mr. Bone to do all he could to prevent Mark having surgery, whether or not he was a Ward Of Court. To prevent this, Mark was to be moved to a designated "Place of Safety."

Unfortunately, it might take a couple of hours before all the paper work could be completed, and there was a chance that Mark's parents would have collected him before then. The ideal situation would have been to have moved Mark to the Children's Ward at the main hospital immediately, but because the roads were blocked, this was impossible.

So, Sister had decided that Mark was to be hidden. As it would be hard for us to hide him on the ward, he was to be taken down to the Isolation Ward. The Sister there could be relied upon to keep any unwanted visitors out!

As soon as Mark was officially a Ward Of Court, he could come back to his old room, and then, when the roads were clear, he would be transferred to the Main Hospital. Sister had already spoken to the Council Road Department, and they had assured her that the road would be passable by midday.

To lessen the strain for us, nurses that had been off duty the day before were to work in the ward. Those of us that had been seen by the Bones were to be kept out of the way. Gale was to go to Isolation with Mark and look after him. I was to go and work with the babies, and the other two that had been on duty when Mark was admitted were to go into the "Milk Kitchen" and prepare the day's feeds. We were to say nothing to any of the mothers on the ward, in case they talked about it outside the hospital. We all agreed that it would be best if the whole sad event could be kept as quiet as possible.

Gale asked how Sister was going to avoid Mr. Bone.

"Don't worry about me. He probably thinks I'm the cleaner!"

She had a point; her flowery apron was hardly uniform! The picture was completed by a pair of fluffy slippers.

As we stood up to leave, Sister said,

"Remember now girls, that child's life depends on you keeping to the plan. That man must not get hold of him."

I wouldn't have been surprised had she said , let the battle commence.

As we left the office, a couple of porters appeared. One was pushing a pram; the other had a snow shovel in his hand. They were, they informed us, bodyguards.

Sister took the pram and wheeled it off down the ward to collect Mark. He was wrapped up, put in the pram and taken off to Isolation.

Once he had gone, we all disappeared to our allotted positions. Sister spent the morning bustling about the ward carrying a mop. She looked a pretty convincing cleaner without it, but perhaps she felt safer with it in her hand, or maybe she was going to use it as a weapon!

I didn't really enjoy working with the babies. I had never had any experience of very small babies, and wasn't able to help with the complicated things. All I could do was feed them, and after some instruction, I was able to change a nappy.

It was a constant round of feeding and changing all morning. By lunchtime I considered myself an expert at both. Sister kept bustling in and out with a running commentary on what was happening about Mark. Just as I was getting ready to go to lunch, she came in and said that Mark was officially a Ward Of Court, and consent for his operation had been signed. As soon as an ambulance could get through, he would be moved.

It was a tremendous relief to know that Mark would be able to have the operation, but I couldn't see that Mr. Bone was going to admit defeat easily. I could imagine him storming into the ward and simply taking Mark. He didn't seem the type of man to be put off by a piece of paper.

I was pleased that I was working a split day, so that I would be off for the afternoon. With luck, by the time I arrived back at 5:30, all the fuss would be over, and Mark would no longer be our problem. I had just reached the ward door when the ambulance drew up.

Mark was still in the Isolation Ward, so the ambulance men were dispatched to collect him. As the road was still icy, they took the pram, rather than get the ambulance stuck at the bottom of the hill.

Sister decided that someone would have to go with Mark in the ambulance. She couldn't go herself, because she had to attend a meeting that afternoon. Gale couldn't go because she would have to stay and look after the ward in Sister's absence. I was the only one that knew Mark that could really be spared. It seemed to have slipped her notice that I was going to be off duty!

"You haven't any plans for this afternoon, have you, Nurse?"

"Yes, Sister, I was going to write a letter to my grandfather, and I haven't had my dinner yet."

I was starving hungry, and if I didn't write to Granddad, I wouldn't get my next postal order.

"You can write your letter when you get back. I'll make you a sandwich to take with you, and I'll get the kitchen to save you something for when you get back."

I resigned myself to losing an hour of my off-duty. Had I known that I was going to lose the whole afternoon, I might have put up a fight. It probably wouldn't have done any good. Sister had decided that I was going, and that was that.

The ambulance men arrived with Mark in the pram. Sister settled me in the back of the ambulance with a packet of sandwiches in my pocket, and Mark cuddled up on my knee. He managed to sit right on top of my sandwiches. Sister handed up a parcel containing Mark's notes, and issued her instructions to the driver. He was to take me and the child to the Main Hospital Children's Ward and then bring me back. I was not to be left alone with the child at any time, just in case.

The driver climbed into the front, and the other man settled himself in the back with me. If there was to be trouble, he didn't look as if he would be a lot of use. He was short, thin and not in the first flush of youth.

I had no idea whether or not the Bones even knew that their son had been made a Ward Of Court, but if they did, there was sure to be trouble. I had visions of Mr. Bone staging a kidnapping or some other devious scheme to recover Mark.

The ambulance man introduced himself as Squirrel, and filled me in on all the missing details on Mark's case. The Bush Telegraph had been active again! I was told that Mrs. Bone had 'phoned the ward during the morning, and had been informed that Mark had been moved to the Isolation Ward for observation, as Sister was worried about him. He would be transferred from there as soon as possible.

He added. "Mother never told a lie. All she said was correct. She *was* worried about Mark, and he *was* being transferred. She just didn't tell the whole truth."

He went on to say that Main Theatres were expecting Mark, and as soon as we got him to the Children's Ward he would be prepared for theatre. Squirrel was nearly right. We didn't actually get as far as the ward.

A porter was waiting for us as we drew up to the hospital doors. We were to take Mark straight to theatre. Mr. Bone had somehow found out that Mark was to be moved ready for surgery, and he was busy causing a scene on the ward.

As I climbed down from the ambulance, Matron appeared.

"Can you manage to carry the child?" she asked.

"Yes, Matron, he isn't very heavy."

"Right then, Nurse, come with me." She turned to the ambulance men,

"I think we will be less conspicuous without you two. I'm sure the porters will be able to find you a cup of tea. As soon as Nurse is ready, she will come and find you. Then you can take her back to the Annex."

Off we went, Matron and I, walking along like two ladies taking a baby out for an afternoon stroll. It seemed miles across the courtyard, and I had to resist the urge to run. I was sure that Mr. Bone was behind me and was going to snatch Mark from me at any moment. My anxiety must have shown, because Matron took Mark from me saying,

"He wouldn't dare to lay a finger on me, or the child."

We reached the theatre at last, and again we were expected. We were shown straight into a small room, and I was told to sit with Mark until the doctors were ready. It would only be a few minutes.

Matron passed Mark to me, and said that she would stay until she knew that he was safe. After a while my arms began to ache with holding Mark. He was getting heavier and heavier. I would dearly have like to have sat down, but I did not dare to sit in Matron's presence unless she suggested it.

I walked up and down talking to Mark, constantly telling him that he would soon be better, and that Mummy would come soon and take him home. I hoped that I was right. I had a horrible feeling that Mr. Bone might refuse to have Mark home.

I was pleased that they were ready for Mark. I found it impossible to know who was whom in theatre. All the male staff wore green cotton suits, and the nurses, green cotton dresses. Everyone had a green hat and a white cotton face mask. It could have been a doctor or a porter; I didn't know which.

As I handed Mark over to the person in green, the poor little chap held out his arms to me and started to cry. Before I could go to him Matron said,

"Would you like to stay and see the operation, Nurse?"

I rapidly declined the offer. I still remembered fainting on bonfire night, and there hadn't even been a lot of blood. To faint in front of all these strangers would be just too embarrassing.

We left Mark to his fate and went out into the theatre foyer. Matron told me that she had to make a 'phone call, and that I was not to leave without her. I immediately thought back over the last few days. I couldn't remember doing anything that might have upset her. Then I remembered that i was wearing my S.N.A. badge as an apron pin.

Luckily; I hadn't taken my cloak off as I entered Theatre, with luck she might not have noticed it. I hastily made sure that the badge was covered by a cloak strap. I couldn't think of anything else I might have done wrong. By the time she returned, I was ready to defend myself, whatever the accusation. Such was my relationship with her, that every time she wanted to see me, I immediately thought that I was in trouble.

For once I was not. Matron had just been checking to see if Mr. Bone was still on the Children's Ward. He was, so it was clear for me to cross over to the Porters Lodge and find my transport back to the Annex. Matron offered to escort be over, but I declined, assuring her that I would manage to avoid Mr. Bone.

Squirrel and his driver had finished their tea, so we climbed aboard and set off. As the ambulance went out of the hospital gate, the radio in the cab started to crackle. A disembodied voice was issuing orders. What it said I couldn't understand. It sounded like a man from Mars.

The driver reached up and touched a switch on the roof and the ambulance bell started ringing. That was in the day before we were forced to accept the sirens that they have now. Squirrel turned and said,

"Nothing much. An old lady has slipped on the ice and broken her hip. She'll be on her way to the Annex, so we can deliver you at the same time."

We could see where the patients was, by the knot of people standing on the pavement. The driver drew up beside them. There in the middle was a tiny little woman laying on the icy pavement. There were about ten people standing looking at her. Not one of them had thought to cover her with something warm. Her hands were white with cold.

The onlookers were bundled aside and she was lifted onto a stretcher and put in the back of the ambulance. Squirrel climbed in the back and we set off again. It was four o'clock by this time. I could see that I was not going to write any letters today. The sandwiches Sister had made me were still in my uniform pocket, and I was very very hungry.

I thought about trying to eat as we went along, but decided against it. Nurses did not eat in public.

The patient was conscious but rather confused, and she kept mumbling away to herself. When I said I was surprised that she was allowed out in that state, Squirrel told me that he knew her well, and that she was normally fine. The shock of the fall and being left to lie in the cold had upset her, and if she recovered she would be fine. I knew very little about orthopaedics then, but enough to know that not many elderly people recovered from a broken femur.

The pavements in the town were made from brick, and although picturesque, were very difficult to walk on. Even in the summer they were dangerous, being far from level. Given a covering of ice, they were absolutely lethal.

I had always wanted to ride in an ambulance with the bell ringing, but now it was happening, I was not enjoying it at all. The roads were still very slippery, and it had started to snow again. Several times it felt as if we were going sideways. I was convinced that we would crash, and Matron was sure to hold me responsible in some way. As far as she was concerned, anything that happened near me was my fault.

The worst moment came as we turned in through the hospital gates. The driver had stopped to wait for a gap in the oncoming traffic, and he was going slowly as he reached the gates and could not get up the hill. All that happened was that we slid backwards down the hill onto the road.

This must have been a frequent event, as the Gatehouse Porter appeared with some road grit, shovelled some under the wheels, and got us going again.

At last the driver stopped, jumped down out of the cab and opened the back doors. I climbed out and made my way down the ward. It was 5:50

P.M., and I had been due back on the ward at five. It had taken all afternoon to move one small boy six miles. I consoled myself with the thought that it had been worth it. The longer he had stayed with us at the Annex, the greater would have been the danger, both from his illness and from his father.

Sister welcomed me back, and took me straight to the kitchen. A feast had bee prepared for me. There was tomato soup, toast, scrambled eggs and rice pudding. It might not have been *Cordon Bleu*, but it was certainly very welcome.

"Sit down and eat. You can tell me how you got on while you eat. Then I'll tell you what has been happening here."

I related the afternoon's adventures, and assured her that Mr. Bone had not been able to prevent Mark's operation, I was able to assure her that I had taken him to Theatre myself, and handed him over to the theatre staff. She was reassured when I told her that Matron had been there with me.

My afternoon had been somewhat boring compared to the happenings on the ward after I left. Mr. Bone had arrived in a taxi, seconds after the ambulance had left, and demanded to see Mark. Sister had told him that Mark has been moved, and that there was nothing he could now do to prevent the operation taking place, as Mark was now in the care of the courts.

He had been very angry and abusive, and had left the ward saying that no one was going to operate on his son, court or no court.

Poor Sister was worried in case he had stopped the ambulance, as he would have passed us on the way. She hadn't dared to 'phone the ward or the theatre, in case they had bad news for her. As soon as she knew that Mark had arrived safely, she started ringing round to find out how he was.

Several calls later, she still hadn't found out, and in desperation she rang Matron, and at last found that Mark had been taken to the Private Wing. It was the only ward that could house him and the Policeman necessary to keep out Mr. Bone. Information as to Mark's condition and whereabouts was being kept a secret, as the newspapers had got hold of the story and Matron was worried about what they might print.

Sister had just put the 'phone back on the hook when it rang. The switchboard operator said that there was an outside call from a public call box, and put the call through. It was Mrs. Bone. She was ringing from a call box because she did not want her husband to know what she was doing. She said that she wanted to thank sister and her staff for all they had done for Mark.

Matron was right; the papers had made the most of the story. The next morning I was able to read all about my ambulance ride with Mark. The story was in all the papers, yet no one from the press had been near the ward, nor spoken to either Sister or myself.

One of the papers even had a picture, supposedly of me, getting out of an ambulance carrying a child. It wasn't me, but I didn't complain. Whoever she was, she was a very pretty girl.

I often wondered what had happened to Mark. We had heard that his parents had moved away from the area soon after he had been discharged from hospital, so we had no way of finding out.

Years later, when I was a Health Visitor, I was asked my a colleague to visit one of her new babies whilst she was on holiday, as the mother was very anxious and tended to panic. This was a normal request, so I agreed. She added that there was an older child by a previous marriage.

I went round to the house, and the door was opened by Mrs. Bone. We recognised each other straight away, and over a cup of tea, I heard all about what had happened since I had seen her last. Mark had been discharged from hospital to her care, but had remained a Ward Of Court for several months.

Her husband was offered a job in the North, and rather unwillingly she went. She stood it for a year, but was so homesick that they agreed that she and Mark should return to live with her parents.

The marriage ended in divorce. Eventually, Mrs. Bone remarried and was now very happy. She was understandably anxious about her new baby; the thought of having to repeat the trauma of Mark's operation worried her. I was at least able to reassure her that the condition was very unlikely to occur twice in one family. I left, having arranged that I would visit another day, after Mark had returned form school.

On my next visit, Mark answered the door himself. A tall muscular young man, he looked so unlike the small boy I had nursed so long ago. He still had very large eyes, and he joked that he was often likened to a *Midwich Cuckoo*.

He remembered nothing of his time in hospital, but his maternal grandmother had kept a scrapbook for him of all the newspaper cuttings.

We talked for a while, and as I was leaving he said,

"You know, you have changed a lot. You don't look anything like the picture in the paper."

I didn't tell him it wasn't me. I would rather leave him with the memory of the girl in the newspaper.

CHAPTER EIGHTEEN

I was off duty the following day, and I braved the weather to walk up to the village. I wanted to buy a newspaper to read all about the saga of Mark. In fact, I bought several, which left me without any spending money for the rest of the month. It was worth it; the entertainment value was tremendous. It was obvious that the reporters had spoken to Mr. Bone, as they were nearly all in his favour. Lurid scenes were painted of tearful parents pleading with the hospital staff to save their baby from a life-threatening operation.

I wished one of the reporters had bothered to contact the ward. Sister would soon have set the record straight. Several times since that occasion, I have nursed patients that were in the news, and not once have the facts been reported accurately.

Newspaper reporters have to accept much of the blame. In each case, they reported the facts in the most sensational way possible. People like to read about dramatic situations; one rarely reads of good or happy events. At the same time the hospital was not without fault.

We were forbidden to give information to the press, and if a caller managed to get past the switchboard operator, we were told to refer them straight to the Hospital Secretary.

This august person sat in state in his office, and ran the hospital. Whilst Matron was responsible for the welfare and behaviour of the nurses, he was responsible for the hospital. Not once during my training period did I ever see the man on any ward. How he knew enough about the patients' conditions to issue statements to the press remains a mystery, unless he read the reports sent to Matron's office twice a day.

Since we all hated doing the reports, and abbreviated them so much as to render them useless, he would not have been in a position to give any worthwhile information.

Had the reporters been told a few honest facts about the patient, maybe they would not have printed quite so much rubbish. I once remember a man sitting up in bed reading aloud to the ward that he was not expected to live.

The mums on the ward were still arguing about Mark's case when I went back on duty. I was regarded by some as the heroine, and others as the abductor. Sister decided that I was best out of the way and sent me down to the Baby ward.

As I was to be working with the babies for a while, I was given proper training on how to look after them. There were only five babies in the ward on my first day, and as there were three nurses on duty, I thought that I was in for an easy day. I was wrong!

First, I was shown how to bath a baby, and then I bathed one under supervision. Bathing a baby is not an easy task. There was as row of special baby baths. They were only shallow sinks with a draining board, but they were supposed to have been designed specially for the job. The sink was filled with warm water and a warm towel was put on the draining board. The baby was put on the towel and undressed, then the towel wrapped round to form a cocoon. Having contained the waving arms, the face and hair were given a wash.

That bit was easy; the next was the difficult part. The baby was unwrapped and laid on the draining board. One lathered one's hands with soap, and transferred the soap suds from the hands to the infant's body. The wet, wriggling, and usually screaming infant, was picked up in wet soapy hands and lowered into the water. After that, it was swished about a bit to rinse it, then scooped out of the water and put back on the towel and dried, powdered and dressed.

I bathed two babies that morning. They both waited until I had put a clean nappy underneath them before emptying both their bowels and their bladders. That meant that I had to clean their bottoms and fold a new nappy. Folding a nappy is an acquired art, and at that time I was far from expert. One had to be very careful how one picked up a baby after it had been changed. As the baby was lifted up, the nappy fell down.

I learnt a very valuable lesson during that bath session. It is unwise to stand directly in front of a naked baby boy. When they pee, the jet of urine comes forward and upwards with tremendous force, wetting anything within a three foot radius. One scored a direct hit on my cap, the other only managed to wet the bib of my apron. I decided that I preferred nursing older children.

Once the little darlings were all nice and clean, we fed them. I liked that; one could legitimately sit down. The baby I had been given to feed was eight weeks old, and had been admitted in the early hours of the morning.

He had a history of vomiting after his feeds for the last few days. The problem had apparently reached crisis point after his 2 A.M. feed.

He had not yet had a feed since his admission, so Sister came to watch him being fed. I gave him half of his milk, then sat him up and rubbed his back to bring up his wind. I was rewarded with a loud burp. He took the rest of the bottle without any bother, then, as I sat him up to wind him again, he was sick.

It came out in a stream that shot across the room. No wonder his mother had sent for a doctor; the poor soul must have been panic stricken. Sister had positioned herself behind me. I now understand why. She had already decided that the baby had *Pyloric Stenosis*, a narrowing of the outlet to the stomach.

Sister emerged from behind me,

"Perfect. Very good demonstration. Get him clean and we'll show him to doctor. Don't clean the floor. I want doctor to see how far the vomit reached."

I was happy about that. It was going to be bad enough cleaning the baby, as he was wet from head to toe, half from the vomit and half from the urine. As we did not have any plastic pants to cover the nappy, I was rather damp myself.

It was back to the sink. I didn't want to chance bathing the infant without supervision, so I just sponged off the smelly bits and changed his clothes. By the time I had him clean and dry, I had reached the conclusion that babies are not unlike horses. They know straight away if their handler is inexperienced and play up.

Dr. Kerr was suitably impressed by the "Area of Projection," and it was arranged that the babe would go to theatre as soon as the parents could be contacted to give their consent. As it was only a minor operation it would be carried out in the ward theatre, and Sister asked me to help her with the preparations.

The theatre was really only two small rooms, one the actual operating room, and the other, a lobby, standing between the ward and the theatre. The operating room contained a small metal table, a large moveable lamp and an anesthetic trolley. The only preparation the room needed was to cover the table with several layers of sterile sheets so that the baby had something soft to lie on. Having prepared the theatre, it was time to get the baby ready.

As we left the lobby, I noticed a pair of black shoes, an apron and a sister's cam hung behind the door. Sister saw my look of surprise;

"That is my emergency uniform. If Matron is on her way down here, the porters ring and warn me, so that I have time to pop in here and get dressed."

I'd often wondered what Matron had thought of Sister's somewhat unconventional dress. She must have heard rumours, but had not yet seen for herself. Brilliant! I approved of any scheme that was out to beat the strict regime imposed on us, and Sister had managed to outwit Matron. I suddenly realised that I was not alone in trying to change things. The only difference was that Sister had just gone her own sweet way, whereas I was trying to effect change by confrontation. Maybe I should be more subtle.

As we went back to the baby, Sister asked me the question I had been dreading.

"Would you like to watch the operation?"

I felt that Sister was perhaps the one person in the hospital that might understand my problem, so I confessed.

"I *would* really, Sister, but I can't stand the sight of blood. I just faint."

Sister roared with laughter. I couldn't see that it was *that* funny.

"They are going to have fun with you in theatre aren't they? Never mind, if you want to watch you can try. The thing to do is to shut your eyes as soon as the surgeon picks up the scalpel and keep them shut until you hear him ask for a clamp. The worst is over then. I'll be there, and if you look like fainting I'll send you out. It helps if you are hungry; you can go to dinner after we have finished. I'll ask the kitchen to keep you a meal."

I agreed to give it a try. I felt confident that with Sister helping me, I might just manage to watch. I was not so sure about being able to eat anything afterwards though.

The baby's mother was sitting beside his cot when we returned to the ward, and Sister explained that he really needed an operation to correct the blockage. It would only take a few minutes, and from then on, he would be fine. The worst bit would be for Mum, as she would have to see her baby in a special splint to keep him still.

The way Sister described everything, it sounded no worse than cutting his toenails! Once his mother had signed the consent form, Sister started to prepare the baby. He was undressed and loosely bandaged onto a padded cruciform splint, then covered over with blankets. He was not at all impressed and screamed his head off. Sister picked him up and gave him to his Mum to cuddle.

After a few minor difficulties, he was quieted. It is not easy to hold a baby in a Rammstedt's splint. One hand has to hold the baby and splint, the other, the nappy.

By the time Mum was happy to be left holding her baby, the doctors had arrived. Sister left to make sure that they had everything they needed.

"When they are ready I'll call you. Bring Clive with you."

It hadn't occurred to me to ask the baby's name. To me they were just babies! Once I knew his name, he became a person, rather than a squalling brat. I began to feel quite fond of him.

All too soon they were ready, and I was faced with the problem of taking the baby from his mother. We tried a direct handover, but there seemed to be too many arms and legs and they kept getting in the way. In the end, Mum put him down in his cot, and I picked him up from there. I found that the only way I could carry him was to hold him against the bib of my apron, with one hand supporting his head and the other under his nappy. By this time he was yelling his head off, and as I walked down the corridor he was sick all down my front.

Sister took the baby off me as I went into theatre, and handed me a mask. Once she had put the baby on the table, she came and stood by me. The small room was full of people. As well as the operating team, Dr. Samuels, the consultant Peadiatrician was there. Sister introduced me to him, and said,

"Dr. Samuels, Nurse wants to watch. We are a bit short of staff; is it alright if she stands by the door so that she can slip out if she is needed?"

I had never seen the consultant before. He was a small grey haired man and reported to be very fierce. He stared at me for a while, then said,

"As long as she closes the door after her."

The anaesthetist put a mask over the baby's face and after a few seconds nodded. That was the signal for the operation to start. Sister stood just in front of me throughout the operation, and told me what they were doing at every step. She kept on leaning forward and obstructing my view, which annoyed me at first. Then I realised that she only did it when she expected blood to flow.

A small hole was made in the lower part of the baby's chest and the pyloric sphincter, the valve at the outlet end of the stomach, exposed.

Dr. Samuels asked me if I could see properly. There was, he said, room for me round the table if I wanted a better view. I declined his offer and stood propped up against the door.

The surgeon made a small incision in the sphincter to cut the muscles, and before the blood had time to flow, had stitched it up again. The rest of the hole was closed, a dressing put on the top and the job was done.

Sister told me to hold the door open for her. She picked up the splinted baby with an ease that showed years of practice, and took him back to his cot. It had taken ten minutes, including the time taken to take him to and from the theatre.

Once we had him settled in his cot, Sister sent me off to dinner, telling me that when I came back, I was to sit with the baby. I was surprisingly hungry, and very proud of myself. With Sister's help I had managed to watch an operation.

When I reached the dining room, all there was to eat was corned beef salad and cold rice pudding. I was not impressed. It was a freezing cold day and I wanted something hot. I refused to eat the salad, and demanded a hot meal. After a great deal of arguing with the cooks, we reached a compromise. I had the salad supplemented with a slice of bacon, an omelette and baked beans. A hot rice pudding was produced from somewhere, and I was happy.

Clive was awake by the time I returned from my dinner, and Sister settled me beside his cot with a list of instructions. He was to be offered a teaspoon full of glucose every quarter of an hour for two hours. If he managed to take that without vomiting, the amount could be increased. I was to assess just how much liquid he had taken at each attempt, and keep a fluid chart.

Giving a baby anything off a teaspoon is not easy, and when it is something with an unfamiliar taste, it is quite impossible. Clive had never met a spoon before, and as soon as he felt the cold hard object in his mouth, he reacted. Instead of sucking the liquid off the spoon and swallowing it, he spat the spoon out. I found that, if I stuck my finger in his mouth and trickled the glucose onto my finger, he sucked and swallowed. How much actually got a s far as his stomach I was not prepared to say.

I was not too worried. Sister had said that he was to be offered, not that he was to have, after all. I had offered him the drink and he had refused.

By the time I went off duty I was managing to get him to swallow most of the teaspoon full, and I was rather pleased. I did not admit this to Sister. I was afraid that she might decide that I should stay, and give him the rest of his feeds.

The Bush telegraph had been busy during the afternoon, and by the time I went for my tea, everyone appeared to have heard about my battle with the cooks. They actually called themselves chefs, but to me a chef was a master cook. The lot we had in the kitchen were a long way from being masters at anything.

As I sat eating my stale bread and butter, two third year nurses came and joined me. I was indeed honoured! They introduced themselves as Mohammed and Carstairs and asked me if I would help them. I said I would, but only if they joined the S.N.A.!

I had enough to do looking after members, without taking up the fight for just anyone that had a problem. They agreed to join, and told me what was bothering them.

Carstairs was a vegetarian, and was having to live mainly on soggy vegetables. Friday was not a problem as we had fish, which she ate. During the rest of the week, the only protein offered was meat. She had asked if she might have an egg or some cheese, but had been refused. Matron had sent for her and told her that she was being stupid; she *must* eat meat.

In the enlightened eighties, we are more conscious of our diet, and a vegetarian is no longer regarded as a crank. Then, it was a different matter. We all had to conform; there was no room for the individual.

Mohammed's problem was not so bad. Most of the time she managed to avoid things that, as a Muslim, she was forbidden to eat. It was during the period of Ramadan that she had trouble, as she needed to observe a fast between the hours of sunrise and sunset. Matron's answer to the problem had been to make sure that all Muslim girls were on night duty during Ramadan.

That was at least *some* help, they were able to eat a meal at midnight, but they did not get any breakfast or supper. Mohammed had asked the cooks if she might have some sandwiches to take on duty, so that she could have something to eat as soon as it was dark. Her request had been refused.

I was annoyed that the kitchen staff were able to dictate our eating habits, and to some extent, how we observed our religion. We all had to eat fish on Friday to please the Catholics, but any other religion was ignored. I decided to take up the cause. It was, after all, a while since I had something worthwhile to fight for. If I wasn't careful, Matron might think that I had become staid in my second year.

I spent the evening composing a letter to the Head cook, setting out our complaints and asking that some consideration be given to individual diets. As the evening wore on, word spread that I was trying to do something about the food, and more and more nurses visited me with their complaints. By the time I had finished the letter it was late, so I just addressed it and left it on the table in the deserted kitchen.

Deserted, that is, by humans. As I turned on the light to see my way to the table, the cockroaches dived for cover.

I spent most of the next morning in Matron's Office. I had hardly started work when I was summoned to her presence. Had I stopped to think, I would have waited and delivered the letter on a day that Matron was not at the Annex. That would have given me a little more time to judge the reaction from the kitchen.

I felt that the points I had made were valid. I had not said that they were rotten cooks; I had simply asked that we be given a choice of meal, and that provision was made to allow the keeping of religious fasts. I would not give way. I explained that it was not me that had complained; I had been asked to act on behalf of members of the S.N.A.

I could see that Matron thought that I was being tiresome, but I was past caring. She could only ask me to leave, and that wouldn't have bothered me too much. I was tired of being treated like an idiot, having no privacy, appalling food and very little free time.

Suddenly, I could stand the system no longer, and I lost my temper. I told her that I had written to the R.C.N. and the G.N.C. asking that out plight be investigated. We were all tired of working long hours and being hungry. We resented the fact that we were unable to lock our room doors, or even to have a bath without worrying that someone might walk into the room.

Matron stood up, and I think came very near to losing her temper.

"Go back to work." she said angrily, "I will consider what to do with you later."

Sister wanted to know what had been happening, so I told her. She was marvellous. I hadn't really written to either the R.C.N. or the G.N.C., so Sister took me into her office and helped me compose both letters. Once they were written, she dispatched a porter to the post box with them. I spent a few days worrying about all that I had said to Matron, and then forgot about it. Eventually, I was called to her office. On her desk were two letters addressed to me. One had the R.C.N. stamp on it, the other, that of the G.N.C. She handed them to me and told me to open them.

I refused, and put them behind the bib of my apron. She was furious, and demanded to see what was in them. The more she demanded, the more I refused. I could see that the interview was not doing either of us any good, so I left. I resisted the temptation to bang the door behind me.

Sister was waiting for me when I got back, and I opened the letters. They both acknowledged receipt of my letters, and promised that they would investigate my complaints.

All was quiet for weeks after that, then suddenly workmen moved into the Home and fitted locks on all the room doors. A notice was put up saying that the hospital had decided to appoint two members of the nursing staff to the Catering Committee. Nominations were wanted, and an election would be held.

The only names put forward were mine and Sister Children's, so there was no need for an election. From then on, we had to suffer the boredom of a monthly committee meeting.

The meetings were always held at dinner times, and a buffet was left ready for the committee members. There were vol-au-vents, salmon and cucumber sandwiches, fresh salads, a hot meat dish, hot vegetables, jacket potatoes, and fresh fruit. I hadn't seen so much as an apple since I left P.T.S.

The surprising thing to me was the high quality of the cooking. Of course, the other committee members had never eaten the food prepared for the nurses. The only experience they had of hospital food was that served to them at their meetings. Understandably, they could not appreciate why we were complaining. The food served to them was superb. Sister solved that problem by bringing a meal from the staff dining room. It was Irish stew, mash and cabbage. It couldn't have been a better meal to bring; the stew was full of fat, the mash had black lumps in it, and the cabbage smelt awful. We won our point, and from then on, the standard of cooking rose dramatically. At every meal, even breakfast, there was a choice of main dish. At dinner there was always a green salad with either cheese or egg.

For once everyone was happy.

CHAPTER NINETEEN

Had I been on any ward other than Children's, I am sure that I would not have survived the fight with the kitchen. The support given to me by Sister was tremendous. She encouraged me when I had moments of doubt and gently pushed me in the right direction. She had won her battle against the system all those years ago, and was passing on her experience to me.

I discovered that over the years, many people have wanted to change the system, but very few have had the stamina to actually do anything about effecting a change. With her help, I decided what would make the greatest improvement to our living conditions, then tried to get things changed. I also learnt that, when dealing with authority, one should start at the highest point and work downwards, never the other way round. The knowledge that I gained from Sister in those few weeks has stood me in good stead ever since. In between writing letters and standing on the carpet in Matron's office, I managed to get some work done.

I stayed in the baby ward for two weeks. Although I did not really enjoy looking after babies, it had to be done as part of my training. I found it very harrowing, not so much nursing the babies, but coping with their parents.

How can one reassure a mother who has just given birth to a baby that has neither arms nor legs, that it was not her fault, when in fact it was, even if indirectly.

We were in the age of wonder drugs, and a new tranquilliser had been developed, heralded as a breakthrough and dispensed with gay abandon.

No one realised that if given to pregnant women, it would prevent the foetus from developing limbs. Thalidomide has become a household name, not because of its medical use, but because of the children that were born deformed as a result of its use. The drug was withdrawn by the manufacturers in the early sixties, but there were still bottles of it in medicine cupboards. Pharmacists tended to write on a dispensed bottle;

"The tablets. To be taken three times a day", or whatever instructions were given by the doctor.

Thus, a woman would go to her doctor and obtain a prescription, take a few of the pills and begin to feel better. The rest of the pills were put at the back of the cupboard in case they were ever needed again. Many women begin to feel unwell at the start of a pregnancy, often before they even know they are pregnant. It is easier to rifle through the medicine cupboard and take the rest of the pills than to visit the doctor. After all, they had cured her last time she took them.

I was lucky. By the time I started my training there were very few Thalidomide babies being born. I saw only one, and that was more than enough for me. The Maternity block rang down to the ward to ask if we would accept the baby as a patient. There was nothing wrong with her, apart from her deformities, but they did not want her in their nursery as she was bound to upset the other mothers.

They did not consider what effect taking her away from her mother would have, on either the child or the parents. At the time, "bonding," or the need to establish a link between mother and baby, was not recognised as being important. Sister however, knew that it was wrong to separate a young baby from its mother, and said so to the midwives.

After a great deal of arguing, she gave in and agreed to accept the babe. A midwife brought her down to us, bundled up in layers of clothes. The notes that came with her said that she had been seen and examined by Dr. Samuels, and was healthy. Her father had seen her and named her Rachael.

When we unwrapped her, she had not even had a bath to remove the vernix, the white greasy substance that protects the baby in the womb. Sister was furious with the midwives, and spent a long while telling them so on the 'phone.

Whatever their feelings about Rachael, they should have spared some thought for those of her parents. Many Thalidomide babies were rejected by their parents, and I feel that, in many cases, the midwives could have done a lot to prevent this from happening.

Neither of the parents knew the extent of Rachael's deformities. Her father had been told that there was something wrong with her limbs, but not what. Her mother had been told nothing, except that Rachael was being moved to the Children's Ward for observation.

Before she was transferred to us, she was wrapped in a shawl and shown to her father, so that all he could see was a mop of dark hair and a pair of blue eyes.

Sister prepared her plan of action. We were all briefed as to what to do and say. We waited somewhat anxiously for Dad to appear. Sister met him at the ward door and took him into her office to explain briefly what was wrong with his baby. Then she came and asked me to wrap up the baby in a shawl and bring her to the office.

I didn't know what Sister had said to him, but as I went in, he was pale and looked very anxious. Sister took the baby from me and gave her to him to hold. After he cuddled the baby for a while, he relaxed and said,

"She looks alright to me; she's a beautiful baby."

Only then did Sister unwrap Rachael's arms from the shawl. On her right side, her forearm was missing; her fingers grew straight out of her elbow. On her left side there was no arm at all, just fingers. So good was Sister's preparation, that he did not recoil. He gently touched Rachael's right hand, and as he did so, she bent her fingers round one of his, and gripped it.

Once he had accepted Rachael's lack of arms, Sister unwrapped the lower half of the baby. All she had in place of legs, were two short stumps. He hardly seemed to notice the lower limbs; his finger was still held fast by the tiny, malformed hand.

Sister smiled at me,

"I think a cup of tea would be nice, Nurse. We'll leave Dad and baby to get to know each other while we make it."

We left them alone together for a few minutes, then I took a cup of tea to Dad in the office. He was still sitting in the same position, his finger held fast by his daughter.

Sister eventually parted them. It was time for Rachael to have a feed, and Sister thought that it was time Dad went to explain about the baby to his wife. The poor man was understandably worried, both about how he was going to explain to her about Rachael's deformities, and of her reaction. Sister offered to do the explaining, and went with him, saying,

"If the midwives can't do their own job properly, they had better not try to stop me doing it for them."

Rachael was only with us for two days. Her mother discharged herself from the Maternity Ward because she wanted to be with her baby. On her way home, she had called into the ward and asked how often she could visit. Sister told her that the only reason that we had the baby was because no one else wanted her. There was no reason why she could not go home. So, Rachael went home to the care of her parents and the District Midwife.

In my third year of training, I spent a week with a Health visitor, who, hearing that I had nursed Rachael, took me to see the family. Rachael was eighteen months old then, and was very mobile. She sat on her bottom and wriggled along at an amazing speed. Her speech was very advanced for her age, her favourite phrase being "Me oshus brat."

Her mother looked embarrassed, and explained that, as neither she nor her husband felt that they could discipline Rachael, she was rapidly becoming a very precocious child, and they often told her so. The nearest Rachael could manage to precocious was oshus!

They were hoping that Rachael would soon be fitted with artificial legs, so that she could learn to balance and walk, and so lead a more normal life.

The one good thing to come out of the tragedy of thalidomide was the tremendous advance it brought about in the development of artificial limbs for children.

One of the duties of nurses on the baby ward was to prepare the daily feeds. Breast feeding was going through one of its unfashionable phases, and all the babies that I helped to nurse were bottle fed. The choice of milk was left very much to the mother.

There were several options, among them National Dried Milk, sold in the Child Welfare Clinics at a very low price. It had been introduced during the war to ensure that milk for babies was readily available.

It was not a popular feed, mainly because it was very difficult to mix. However carefully it was done, it was nearly impossible to mix without getting lumps of powder, and thus had to be strained into the bottle. Fortunately we had only one baby having National Dried. One of the babies was having a proprietary dried milk that *was* easy to mix. One measured out the water, then dropped in the appropriate number of scoops of milk powder into the water and gave it a stir; instant food and no lumps. The others all had tinned milk.

I shudder to think of it now, feeding very small babies on diluted evaporated milk! High in fat, sugar, salt and all manner of things that we have since been told mean certain death to an infant. Since we were unaware of the dangers, we happily fed it to the babies, and they thrived.

I liked mothers who had decided to use evaporated milk, as it was the easiest to mix. They chose it because they could get it from their local shop. They did not have to make a trip to the clinic, or to the chemist. They could just pop down the road and get a couple of tins at a time, rather than having to buy a week's supply.

Each baby had six feeds a day, and all the feeds were mixed in the morning and measured into glass bottles marked with the baby's name. A rubber cap was fitted over the neck of the bottle, and the bottles put in the 'fridge. The feeds were warmed before being given to the babies by placing them in a jug of hot water. It was the responsibility of the "Milk Kitchen Nurse" to see that the feeds were taken out the 'fridge half an hour before each feed time, so that the bottle warmed up a little. If this was not done, the bottles tended to crack as they were put in the water, and another feed had to be mixed. I soon found it prudent to mix an extra feed than to have to mix another one because I had cracked a bottle.

Once used, the bottles and teats were cleaned and boiled for ten minutes, then stored in a bucket of Milton. Since Sister was generally very progressive, I could not understand why she insisted on boiling; Milton was in itself a steriliser. Nothing would convince her that the bottles would sterilise in a solution.

I had been told that I was to stay with the babies for a month. After two weeks I was counting the remaining days. I couldn't wait to go back to the older children.

When Sister asked for a volunteer to help in the Isolation ward, I saw it as a chance to escape from nursing babies. There was an outbreak of whopping cough, and the nurses were rushed off their feet. I rapidly volunteered, as I knew that I was immune to the disease, having had it as a child.

The Isolation Ward consisted of a long line of small rooms, either side of a central corridor. Each room had been designed to house one bed. The ward was so busy that there were either two beds or four cots in most of the rooms. As I had no experience of "Barrier Nursing," the nursing of infectious cases, I was sent to work with the staff nurses for the morning.

As Staff described our first task of the day, I thought that she was joking. We had to remove a patient from an iron lung! In my innocence, I had thought them to be a thing of the past.

We entered a room dominated by a metal cylinder. All that was showing of the patient was a head sticking out of one end. As we entered the room, I could see a face reflected in a mirror above the cylinder. Staff looked into the mirror and introduced me to Paula, the patient. I watched fascinated as Staff turned knobs and twirled levers. Then she pulled on a bar behind the patient's head, and slid out a stretcher, complete with patient.

Staff explained that Paula was a victim of Polio. She was no longer able to rely on her body to breathe naturally; each breath was a conscious effort. That was fine all the while she was awake, but when she fell asleep, she stopped breathing.

I found nursing Paula very difficult. She had been a ballet dancer, and the room contained several photographs of her on the stage. A once vibrant and talented woman was now reduced to having to think about every breath. Even her speech was laboured; she had to stop after a few words and breathe.

I was glad when we had her settled in a chair, and I could leave her. During the time I spent on the Isolation Ward, I tried hard to avoid Paula. I did not find it easy to see her as just another patient. I was unable to forget that such a promising dancer was reduced to sitting in a chair, or lying in a machine, viewing the world through a mirror.

I knew the theory of barrier nursing. One put on a protective gown before approaching the patient. The gowns were kept inside the room door and labelled with the patient's name. After treating the patient one hung up the gown, washed one's hands, then moved on to the next patient before repeating the process. So much for theory.

I spent the rest of my first morning in a room with four very small children that were at the whooping stage of Whooping Cough. I don't think I changed my gown once. No sooner had one child stopped whooping than another would start.

Whooping Cough is one of the nastier of the childhood diseases. It starts innocently enough; the child gets a runny nose and slight cough. The cough worsens and then the characteristic whoop appears. By then, the child is very ill. Each coughing fit can last up to ten minutes, during which time the child is literally fighting for breath, and very often goes blue as a result of oxygen starvation. Eventually, the child is exhausted and the coughing stops. Often the child vomits at the end of each bout of coughing. As these attacks may occur at frequent intervals, often as many as twenty times a day, the child rapidly becomes very weak. The force of the cough can result in rupture of lung tissue and the lack of oxygen may cause brain damage.

The only way in which we could help, was to hold the child during a bout of coughing, mainly to reassure him. There was nothing we could do to stop the cough. We just had to sit and hold the child, and always be ready to run for the oxygen bottle, there was one in every room, should a child get too blue.

At first, I found it difficult to assess when to give oxygen. After a couple of hours, I learnt the meaning of the different shades of blue. Pinky blue indicated that a child was able to recover on his own. Dark or navy blue meant that he needed oxygen, and fast.

I noticed that the main tap on the top of the cylinder had been left turned on. They were supposed to be kept tightly closed, in case the valve leaked and the gas was wasted. Staff explained why it was left on,

"If you have a blue child in your arms, you haven't the time to fit the spanner and turn on the main tap. Sometimes that is only just enough time to turn on the valve."

Beside each oxygen bottle was a pile of disposable polymasks, and one was already connected to the tubing. These masks were made of perforated polythene; they were easy to use, and comfortable for the patient to wear, yet were unpopular with most sisters.

I spent six days on the Isolation Ward. During that time, the longest break I had was two hours one afternoon. Sister had given me the afternoon off, but I was called back to the ward early, as they were expecting an admission and there was no one free to deal with it.

When it arrived, it was a baby covered in spots. It was quite usual for a ward to be expecting an admission about which they knew nothing. It was worse on the Isolation Ward, as the patient could have been of any age and either sex. All we knew on this occasion was that we were expecting an admission, and that the patient had spots.

Helen was two weeks old and was suspected of having *Pemphigus Neonatorum*, a highly contagious condition caused by a *Staphylococcus aureus* infection. She was covered in large watery blisters and looked a very sorry sight. It was back to nursing babies! Helen was given antibiotics and the blisters painted with Gentian Violet, a purple antibacterial liquid.

Despite the antibiotics, Helen did not improve, and by the next morning she was a very ill baby. Dr. Kerr had spent most of the night with her, and had commenced an intravenous drip, as she was unable to swallow. The only vein that he could find was on the side of her head, so the poor mite had been shaved and her head was supported on a splint to stop her moving and dislodging the canula.

Her parents had been called, and they had asked for a priest to baptise her. Dr. Samuels arrived before the priest. He asked the parents if he might try a new drug on Helen. He explained that although other doctors had used Cortisone on similar cases, he had never used it himself. It might save Helen or it might not, but he felt that the risk was worth taking. They agreed, and I was sent to prepare an injection tray.

I felt very honoured to be present at the administration of a new drug. New, at least to us, other hospitals had probably been using it for years.

Dr. Samuels had a vial of the drug in his pocket, and he drew a minute amount of it into the syringe, then injected it into the top of Helen's leg. Nothing happened. Helen was too ill even to cry at the pain. We all stood and watched, half expecting a miracle, half expecting Helen to stop breathing.

While we were waiting, the priest arrived and rapidly baptised Helen. Despite the drama of the situation, I was amused that a Catholic priest was conducting a baptism in the presence of a Jewish doctor and an agnostic nurse.

No sooner had the priest left the room, than Helen opened her eyes and began to cry.

Dr. Samuels repeated the Cortisone injection in the afternoon, and again in the evening. By the end of the day she was taking her feeds from a bottle and the blisters were drying up. The next day she had only a few crusts to show where the blisters had been. The day after that, she was discharged, a fit and happy baby. All that there was to show that she had been ill, was a large area on the side of her head without any hair, and a few dry spots on her skin.

I was convinced that Cortisone was a wonder drug, and plucked up the courage to ask Dr. Samuels to explain what it was and how it worked. He told me,

"It is an artificial steroid. How it works I do not know. Nor do I know if it was the drug that saved her. It might just as easily have been the priest."

I was convinced that it had been the drug, not the priest, that had caused the sudden change in Helen, but as I progressed through my training, I was not so sure. I have several times seen a moribund baby unaccountably recover after baptism.

Matron insisted that every nurse be sufficiently familiar with the baptism ritual to be able to baptise an infant in an emergency. On the Maternity Wards and on the Children's Ward, there was a bottle of Holy water, reputed to have been sent to us from Lourdes. It was there to be used by the nursing staff in an emergency. It was only to be used if a clergyman was not available.

I thought that the whole idea was too stupid for words. What difference was one of us going to make by sprinkling the baby with water and making the sign of the cross on its forehead? Half of us weren't even Christians!

When I returned to Children's from Isolation, Sister asked me to go on nights for a week. On my second night, I was the senior nurse; the whole ward was my responsibility and I was terrified.

In the middle of the night, the Maternity Block sent down a baby of three days old that was having continuous convulsions. The mother came down with the baby. Convinced that it was going to die, she had insisted on being allowed to leave her bed. One look at the baby, and I agreed with her.

Dr. Kerr injected all sorts of things into the baby, but it refused to come out of the fit. The mother was worried that the baby would die without being christened. Dr. Kerr explained that we could not christen the baby, but we could baptise it, thus making it acceptable to God. I thought,

"What about the bit in the bible that says, Suffer little children to come unto me." It doesn't add, but only if they have been baptised.

Dr. Kerr added that I would baptise the baby. He couldn't, as he was not a Christian. I fetched the water, sprinkled it on the baby's head and repeated the words taught me by Matron. I had no idea what the parents were going to call the child. I looked at the mother, hoping that she would supply at least one name, but she was in deep prayer. There was only one thing to do; I gave the baby my own name.

As I made the sign of the cross, the fit stopped. The baby did not have another fit that night, and was sent back to the Maternity Ward the next day.

When we had all got over the shock, I asked the mother if she had chosen names for her baby, as I had given it my own Christian names, those being the only ones I could think of in the heat of the moment. She had, in fact, decided on some names, but thought that it might be tempting fate to change the names given at baptism.

I stayed on the ward until Sister arrived the next morning. I wanted her to reassure me that I had done the right thing. All she said was,

"It was a jolly good job the baby was a girl. A boy would have had a difficult time in life with *your* names."

CHAPTER TWENTY

The following night, I was again in charge of the ward. The early part of the night was quiet, and by midnight we had done all our chores. As all the dressings now came direct from C.S.S.D., there were no drums to pack, and we used only disposable syringes. It made a terrific difference to the work load, as there were only the two sterilisers to empty, clean and refill. I sent my junior to her meal, then crept round with a torch to see that all *my* children were asleep.

I stood for a while looking out of one of the windows. There was still a sprinkling of snow on the ground. Not enough to be a nuisance, but just sufficient to reflect the moonlight and give everything an eerie quality. It was a beautiful clear night, and I could see the lights twinkling in the distant town.

I began to feel cold, so I went and settled myself in the office with a book. It was possible to position a chair so that one could see out into the ward through the office door. I had never found the time to read on duty before, but had always carried a book, just in case. The book I had with me was one of Dennis Wheatley's Black Magic stories.

As so often happens, I became totally immersed in my book. Just as the hero was preparing to defend himself against all manner of unspeakable manifestations, I heard stealthy footsteps in the corridor. I leapt out of the chair and hid behind the door, grabbing the torch to use as a weapon!

The door opened wider, and there stood Night Sister. I felt an utter fool. My embarrassment was increased when she asked me if I would like her to stay until the junior got back from dinner. I could not explain that I was not afraid of being on my own, but that I was frightened because I had thought she was the Devil! For a start, I should not have been reading on duty.

Since then, I have always taken a light novel to read at night. Nothing more scary than Georgette Heyer.

Sister had come to warn me that there was a baby on its way down from maternity, and it was going to need an exchange transfusion. That was fairly typical of the midwives. They so often treated the Children's Ward as a dumping ground for all their unwanted jobs. There was no reason at all why the baby could not have been transfused on their ward, except that it was a long and tedious process.

In those days, when a baby was born to a mother with Rhesus Negative blood, and if the baby's father was Rh. Positive, the baby often developed severe jaundice shortly after birth. The only way to save the baby was to exchange a large proportion of its blood.

I explained to Night Sister that I had never seen an exchange transfusion and had no idea what to do. She simply told me that we all had to learn sometime.

After she left, I consulted the ward Book of Procedures and found a list of things that would be needed. I managed to find most of the items on the list, set up a trolley and took it into the operating theatre.

Dr. Kerr arrived before the baby, and checked the trolley. He said that all he needed was a small blood canula, a three way adapter, three pieces of tubing, a Y connector and a syringe. Most of the equipment I had prepared was redundant.

The baby arrived at last, accompanied by a midwife and a porter. Fortunately, the porter had thought to collect the bottle of blood on his way down.

The baby was put on the table, and sedated. Then we started to change his blood. The canula was passed into the umbilical vein and connected to the syringe. This was then joined via a system of tubes and valves, to a bottle containing the new blood, and another one to take the old blood.

Ten c.c.'s of blood was withdrawn from the baby, and replaced with 10 c.c.'s of fresh blood taken from the bottle. Then we waited for five minutes. At the end of that time, I had to count the baby's pulse and respiration rate. After that, Dr. Kerr repeated the exercise. I had to write the figures on a board so that we did not lose count. There were two columns, in and out.

The baby weighed six and a half pounds. He was to receive 80 c.c. of fresh blood for every pound of his body weight. That meant 520 c.c.'s at the rate of 10 c.c.'s every six minutes. The whole operation took over five hours. No wonder the midwives had passed the job to us. There had to be a gap of five minutes between every 10 c.c.'s transfused, in case the baby reacted to the fresh blood. Any increase in the heart or respiration rate indicated that the baby did not like the new blood. The transfusion would then be stopped.

I learnt a great deal in those five hours. Dr. Kerr explained all about Rhesus factor, what happened to babies born to Rh. incompatible parents, and why so many of them were stillborn. Basically, the mother developed antibodies to her own child, and her blood destroyed that of the baby. The lucky babies were born early and transfused. The unlucky ones had their blood digested and were born dead.

I was pleased that I knew my blood group. I was Rh. Positive, so my babies would be alright! He went on to tell me about all the other congenital abnormalities. Hydrocephalus, anencephaly and spina bifida to name but a few. In those days, there were no intra-uterine tests for foetal abnormality, so a far higher proportion of babies were born with congenital defects.

I decided then that I would not have any children. It was altogether far too chancy.

In the late sixties, a way was discovered to prevent the formation of Rhesus antibodies, and from then on, any Rh. Negative mother was given an injection as soon as her first baby was born. The horrors of the Rhesus baby were then over.

It had been a long night and it wasn't over yet. I had to clean up the theatre, get the baby properly admitted, write the Kardex reports on the rest of the children and fill in the Night Report for Matron. I left the ward at eight-thirty, an hour late.

Breakfast had been cleared away by the time I reached the Home, but I was almost too tired to care. My junior had told the kitchen staff that I would be late, and they cooked me a proper supper. I had soup, bacon, omelette and chips followed by a fruit salad. For once I did not go to bed hungry. Instead of being grateful to have any food at all, it started me thinking. If they could cook a meal for one, why couldn't they cook for all the night staff. Why were we only offered cereal and dried up fried breakfast for our supper?

I started a long, drawn out campaign. It took a year before the cooks gave in, and the night staff had breakfast and supper cooked for them at the appropriate times of their day.

The rest of my week was spent as junior, and I enjoyed being able to ask someone else to make the decisions. I had found out how little I really knew!

It was nice to be back on day duty. I had found it difficult to adjust to nights, knowing that it was only for one week. During the past two weeks, several nurses had been moved off the ward. There was now only Gale and a third year called Ellerman that were my seniors.

I realised that there would be times when I would be left in charge of the ward. I was nineteen years old; I had been training for one year and three months, and had been nursing children for just over one of those months. Yet I was going to be expected to assume responsibility for the lives of young children and babies.

It was one thing to be left in charge at night. There was always Night Sister to call on in times of crisis. During the day, there was no one other than Matron's office staff. Only the feeble rang them for help.

Being in charge of the ward meant that I held the keys to the drug cupboards and was responsible for giving out medicines. I also had to organise the work of the other nurses, cope with telephone calls and deal with relatives. There was always the chance of an admission as well.

It was one hell of a load to put on young and inexperienced shoulders. Sister managed the off-duty list so that I was only left in charge at the weekends, and then, only for the afternoons. Things were a lot quieter at these times. Eventually, the time came when I was left "on my own" one evening in the week. The ward was very busy, and Sister stayed until 6:30 P.M. to get as much of the paper work done as possible. Before she left, she gave out the six o'clock medicines. I was left to report any changes between then and the time I went off at 8:30 P.M., also to write out Matron's report and help with the ward work.

No sooner had Sister gone than the 'phone rang. It was a local G.P. to say that he was sending in an eight year old boy in *Status Asthmaticus*, an uncontrollable asthmatic state. I was given the child's name and address, and told which drugs he had already been given. The parents were bringing the child by car. He had been a patient before, so they knew how to get to the ward. The doctor apologised for organising the admission himself, but he had been unable to contact Dr. Kerr.

I tried to find Dr. Kerr, but the switchboard operator said that she had been trying to contact him for over half an hour. The last she had heard of him was when she gave him a message from Maternity. Since then he was not answering his bleep.

I really *was* on my own. My only hope was the child's old notes, so I rang the Porter's Lodge and asked if one of them would be kind enough to dig out the notes from Medical Records. I could not go myself, and there weren't enough nurses to go round as it was. I could not spare one to go searching for records.

The porter arrived seconds before the child. I had just enough time to thank him, and to ask him if he saw Dr. Kerr to tell him that he was wanted urgently. Dr. Kerr appeared within five minutes, confirming my belief that the most useful people on the hospital staff are the porters.

The child's name was Edward, and he was a frequent visitor to the ward. His folder of notes was very thick. He had been a patient five times in the last year. I didn't have time to admit him properly, so I just settled him in bed ready for Dr. Kerr to treat, and laid out in the clinical room a few things that I thought might be needed.

Doctor examined Edward, then asked me to get him some adrenaline and some ephedrine. I didn't know where to look for either, and said so. There was not time for me to begin a slow search through the drug cupboard. Luckily, he knew where they were, so I handed him the keys and let him look.

Had anyone come into the ward and seen a doctor with the ward drug cupboard keys in his hand, I would have been in very serious trouble. The keys were to be kept "pinned to the person of the nurse in charge of the ward." She, and she alone, was the only one authorised to unlock the cupboards.

Whilst I could see the logic behind this rule, there were times when it added an extra burden. I should really have found a nurse to look after Edward, and then gone with Dr. Kerr. There was not time. The child was blue, his breathing very laboured, and he was rapidly losing consciousness. Every second counted; there wasn't time to waste minutes. It was just one more example of bureaucratic stupidity. I had not even had the results of my prelims, yet I was expected to guard the drugs. Dr. Kerr, a qualified doctor in his third year of post-graduate training, was not considered a responsible person. I knew which of us was most likely to make a fatal mistake, even if the Office didn't.

I was a bit surprised when Dr. Kerr walked into the room with two syringes in his hand, and even more surprised when he put them down on the top of the bedside locker, rolled up Edward's sleeve and gave him the first injection. He hadn't even wiped the skin. Then, he disconnected the syringe from the needle, leaving the needle in the child's arm, fitted the second syringe to the needle and gave the second injection.

I stayed with the boy until his breathing settled down and then went to find Dr. Kerr. He was sitting, writing up Edward's notes. I asked for the keys, and he felt through his pockets until he found them. As he handed them over, he said,

"You face was a picture; all this nonsense about injection trays is only to give you nurses something to do. All you need to give an injection is the drug, a needle and a syringe. It is a far more sterile procedure done that way than the way you lot do it."

I had never thought about it before, but he had a point. There really wasn't any need to take a syringe out of its packet, put it in a receiver, fill a gallipot with spirit, fill another one with cotton wool swabs, then cover the lot with a towel. If the things had been sterile to start with, by the time we had finished, they probably weren't.

The ward was in chaos when the night staff arrived. In between checking Edward to see that he was still breathing normally, I had managed to write the report for Matron and send it up to the Office, but I had not written out Edward's admission forms, nor had I done the Kardex reports, checked any of the other children, or written out the order to give to pharmacy the next day. I had at least an hour's work to do.

There is usually a terrific animosity between day and night staff. Neither shift will lift a finger to help the other, and rude notes about unfinished work abound. I never have understood why, although I have often been as guilty as the rest.

It was different on Children's, and I can only think that it was because we were all part of a team. We might be on day duty today, but tomorrow, Sister might move us to nights. Each shift did as much as they could to help the next.

While I wrote out the Kardex, one of the night girls filled in Edward's admission forms, and another did the list for pharmacy. I was only fifteen minutes late going off duty. Had I been any later, there would have been yet another argument with the kitchen staff.

As I left the Home the next morning, Home Sister stopped me to say that Matron wanted to see me at ten o'clock. My heart sank. She must have heard that I had handed over the keys the day before. It was the only thing that I could think of, unless I had again broken a rule that I did not know existed.

I presented my self at her door on the dot of ten, and was made to wait for ten minutes. When I went in, she handed me a letter and told me to open it. I refused. I was not going to open my letters in front of her. It was addressed to me. If the letter in it was for her to see, then she would have received a copy.

Surprisingly, she gave in without a fight. Then she said,

"The local Carnival Committee have asked if the nurses would provide a float for the carnival this year. The carnival is to coincide with the end of the college rag week, so I thought that it would be nice for the student nurses to man the float. I will organise a lorry for you, and I have here a list of suggested themes. I'll leave the rest for you to arrange."

She handed me a sheet of paper and dismissed me. I pushed the paper behind my bib and forgot about it. I was more interested in the letter. As soon as I had shut the door behind me, I opened the envelope. It contained a scrappy piece of paper on which was a duplicated letter. It said that I had been successful in passing parts one and two of my Preliminary State Examination. My name was written at the bottom of the letter.

One year of blood, sweat and tears, and all I had to show for it was a cheap bit of paper, eight inches long by four inches wide, with a duplicated message on it. It was not even addressed to me, only "Dear Madam." After all the effort I had put in, I thought that they might have managed something a little better than that.

The letter was dated twenty-fifth of March; it was then the thirtieth. Matron must have had the letter for days. I resented the way she sorted through our post, and removed anything that looked official to give to us personally. I was even more angry when I realised that she already knew what was in it, because she received notification of the results from the G.N.C. The old bat didn't even congratulate me.

Sister did though, and she made sure that all the children knew I had passed a very important exam. They spent the day drawing "Well Done" cards. I still have them in my box of treasures. They mean more to me than the bit of paper from the G.N.C. After all, a lot of effort went into those cards.

I forgot about the carnival until I took my apron off that evening, then Matron's list fell on the floor. I was not very impressed with any of her suggestions, so I put it ready to take on duty the next day. I was sure that Sister would have some better ideas, and if not, there was until the end of May to think of something.

Sister said that it would be unwise to upset Matron by ignoring all her suggestions. One of Matron's ideas was a float to depict nurses at work. Why not expand on the idea, using Children's Ward as a theme. I wrote to Matron saying that the S.N.A. would prepare a float showing nurses caring for children. I had a lovely letter in reply, agreeing to the theme and offering help should we need any.

It was now April, and the weather was improving daily. The grass in front of the ward was used as a play area for the children, and as they were not allowed to play unsupervised, we had a chance to sit in the sun. Sister was a great believer in the healing properties of fresh air, and any child fit enough was sent out to play.

The babies were put into prams and pushed round the grounds. It was marvellous to be out for a walk whilst still on duty. Instead of forcing myself out in free moments, I was actually being sent for a walk.

In the middle of April, the change list went up with my name on it. I was to move back to the Main Hospital and work on the Female Surgical Ward. I was not at all pleased. I liked the freedom of the Annex Home, and I had become used to having my own room. Now I would have to share, and worse, I would be nursing women. I was feeling very depressed.

My depression deepened as the week wore on. Even the plans for the float filed to cheer me up. Sister had given me two days off at the end of my last week, so I had the whole weekend to move. She promised to find some packing cases for me, as I had far too many bits and pieces to fit in my suitcases.

My last afternoon on Children's was one of those hot sunny April days. I was hoping that I would be sent out for a walk, as it was far too hot to stay indoors. Sister told me to take one of the older babies out for a walk. I was just going out of the door with the pram when she called me back.

"Nurse, I forgot to collect my bread from the baker. Would you be an angel and walk up and get it for me?"

"I'll go, Sister, but I'll have to get changed first."

The bakery was in the village. It was at least a mile away, and we were not allowed out of the gates in uniform.

"Nonsense," replied Sister, "You are on duty, therefore you will go in your uniform."

So, off I went in my uniform, without even a cloak. As I left, my depression lifted. I had been ordered to break one of the hospital rules.

I didn't hurry on the way to the village. The baby was nearly a year old and was sitting up in the pram waving its hands about and chattering. I parked the pram outside the bakery and went inside to collect Sister's bread. The baker was very chatty, and when he saw the pram outside the shop, he gave me some stale bread to feed the ducks on the village pond.

I lifted the baby out of the pram, and between us we scattered bread over the village green and the ducks came and gobbled it up. It was great fun. On the way back to the Annex, we stopped and picked some flowers from the side of the road to give to Sister. I was very pleased to see the hospital bus go past. I hoped that Matron was on it!

I gave Sister her bread and the flowers, then settled the baby back in its cot. Then I asked Sister if she would sign my Schedule. She apologised, but said that she was far too busy. If I went down with it the next morning about ten, she would do it then.

I went round the ward and said goodbye to the children and the mums, collecting several pictures that the children had drawn for me on my way. I was not sorry to leave the ward. I had enjoyed working for Sister, but I did not like nursing children.

I was not sure whether to wear my uniform the next day. I was not on duty, but I would be going onto the ward. In the end, I decided against it. Sister was not a great one for uniforms herself; she probably wouldn't even notice what I was wearing.

Sister was in her office with a tall young man. She introduced him as her son, Henry.

"Nurse, I hope you don't mind, but I have organised Henry to take you and your things down to the hospital. You will be able to get them moved then in one trip. While you are doing that, I will sign your book. Henry will bring you back to collect it when you have finished moving."

Henry and I toiled up and down stairs carrying cases and boxes. We packed the car, drove to the Main Home, then unpacked. The Home Sister was not inclined to allow a man into the Home, but Henry was unmoved. He explained that he had been told by his mother to help me move. If Home Sister would not allow him to help, then would she please 'phone his mother and tell her.

Once it was established that he was not my boyfriend, but was Henry, she gave way and let him in. Having unpacked the car, we returned to the ward and I collected my Schedule. It had been signed in my absence, and Sister had marked me as proficient in everything that I had put on the list, although some of the things I had clearly marked as only being observed.

I pointed out to her that she had credited me with far more than I was due. She wasn't bothered; she simply said,

"I've only done it to make sure you don't come back!"

As Henry drove me back to the town, I wondered whether or not she had been joking.

CHAPTER TWENTY-ONE

Ward Six was even worse than I imagined. As it was an acute ward, as soon as the woman were well enough, they were moved to a convalescent ward. All the patients needed constant care.

The ward was on the ground floor of the wing that had been added in the late thirties, and was behind the main courtyard, between the Operating Theatere and the Mortuary. Since all of the patients went to the former, and a horrifying number ended up in the latter, it was well placed.

Officially the ward had forty-one beds, eighteen down each side, four across the top in a large bay window, and one in a side ward. The side ward was used for patients that needed the constant attention of a "Special," or for members of staff that had been to theatre and were not well enough to return to the Sick Bay in the Home.

As it was the only female surgical ward for miles that admitted major surgery cases, there were frequently more patients than beds. On these occasions, extra beds were put up down the middle of the ward, and at one time there were six extra beds, making forty-seven patients.

A sister, two staff nurses, four student nurses and a ward maid were expected to be able to manage everything, from giving out meals to taking the bodies to the Mortuary. To say we worked hard would be the understatement of all time. Apart from a day and a half off each week, well some weeks, I do not remember having any time off during the month that I was there on day duty.

Sister spent ages each week working out an off-duty rota, but when the time came, there was just too much to do, so, we stayed until it was done, or the night staff came and took over from us. This did nothing to ease the already strained relationship between the shifts; the night staff had enough to do without having to finish our work.

There were two teams of doctors, each consisting of a Houseman, a Registrar, and a Consultant. One team operated on routine admissions on Monday and Thursday, the other on Wednesday and Friday. Emergency cases were dealt with as the need arose, so that it was rare for a day to go by without at least one patient going to theatre.

On my first day I was given the job of preparing the patients for theatre and going with them as far as the Anaesthetic Room. There were seven patients to prepare, six for abdominal surgery, and one for a thyroidectomy.

The thyroid patient was first on the list. All I had to do for her was put her onto a theatre bed, and see that she had a label on her wrist stating her name, age, ward, and expected operation. I then had to make sure she was not wearing false teeth, jewellery, make up or nail varnish, and that she had signed a consent form.

When all that was done, Staff checked out the pre-medication and gave it. Then on to the next. All the others had to be shaved, so that there was not a hair left between their armpits and their groin. The approved method was to dry shave. That is, to scrape a safety razor over the skin and remove the hairs. Can you imagine it?

It was not so much shaving the patient as pulling out the hair. Not too bad on the fine hair of the trunk, but torture when it came to the pubic hair.

I persevered with the first poor woman. It wasn't too bad because she was not very hairy, but after that, I used soap and water. No one came to check what I was doing; being half way through my second year, it was expected that I knew what to do.

As long as the patients arrived in theatre without hair, no one complained. There were far more important things to worry about than whether or not nurses were carrying out procedures in the approved classroom manner.

I was getting on fine. I had started at 7:30 A.M., and by 8:45 I had three patients ready, although only the first two had been given their pre-meds. Then the porters arrived for the first patients and I had to take her to theatre. As soon as she was anaesthetised, I fled back to the ward to carry on with my preparations.

The rest of the morning was a race against the clock. In between preparing the patients, I had to keep an eye on my watch to make sure that I gave the pre-meds an hour before the time the patient was due for theatre. I wondered what would happen if the porters arrived for a patient before I had her ready. By the end of the morning, I was so far behind that the last patient had her pre-med before she had her shave. I had only just finished when the trolley came into the ward.

It was a classic case of bad management. The women always went to theatre in the morning, and the men in the afternoon. It had always been done like this, and no one was going to alter the system.

Had anyone stopped and thought for a moment, they would surely have realised that it would have made sense to have alternated the patients; one from the women's ward, the next from the men's. That way we would at least have had time to breathe between mad dashes to the theatre.

As it was one o'clock when I took the last patient to theatre, Staff told me to go straight to dinner from theatre. The doctors were having a break when we got there, so I had to stand and wait with my patient for half an hour before they emerged. I had only fifteen minutes left on my break; it was back to bolting my food. I did not have the nerve to take my full forty-five minutes.

The afternoon was not so much of a rush, at least not for me. I wasn't a great deal of help as I did not know the ward routine. I was left to take round the tea and help with the bedpans.

As most of the women were unable to move themselves, they had to be lifted onto a bedpan. It must have been agony for them, but if they wanted to spend a penny, then they just had to suffer. We had been told in P.T.S. that if a female patient wanted to pass urine, she could be given a slipper pan. We even practiced giving them to the dummies.

The last time I saw a slipper pan was the day I left P.T.S.. They were wedge shaped pans that slid between a patients legs and under the buttocks. Why on earth they were not used on the wards I do not know. It would have saved one hell of a lot of lifting, not to mention time and pain.

Every patient on the ward that had been on a drip, and that was over half of them, was "on a fluid chart" until they were discharged. That meant that every drop of fluid, in or out, had to be measured and recorded on a chart kept at the end of the patient's bed.

The patient's fluid intake charts were a joke. It was fine all the while they were having intravenous fluids, but as soon as they were allowed to drink as much as they wanted, we were wasting out time. We were so busy that only the very ill patients had their urine measured. For the rest, we just looked into the pan and estimated the amount.

Every now and again I would make an estimate of the amount of urine in a pan, and then measure it as a check. It was surprising how accurate one could become; I was never more than twenty c.c.'s out.

The water jugs on the lockers were collected, washed, and refilled three times a day by the maid. We were supposed to go round with her and measure how much was left in each jug, deduct it from the amount that the jug held, and thus calculate the amount that the patient had drunk.

The maid would never have finished her work if she had waited for us to fiddle about like that. In practice, one of us rushed round ahead of her and asked the patients how many times they had refilled their glasses.

Way back in the mists of time, it had been decreed that patients having major surgery should remain on fluid balance charts for the whole of their stay on the ward, so we had to keep filling them in. Even the doctors thought that most of the charts were a waste of time, and once the patient came off a drip, they never looked at the charts. The only person that liked them was Sister; and she had an addiction to paperwork.

The fun came at the end of the day when the intake and output sides of the chart were added up; they were expected to almost balance. Too much or too little urine and there was something wrong with the patient's kidneys. So great was out distrust of the accuracy of the charts that they were referred to as the "Daily Lie Sheets!"

On this, my first day, I was due to finish work at 5:30 P.M. In fact, I left the ward at eight P.M. Counting the half hour that I had worked during my dinner break, I had worked three hours overtime. There was never any thought that we would get paid for working overtime, or even have the time that was owing to us as an extra day off. The Hospital came first; if we were needed, then we worked. Half the time we were not even asked, just told that we would have to stay on duty until the work was done. I noticed that the only person to go off duty on time was Sister!

Tuesday was an easy day by comparison, as there were no routine operations. Sister Ward Six was a great believer in work books and lists. There was a book for everything, baths, dressings, temperatures, and even bedpans. Every morning she wrote down in her collection of books, what was to be done and by whom. The dressing book was the worst, as she had a nasty habit of adding to it as the day went on. One minute you thought that you had finished, only to find that she had put in half a dozen more.

The work list informed me that I was to help Staff Nurse Dennis to do the dressings. There were eighteen of them, ten to be done before lunch time, ready for the consultant's afternoon round.

Dennis was a happy red-haired woman in her mid-twenties. She had only been qualified for two years, and could still remember what it was like to be a student, unlike Sister who was in her early fifties.

Without Dennis, I'm sure the work would have ground to a halt, smothered by the reams of paper that Sister produced every day. Her sense of humour helped to keep us all sane. She also acted as a buffer against Sister's very acidic tongue.

Sister looked as if she had once been very pretty, but constant worry and pressure of work had given her face a drawn pinched look. Years of spending all day on her feet had affected her legs, and they were swollen and knotted with varicose veins.

Having seen Sister's legs, at least the little that showed below her apron, I determined that I would never let mine get in such a state. From then on, I slept with the foot of my bed raised up on two inch blocks "borrowed" from the ward store.

It took a little while getting used to sleeping on an incline. I used to wake up squashed against the top of the bed, but determined to preserve the shape of my ankles, I persevered.

I had seen dressings done on Ward One, and I had laid up trolleys in P.T.S., but never on a ward. In theory one put on a face mask, scrubbed one's hands and prepared the trolley with everything one might need. The bowls had to be removed from the boiling steriliser with a long handled tool, called Cheatle's forceps.

One peered into the boiling water, tried to locate the right size of bowl, then fished it out with the Cheatle's. It was not easy, especially as I wore glasses. As soon as I lifted the lid of the steriliser, my glasses fogged up with steam!

Once loaded, the first, or dressing nurse, wheeled the trolley to the bedside. The second nurse drew the screens round the bed and prepared the patient, making her comfortable and loosening the dressing, whilst the first nurse went and scrubbed her hands.

The first nurse then returned and changed the dressing in as sterile a way as possible, the second nurse doing all the "dirty" parts of the procedure. It was known as an "aseptic technique."

As usual, practice was very different. We started with the ladies that had been to theatre the day before. The first dressing to be done was the thyroidectomy, and was fairly simple. All that was needed was to remove the old gauze and plaster, wipe away the worst of the mess underneath, and put on a clean covering.

Dennis stood and watched me lay up the trolley. As we left the clinical room, she asked me if I had ever seen a thyroidectomy. When I told her that I hadn't, she said,

"It is important that you do not show disgust or horror at the mess under the dressing. The patient will have to live with the scar for the rest of her life, and your reaction might affect her acceptance of it. The same thing goes for any operation. The first time you do a dressing, always tell the patient what a nice job the surgeon has done, however awful it might look to you."

Dennis wheeled the trolley down the ward and I went to scrub my hands. The "scrub" sinks had taps with long leavers, designed so that they could be turned off by elbows rather than hands. Once I had clean hands, I held them above my waist, palms together in the approved fashion, and walked to the right hand side of the patient's bed, dripping water as I went. Dennis lifted the lids off the bowls and I took out a towel to dry my hands.

"Towel" was simply a term applied to a square of linen; its drying properties were nil. All it did was remove the surplus water. I watched as Dennis removed the old dressing and uncovered the wound. It was a good job she had warned me; it was not a pretty sight. The thyroid is a T-shaped gland situated just in front and slightly below the "Adam's apple." The patient had a horizontal slit in her throat about six inches long, and it was held together with large metal clips.

Using forceps, I lifted out a towel and draped it over the patient's chest. Then, still using forceps, I carefully picked up a piece of cotton wool, dipped it in cleaning fluid and wiped the dried blood away from the wound. Remembering my training, I started at the middle and worked outwards, using a fresh piece of cotton wool for each wipe. I made no comment on the beauty of the scar; I left that to Dennis; she was a far more accomplished liar than I. The ability to tell a convincing lie is an art that I had not yet acquired.

When the wound was all nice and clean, I covered it with a neat layer of cotton gauze, and then stuck some sticky tape on the top to hold it in place. I was rather proud of my first dressing.

The dirty towels were put in a tray on the bottom of the trolley and we were done. As we left the patient's bedside, Dennis took a covered dressing tray off the top of the patient's locker and replaced it with a similar one from the trolley.

While we were clearing away and starting on the next dressing trolley, I asked her what was in it.

"Only a fresh scalpel, clip removing forceps and a tracheostomy tube. Sometimes the thyroid cases bleed internally, and the pressure of the blood cuts off the airway. That is why the wound is closed with clips instead of stitches; they come out quicker. If ever you see the patient going blue, just rip off the dressing and take out the clips to let the blood escape. If that doesn't work, the doctors make a hole in the trachea with the scalpel and put in the tube."

From that point on, I developed a phobia of thyroid patients, convinced that they were going to bleed. I have nursed dozens, all without incident. The procedure was probably yet another remnant from the early days of surgery.

The next dressing was even more horrifying. The patient had been to theatre for an "apronectomy." I had found it very difficult to shave her the day before, as she had an enormous pendulous abdomen. When she had stood up, there was great rolls of fat hanging down.

The surgeons had simply cut out the bit that had hung down and then sewn the edges together. She had a wound that stretched from one side of her abdomen to the other. How one could say that the surgeon had done a good job and left a neat scar, I could not imagine. I doubted that the scar would ever be on show; even without the layer of fat, she was still obese. I couldn't see her ever wearing a bikini.

It was well past eleven o'clock by the time we had finished the dressings of the previous day's operations. Staff announced that she considered me competent, and we could speed things up a bit if we worked singly. She offered to come with me to explain what to do, then leave me to carry on alone.

Sister's Dressing book was consulted, and a star put by the ones that I was to do. Of the eleven remaining, there were five that she judged simple enough for me to manage on my own.

I had often heard a saying, "It's a good thing that God gave nurses elbows, bottoms and feet." Now I was about to find out the truth of the saying.

All was well at first. I settled the patient in a comfortable position, pulled off the sticky plaster that was holding the dressing, lifted the lids off the trays on the trolley, then went to scrub my hands.

On returning, the first problem was how to get behind the screen round the patient's bed without touching anything. Dennis explained that the best way was to push the screen forward with a foot, slide through, then push it shut by leaning slightly forward and backing into it.

We were still using the old metal-framed screens covered in material; there was nothing as sophisticated as curtains round the beds. Having negotiated the screens, the rest was fairly easy. I managed to maintain the aseptic technique reasonably well by getting the patient to help.

The only problem I encountered was opening the swing door into the Clinical Room. If I had used the trolley as a battering ram, I would have marked the wooden door, and incurred Sister's wrath. So, using my newly acquired knowledge, I reversed into the door, using my backside to push it open.

Nurses are often caricatured as buxom, large bottomed creatures. At the risk of offending several of my colleagues, I agree that many nurses have large behinds, caused I am sure, by using them as battering rams. Pads of fat appear to protect the underlying bones. That is my excuse anyway!

As the morning wore on, I began to wonder if I was going to get any off-duty. I was due to work a split shift, but the dressings had to be done first. Sister sent Dennis and me to first dinner, saying that, if we came back early, we could finish the dressings and then go off duty.

It was two-thirty by the time I had completed all the dressings that Staff had marked for me to do. Feeling generous, I helped her with her last one so that we could both get a couple of hours off. Luck was not with us. The consultant was working his way round the ward, removing dressings as he went, and we had to follow him and put on fresh gauze and plaster.

It was four o'clock by the time we had finished, and I was in a filthy mood. Agreed, he had not taken off every patient's dressing, but why we had to do them twice in one day, I could not understand. It would have been easier to have waited until he was on the ward, and then start. He could then have seen the wounds as we did the dressings.

As we left the ward for a shortened afternoon off, I complained to Staff that I thought the system wrong. She explained that Sister liked the doctors to see the wounds looking clean and tidy. I decided that it would have been better for them to see the results of their handiwork "warts and all." That way they might have taken a bit more care.

Staff disagreed, and said,

"All surgeons are slap happy with the knife. It dates back to the days before anaesthetics, when speed was vital. They don't know how to do a tidy job."

The more dressings I did, the more I agreed with her.

CHAPTER TWENTY-TWO

In the hour and a half that I had been away from the ward, Sister had managed to admit three new patients. The superstition that things ran in threes was again proved right!

One had gone to theatre, and the other two would be going as soon as possible. As the ward was already full, three extra beds had been put up in the centre of the ward.

It was going to be a busy evening with only two of us on duty. Staff Nurse Peters took pity on us, and offered to stay until the patients had all returned from theatre. Dennis quickly accepted her offer.

Peters was a very attractive dark-haired girl. She had become engaged to be married just before she took her State Finals. As she was under twenty-one, she had asked Matron's permission. Peters passed her Finals, but was not allowed to wear a staff nurse's uniform simply because she was engaged!

It was never suggested to her that she might like to continue working after her marriage. It was just assumed that she would leave. Peters had committed the cardinal sin of letting a man come between her and the hospital. I only worked with her for three weeks, but in that time, she showed me how treatments and procedures could be carried out to make a patient's life a great deal easier.

For example, dressings were held in place with sticky plaster. We were taught that the easiest way to remove the plaster, was a sharp pull. Peters taught me that soaking the plaster with Ether Meth. softened the sticky backing, and one could then simply lift it away from the skin. It might take longer, but it was a lot less painful for the patient.

One of the new admissions had an intestinal obstruction and was vomiting vast amounts of foul-smelling fluid. Peters decided that it would be better for the patient, and us, if we passed a Ryle's tube. A Ryle's tube is a thin plastic tube that is passed down into the stomach via a nostril, so that the stomach contents can be aspirated by suction.

I asked if I could watch, never having seen a tube passed before. Peters said,

"No, I hate being watched. I'll tell you what to do and watch while you do it."

I should have kept quiet. I had heard all sorts of horror stories about the passing of Ryle's tubes. The end of the tube that rested in the stomach contained a small weight, the theory being that the weight aided the passing of the tube. One lubricated the end with liquid paraffin, then pushed it into the patient's nostril. The difficult part was getting it past the back of the throat and into the stomach. It could just as easily go down the wrong way and end up in the patient's lungs.

Peters watched me lay up a tray with all the things that I thought I needed. When I had finished, she added a twenty c.c. syringe and a gallipot of water. We drew the screens round the patient's bed, thus blocking the way up and down the ward. Peters sat on the side of the bed and took hold of the patient's hand.

"Now, Mrs. Pearce, we are going to stop you being sick. Nurse is going to pop a tube down into your tummy, so that we can pull out all the nasty stuff that you have got in there. It is a pretty beastly business, but if you help us, it will make things a lot easier. At each stage I will tell you exactly what to do, and then what Nurse is going to do.

"Now, Nurse is going to take the tube out of the packet, and using the syringe, fill it with water." I took the hint and did as I was told. I appreciated her not telling the patient that I had never passed a Ryle's tube before.

"Now," continued Peters, "I want you to take the tube from Nurse, and gently push it up your nose until you feel it at the back of your throat. As soon as you can feel it, you must stop pushing. All you need to do then is nod. If you try to speak the tube might move, and we'll have to start again. Nurse is going to hold onto the syringe to make sure that it does not become disconnected from the tube at her end."

Mrs. Pearce and I both did as we were told, and the end of the tube disappeared. Eventually Mrs. Pearce stopped pushing and nodded.

"The worst bit is over now. Nurse is going to very, very slowly, push some water down the tube. As soon as you feel the water, then swallow. When Nurse sees you swallow, she will push the tube down into your stomach. You keep swallowing until I say stop."

It worked like a dream. I pushed a minute amount of water into the tube, then, while Mrs. Pearce swallowed, I eased the tube further up into her nostril.

When Peters announced that Mrs. Pearce could stop swallowing, I stopped pushing. It had all been so easy, but the procedure was far removed from the classroom teaching.

Peters remained sitting on the side of the bed,

"That wasn't too bad an effort, well done." Was she talking to me or Mrs. Pearce, I wondered.

"Now, Nurse is going to pull all that nasty stuff out of your stomach and put it in the jug. As soon as that is gone, you will begin to feel better."

When I had emptied the patient's stomach, I stuck a spigot in the end of the tube to close it off. Then I stuck the tube to the side of Mrs. Pearce's nose with sticky plaster, looping the end over one of her ears. It must have been very uncomfortable. I took the jug full of revolting looking fluid into the sluice to measure it, and Peters followed me in, closing the door behind us.

"Whatever you do, never, ever put a Ryle's tube down like that if any of the sisters or tutors are watching. There is always a danger that the tube will end up in the lungs, and pouring water down the tube will only drown the patient. I've always done it my way, and I've not drowned a patient yet. It is best not to argue with them though."

Since that day, I have put down countless Ryle's tubes, with and without the patient's help, both on conscious and unconscious patients. Only twice have I had any trouble. On both occasions, I had a sister watching me, and the tube ended up coiled in the patient's mouth.

I don't, for one moment, think that Peters and I are the only two nurses that have adopted that particular method, because to me, it seems the obvious way to do it.

As soon as you feel a strange object at the back of your throat, you cough to move it. If, on the other hand, you feel a liquid trickling down your throat, you swallow. If the object is a tube destined for your stomach, then it is swallowed with the water.

As a check against the tube having taken the wrong turning, and entering the lungs, I do however, hold the end of the tube under water to check that there are no air bubbles coming out, unless of course, as in Mrs. Pearce's case, the stomach contents fill the tubing as soon as it reaches the stomach.

Dennis came in and asked Peters to check Mrs. Pearce's pre-med, as theatre had 'phoned to say that they were going to be ready for her fairly soon. I was to make sure that a bed was ready for the patient still in theatre, and move it down to the end of the ward, so that it was near the office door.

There were no intensive care or recovery units in those days. Patients came straight back from theatre to their original ward, however ill they were. It was best to have the very ill patients near the office door so that they could be watched more easily. It also meant that if they died, they could be wheeled into the side ward out of the way.

It was easier for us to lay out a body in the peace and quiet of the side ward, and was better for the patients not to see the Mortuary trolley coming and going.

It was often very difficult on Ward Six to decide who was well enough to be moved away from the door. We spent hours playing "musical beds." It was never just a case of moving two beds. First, we had to move one bed into the middle of the ward to create a space. Then we moved a bed into the space, thus creating another space, and so on, until we had managed to get the right patient by the door. It was often made more difficult because there was only one nurse free to do the moving. Beds are not the easiest of things to move single handed.

Dennis decided that the other two beds would have to stay in the middle of the ward, because none of the other patients were fit enough to be moved.

Theatre rang and asked for a nurse to collect the patient. They also asked that the nurse bring the patient's bed. That meant that the patient was not expected to survive. If she was lifted straight off the operating table onto her bed, it made one less move and increased her chances a little. It also meant that, as soon as she was on the bed, she was the responsibility of the ward and not the theatre. Thus, if she did die, it was us and not them that would have to lay her out.

I helped Dennis to push the bed as far as the theatre door, then went back to continue with some of the routine work. Luckily there was no worry about giving out meals, as Ward Six had the most wonderful ward maid. She had long since taken over the responsibility of serving meals.

Elsie, the maid, was as thin as a rake and had the strength of an ox. She came on duty at seven, and went off when there was nothing left for her to do. She even came in on Sunday evenings, (Sunday was her day off) to make sure that we had remembered to order the food for the next day. Elsie would do anything for the patients, except empty bedpans. She was perfectly happy to give a patient a pan, but remove it, she would not!

I teased her about it one day, and she became very upset.

"It is not my job to empty bedpans."

I could have pointed out that it was not her job to serve meals, wash patients, answer the 'phone or make beds, but she might have taken offence and left the jobs for me to do! Elsie was wasted as a maid; she would have made a very good nurse, but when she had started working at the hospital, nurses had to pay for their training, and Elsie's parents could not afford for her to train.

As I went down the corridor, I heard the theatre porters behind me. They were coming to collect Mrs. Pearce. It was a good thing Peters had stayed on duty. Dennis was still in theatre, and someone would have to accompany Mrs. Pearce. That would have left the ward without a nurse.

Peters asked me to take Mrs. Pearce to theatre. As we left the ward, Dennis appeared with her patient. I was very annoyed to see that the houseman and the registrar were helping to move the bed. That meant that I would have to stand around for ages waiting for them to return and prepare to operate on Mrs. Pearce.

Twenty minutes passed before they were ready for her. That was twenty minutes wasted, not to mention the fact the Mrs. Pearce had been laying on a cold hard trolley for a lot longer than she need have done.

The theatre nurses must have known that the doctors were going onto the ward. They could just have easily waited until the doctors returned, before sending the porters for the next patient.

It was eight o'clock when I arrived back on the ward, and there were still all the fluid charts to do, and several blood pressures to take. Also, the patient that had just returned from theatre was bound to need something done. Dennis would be busy writing the reports, and Peters should have gone off duty at 5:30 P.M.

I was tired and very fed up. I had worked for most of my off-duty that afternoon, but I was still a long way behind in my work. How ever long I stayed on duty past the end of my shift, I was unlikely to get any thanks. The whole system was so unfair; the only person on the ward that went off duty on time was Sister.

I was supposed to be training to become a nurse, yet as far as I could see, I was being used as cheap labour. One minute I was cleaning bedpans, the next, I was trying to keep someone alive. On the odd occasions that there was time, I was being taught, but that was only so that I would be of more use, and could be given yet more work.

I longed to be able to sit down and relax, or have the energy to go out to a dance. I had been on Ward Six for just two days, and it seemed a lifetime. I made up my mind to go and see Matron, and tell her that I wanted to be moved. If she wouldn't move me, then I would leave.

I hadn't even started on the charts when Dennis sent me over to Matron's office with the Report. That was another five minutes gone. As I put the report on the desk in the outer office, Matron came in. I said good evening and turned round to leave. She called me back,

"Are you busy over there, Nurse?"

I thought that the truth wouldn't hurt her for once, so I said,

"Matron, it is frantic. I have had to work through my off-duty for the two days that I have been on the ward, and so have most of the others. We are short of staff, and there are far too many patients for us to be able to look after any of them properly."

I waited for the blast; I should just have told her that we were busy, and left it at that. Instead of lecturing me on my outburst, she turned round and moved towards the door.

"I think I had better come and see for myself."

My immediate thought was, Dennis will kill me for bringing Matron back.

When we reached the ward, there was not a nurse in sight. Both Dennis and Peters had left the ward in a panic to take a patient back to theatre. Matron was marvellous. She asked me what there was to do, and looked horrified when I listed all the things that I had to do before I went off duty. As I finished the list, one of the previous day's theatre cases sat up in bed and vomited.

Matron reached the bed first, and before I knew what was happening, she had started to clean up the mess. I didn't know what to do. I could hardly leave her to it, so I went to find the linen trolley and a billy. She stopped me, saying,

"I *have* changed a bed before, you know, Nurse. I will deal with this while you get on with some of your jobs. You have enough to do as it is."

Strangely, I had never thought of Matron as a nurse! Dennis and Peters came back to find Matron on her way to the sluice with a billy full of soiled bedding. Matron was still on the ward when the night staff came on duty, and instead of leaving us to get on with our work, she called us together.

"The night staff will take over and do the rest of the day's work. I will see that Night Sister sends two more nurses to help them. Dennis, you give the night staff the report. Peters and Wallinger, you are to leave the ward, now, with me. Dennis, you are to report to my office within ten minutes. I want to know that you too have left the ward."

I didn't stop to argue. I just followed her out. The night nurses did not look all that pleased. We had left an awful mess. Not to mention two patients in theatre.

I was far too tired to even think about supper. I just went straight up to my room. As the rest of the nurses were in the dining room, the bathrooms were free, and I was able to enjoy a long hot bath. Well, as long and hot a bath as one could manage in the six inches of water allowed. As I walked back to my room Sue was on her way up from supper. She burst out laughing when she saw me.

"Have you just had a bath?"

"Yes, why?" I asked.

"You fool, you've still got your cap on!"

I had been so tired that I had taken off my uniform and left my cap on. Fortunately, it hadn't suffered too much; it was just a bit soggy at the edges. I couldn't be bothered to fold a new one; I just collapsed into bed.

The next morning, I found that Sue had taken pity on me and folded me a cap. That was jolly lucky, because when I got on duty, there was a message from Matron saying that she wanted to see me at ten o'clock.

I didn't leave the ward until well past ten. Sister was in one of her difficult moods and wouldn't let me go. I wasn't too worried, as Matron sent for everybody at ten. Arriving there on time only meant a longer wait. For once, there was no one waiting in front of me, and her door was open. I knocked and was told to enter. I was greeted with,

"I said ten o'clock. Where have you been?"

Despite a very early night, I was still tired. The last thing I wanted was a lecture on punctuality, especially when it had not, for once, been my fault.

"I tried to get here earlier, Matron, but Sister said it was not convenient for me to leave."

What she had, in fact said, was that she had a ward to run, and she couldn't do it if Matron kept interfering. I thought my interpretation sounded better. Sister was not very pleased that Matron had been on the ward the night before, and was blaming me for telling tales. If I had repeated Sister's actual words, I would have been in even more trouble.

Matron told me to sit down. There were, she said, several things to discuss.

For once, I was not in trouble. Matron just wanted to know how the plans for the carnival were going. During the last few days, I had not thought about the float very much. I had been far too busy, or just too tired.

It looked as if I would not be able to take part anyway. I had asked Sister if I might have a day off for the carnival, and her reply had not been very encouraging. I decided that I had better admit that I had not made any plans, so I said,

"I'm very sorry Matron, but apart from the initial idea, I have not had the energy to make any definite plans. I rather lost heart when I found out that I would not be able to take part."

Matron did not seem too pleased.

"Why not?"

"I asked Sister if I could have the day off, and as it is not her policy to give students time off at weekends, she refused."

If that remark found its way back to Sister, I would be lucky to get any off-duty at all.

Matron sat and looked at me for a while, then said,

"You look tired. Perhaps Ward Six is too heavy. I'll have to see what can be done. You may go."

My depression lifted instantly. It sounded as if I might be moved. I didn't think of all the grim wards I might be moved to, only that I would not have to slave away any longer on Ward Six.

My joy was short lived. Sister was called to see Matron after dinner, and came back with the information that there were to be some emergency staff changes on the ward. There would be two more staff nurses and two students moved to the ward the next day.

The old bat was leaving me where I was.

CHAPTER TWENTY-THREE

Having four extra nurses on the ward made little difference to the work load. It just allowed us to do things properly for a change. Sister spent more and more time organising the work books, then changing her mind, crossing one thing off the list and adding another.

It was very frustrating to spend half an hour giving a patient a blanket bath, then, when you signed the bath book to say that it was done, you found the patient's name had been crossed off and another inserted.

Sister resented any change. She had refused to accept any of the packs from C.S.S.D., so we were still using dressings from drums. Urine had to be tested by the old method of boiling and playing about with chemicals, taking up twice as much time as it need have done. She had, however, agreed to the use of disposable syringes, but only if there were no glass ones available.

Sister was a prime example of a person "promoted to the level of incompetence." As a nurse, she was probably very good, although I never actually saw her do any nursing. She spent all day sitting at her desk orgainising work books and the off-duty rota. On the odd occasions that she left her office, it was only to rush about complaining that we were too slow.

As a manager, she was totally ineffective. A week on a management course would have done her the world of good, and halved our work load as well.

Management courses were then unheard of, and even if a course had been suggested to her, she would probably have refused to go. She thought that the ward was very well run. The only thing wrong in her opinion, was that there were too many patients. I agreed with her on that point. There were far too many.

Sister was not alone in her inability to manage a ward. We were trained to nurse; we were not encouraged to think, only to obey orders. The ability to delegate responsibility, and to organise the care of the patients was something one was supposed to acquire. In my experience, few did.

I am sure that the same ward today is a great deal lighter. Patients are now sat out of bed as soon as they are fit enough to be moved. Even major surgical cases are up and about by the end of the first week. In the sixties, we kept all except very minor cases in bed until the tenth day after operation, when the stitches were removed.

Apart from making extra work for the nurses, it increased the danger to the patient. Deep vein thrombosis following surgery was common. Blood tended to collect in the patient's legs and clot. A daily walk would have prevented this from happening.

One of the commonest causes of death following an operation was a pulmonary embolism, again a result of nursing the patient in bed. "Pulmonaries" were so common that we could almost predict them. They often happened on or around that tenth day following surgery. The patient would sit up in bed and ask for a bedpan, if you were quick, you could actually get them onto the pan before they died. Mostly we were too late.

The explanation we received, was that the clot passing along the Mesenteric blood vessels caused a spasm in the colon. Thus the call for a pan.

We all had a phobia about giving ten day patients a pan. It was very upsetting to find the patient dead, when you went to collect the pan.

Finding a patient dead was a cardinal sin. Matron insisted that any patient dying had a nurse with them, and we often had to abandon ill patients, just so that we could sit and wait for someone to die. There was a very rigid set of rules concerning our behaviour at the bedside of the dying. We had to sit, not stand, on the left side of the bed. How ever many nurses there were, they had to all be at the same side of the bed.

Matron believed that there was a spirit guide sent to collect the departing soul, and she did not want any of us to get in the way. At that time, I was not very sure about her theory, but it certainly meant that the terminally ill patient was never left alone. It was not a lot of fun to sit watching a patient die, especially when you had seen them admitted, hopeful that the surgeons would cure their disease.

Fortunately we were saved that with the pulmonary cases, as they died suddenly. The ensuing interview with Matron was always the same:

"Why did you find that patient dead? Why were you not there with them?"

I once protested that I had not expected the patient to die; that she had been perfectly alright ten minutes before. All I received in reply was,

"Every patient in this hospital is likely to die; it is up to you to see that they do not die alone."

I gave up trying to reason with her. From then on, if a patient in the danger period asked for a pan, I stayed with them until they had used it. That might have saved me one or two trips to Matron, but it did nothing for my popularity with the patients. They were, understandably, not very happy about having an audience.

I gave up any hope of being moved to another ward, and somehow managed to find time to persuade nurses to volunteer to man the carnival float. At first, it was a very difficult task, as none of the Sisters would commit themselves to giving a student a day off on a Saturday.

Students were never given days off at the weekend, and Sisters were afraid of setting a precedent. Matron, bless her heart, stepped in and said that as the students would be representing the hospital, we would be considered to be on duty. After that, I had more volunteers than I could cope with. More, I thought, were volunteering for the free Saturday than for the fun of the carnival.

Convinced that I would have to stay on Ward Six for at least another six weeks, I gave up looking at the change list. I was surprised when Sue told me that my name was on the list, and I became annoyed with her when she wouldn't tell me where I was going. When I went to see for myself, I understood her reluctance.

I was going to Ward Six night duty as third nurse. The very heavy wards had three nurses on duty every night, the third nurse was always a second year student, and when the senior had her nights off, the third was in charge.

Nineteen years and six months old, not yet half way through my training, and I was going to have to make decisions that might mean the difference between life or death to any one of forty or so women.

Fortunately, I would only be left in charge for two nights a week, and I would have a Friday and Saturday night off every other week. By chance, I would be off for the carnival. Perhaps Matron was capable of running a hospital after all!

On my last day, I asked Sister to sign my Schedule. She refused saying, "I have not seen you do anything while you have been on this ward."

She made it sound as if I had sat on my backside for the whole month. I couldn't be bothered to argue with the woman, as I would be able to get Night Sister to fill up the empty page. It was lucky that I was going to have a spell on nights. Otherwise I would be taking my final exams with no record of having any surgical experience.

It was unbelievable how different the ward was at night. The work was the same, the patients the same, but the atmosphere was very different. For a start, we did not have to cope with Sister and her moods. She was the most moody, bad-tempered woman I have ever had the misfortune to work for. Even on one of her infrequent "good" days, she made our lives hell. When she was having a bad day, then nothing was ever right.

Sister always left a list of things for the night staff to do, but at least she was not there to keep adding to it.

Bailey, the senior nurse, was in the middle of her third year, and she was a born organiser. As soon as she had taken the report from the day staff, we were given our orders for the night, then left alone to get on with the work.

The first night I was told to help the junior to make all the patients comfortable. Then I was to take over the observations. For twenty-four hours after surgery, every patient had their pulse, respiration rate and blood pressure checked, or observed, every fifteen minutes. On a theatre day it was a full time job doing just that, without all the other work.

I was fortunate because, as there had been three very long operations that day, only four patients had been to theatre. There had been a radical mastectomy, a nephrectomy, a resection of bowel and a ligation and stripping of varicose veins. I knew which patient had the veins, as she was a staff nurse and in the side ward. Of the others, I had no idea which was which. I was not concerned with the quality of the surgery, only the quantity.

I didn't question the need for quarter hourly observations following the stripping of varicose veins. I did them because it was the rule. I had just finished taking the blood pressure of the Staff Nurse, when Dr. Patel, the Registrar, came into the room.

He said that I was wasting my time. The patient was fine and would be better left alone to sleep. The best thing to do was to take her pulse every hour and her blood pressure every four hours. That way she might at least get some sleep.

I could imagine what Sister would say when she saw an empty chart in the morning, so I said,

"Sister says that they should be done every fifteen minutes."

He might think that he was in charge of the patients, but it was Sister that I was going to have to answer to, not him.

"If you had any sense at all, you would just fill in the chart. *She* isn't going to know is she? As long as there are a few dots for her to look at, she'll be happy."

I wasn't too sure of that, so I asked Bailey if it would be alright to do as he had suggested. She said that she always took all the blood pressures as soon as she came on duty, then decided which of the patients really needed to be watched, and which ones left. That was fine for her. She was near the end of her training and had three years experience of blood pressures. How was I to know who needed watching?

By the end of the night, I was able to tell from the feel of the patient's pulse, whether her blood pressure was worth taking or not, and from then on, I cut down a lot on the observations.

All three of the major cases were having blood transfusions. Bailey was managing the transfusions; my job was to make sure that the blood was still dripping in, and that there were no air bubbles in the tubes.

The night passed very quickly, and for once, I did not have any trouble staying awake between 3:00 A.M. and 4:30 A.M. I was far too busy to even notice the time. Apart from the observations, there were bedpans to give, and patients to turn from side to side. In my spare time, I helped the junior to pack the dressing drums and clean the syringes. That first nights, there were thirty-five syringes to wash and pack.

I managed to break five of them. It was fairly easy to drop them, and the floor was very hard. The first one was a genuine accident, but as I picked up the pieces, I remembered that Sister had said that she would only use disposable syringes when there were no glass ones left. The sooner that happened the better, and as the glass ones were no longer being replaced, the more I broke the better! In my hands even the glass syringes became disposable.

I went off duty in the morning convinced that Sister would know that I had falsified the observation charts, and that she would call me back to the ward. I waited until ten o'clock before I changed out of my uniform and went to bed.

The next night was an easy one by comparison, as there had not been any operations at all that day. We even had three empty beds. I was beginning to panic about being left in charge the following night, so Bailey wrote out a list of things that could possibly go wrong. Then, as we worked through the list, I made notes on how to solve the problems.

One of my main worries was what to do if a drip went wrong, which they frequently did. Bailey told me to ring for a doctor, as it was really their problem, not ours. She suggested that if there were any problems, it would be best to call the doctor first, rather than 'phone Night Sister. It would save time in the long run, because Sister usually ended up sending for him anyway. I wondered what sort of reaction I would get when I dragged one of them out of bed in the middle of the night.

Bailey made sure that I knew how to replace an empty blood bottle with a full one, that I knew where all the emergency drugs were kept, and how to fill in the D.D.A. book. There was nothing else that she could do to help; from then on I was on my own.

I hardly slept on Wednesday; I found myself going over and over all the things that might happen, and rehearsing what I should do if they did. I went on duty feeling rather apprehensive. It was one thing to be left in charge of the Children's Ward, another thing entirely to have to take the responsibility for a heavy surgical ward.

The first thing to be done was to count the D.D.A. drugs. Box by box, Staff Nurse Dennis removed the drugs from the cupboard. We checked that the number remaining in the box tallied with that of the drug book, then wrote across the appropriate page: "Checked and found correct." Then we signed our names. From that point on, any discrepancies would be my responsibility.

Counting the boxes of ampoules was easy, as the ampoules were all arranged neatly in rows. It was counting the pills that bothered me. Dennis tipped them into her hand and we counted them as they were dropped back into the bottle, one at a time. I was glad I would not be taking any of them. They were dispensed twenty at a time, and by the time the last one was given to a patient, it would have been in several different hands.

The pharmacy had special trays for counting pills, but it was a long while before we were given them to use on the wards. It was cheaper for us to use our hands, and never mind what germs we might have passed on to the patients.

There had been six operations that day. Only two of them were major, one a nephrectomy, the other an abdomino-perineal excision of rectum. It was Miss Patterson, the patient that had the latter, that caused me concern. It was a very nasty operation, and only performed as a last resort, usually for cases of bowel cancer when the growth had blocked off the bowel. A section of bowel was brought to the surface of the abdomen and formed into a colostomy; the rest of the bowel below the colostomy was then removed.

Miss Patterson was in her late sixties, and had been admitted with an intestinal blockage the week before, while I was on day duty. She was a nice happy little person, and had great faith in the doctors. She was convinced that she would be able to walk out of the hospital a new woman.

She had already been given two pints of blood since she came back from theatre, and was to have at least three more during the night. She had a Ryle's tube that was to be aspirated every half hour, and a drain in her wound that was connected to a vacuum pump. I made sure that I did her observations myself; I was not going to chance those being done every four hours!

My first task was to decide which of the patients would be needing Pethidine to relieve their pain, and then prepare everything so that Night Sister could check the drugs with me when she came to do her first round.

Having set out the treatment cards and injection tray, I collected the medicine trolley and the remaining treatment sheets, and set off to give out the routine medicines and the sleeping pills. The trolleys were a recent introduction. Before their arrival, the medicines were dispensed from the cupboard on the office wall. They were really a mobile cupboard, and the bottles were supposed to be arranged in groups, so that, for example, all of the antibiotics were stored together.

I had trouble reading the sheets, as only one of the doctor's handwriting was legible. Then, I had to find the pills. There must have been some sort of system, but I could not decide what it was. I was still battling with the medicine round when Night Sister came in and took pity on me. She dispensed the pills and I took them to each patient. Even she was amazed at the disorder in the trolley.

With the medicine trolley safely parked in the office, Sister asked me to take her round the ward. I had been dreading this, as I was expected to know the name, diagnosis and current state of health of each of the patients. It was not unreasonable to expect the nurse in charge of a ward to know all about her patients, but it was very difficult to remember everything about everybody.

When we had finished the inquisition, Sister checked out the doses of Pethidine. The patients' names were entered in the D.D.A. book and I was left to give the injections and then sign the book. Even in those days, *that* was highly illegal. The two nurses that had checked the drug, one of which had to be S.R.N., were supposed to go to the patient together, and administer the drug. It took me twenty minutes to give the injections, and Sister just had not the time to stand and watch. If she had stuck to the rules, she would never have managed to complete her round of the hospital.

I still had two injections of Pethidine to give, when Mr. Harris, one of the registrars, came into the ward. He sauntered into the office, sat down at the desk, and said that he wanted the notes of the patients that were going to theatre the next day. I pointed to a pile of notes on a shelf, and told him that they were all there.

I had heard all about Mr. Harris, and although I had often seen him on the ward, he had never spoken to me before. He was a tall handsome man, half Italian, half Australian, and he looked a bit like Frank Sinatra. He was well aware that he was a heart throb; he also thought that he was God.

He looked at the pile of notes and said,

"I said that I wanted the notes; I did not ask where they were."

I was furious. If he was too idle to take them down off the shelf, he would have to do without them. I decided that he would have to be put in his place. I was not going to run around for him like a slave, or any other doctor for that matter.

"If you want the notes, that is where they are. I am here to nurse the patients, not to run about after doctors."

Before he could answer, I grabbed the last two ampoules of Pethidine and the treatment sheets, and disappeared into the clinical room. I would do the rest of the work from there.

Having completed the injections, I had to return to the office to sign the D.D.A. book. By then I was feeling rather sorry for my outburst, and to make amends, I asked if he wanted to examine any of the patients. He was obviously as angry with me as I with him, because he replied,

"I wouldn't dream of putting you to any trouble."

If he could be sarcastic, then so could I. I replied,

"It's no trouble; I have nothing urgent to do."

"In that case, I would like to see Mrs. Patterson. I have already found her notes myself."

He had obviously learnt one lesson. I walked out of the office ahead of him, and drew the screens round Mrs. Patterson's bed. Once he had satisfied himself that she had not deteriorated any further, he asked it I was happy about the management of the blood transfusion.

My opinion of him rose when he offered to show me how to change the "giving set." Not only did he show me but he explained what I could do to restart a drip that had stopped, and how to expel air from the tubing.

As we left Mrs. Patterson's bedside, I pushed back the screens and walked ahead of him into the office.

He sat down at the desk and glared at me.

"There are two things that you should know. One, I am usually addressed as Sir. Two, you should hold doors open for me and let me pass through first."

He had to be joking! I was not going to put up with that sort of treatment, and I said so.

"In England, Doctor, ladies go first, and gentlemen hold the doors. Whatever you think of yourself, I consider myself to be a lady. Also, I save the title of Sir for those that have been knighted, or for those men that I think deserve it. You do not, in my opinion, fall into either category,"

I waited for the explosion, but instead he just laughed, and added, "You won't last long around here. You have too much to say for yourself."

"I have lasted for nearly eighteen months," I replied, "and I have every intention of lasting out the next eighteen."

From that point on, we became very good friends, and he even invited me out for a meal one evening. It was not the most enjoyable evening I had ever spent; he was the most crashing bore.

For once I was glad of the ten-thirty curfew.

CHAPTER TWENTY-FOUR

I lost my first patient that night. Although there was nothing I could have done to save her, I still felt very responsible.

Just as I was about to go to dinner at 1:00 A.M., Casualty 'phoned to say that they had a patient for us. They admitted that they knew little about her, apart from her Christian name, which was Veronica. She had been examined in the ambulance by the duty doctor, and taken straight to theatre.

I left instructions with the junior nurses to prepare a bed as near to the office as possible. That in itself presented a problem, as there were not that many patients that were well enough to be moved too far away from the door. I also asked them to 'phone the dining room when the patient was ready to return to the ward.

I ate a very hurried meal, and was back on the ward within twenty minutes. There was really no need for me to hurry; both of the juniors were perfectly capable of admitting a patient. However, this was my first emergency admission, and I didn't want anything to go wrong.

I need not have hurried. It was 2:30 A.M. before theatre rang, asking for a nurse to bring a bed to collect the patient. Two of us took the bed to theatre, and I waited to accompany the patient back to the ward.

The report I received from the theatre nurse was not very good. "Miss Smith" had somehow managed to get in the way of a load of shot gun pellets, the majority of which had hit her in the stomach and abdomen.

Mr. Harris and Dr. Piper, his houseman, had done as much as they could to stop the bleeding, but the patient was too weak for them to do anymore. They planned to operate again just as soon as the patient was strong enough.

Both doctors came back to the ward with the patient, and stayed until she was settled. Then Harris left. He said that he was operating at nine the next day, and needed to get some sleep. Piper would have to cope, unless the situation was desperate. It seemed to have slipped his memory that Piper would also have to be in theatre at 9:00 A.M.

Dr. Piper stayed on the ward until nearly 4:00 A.M., and then he too retired to bed. He had been on duty since 8:00 A.M. the previous day, and despite the strong cups of coffee we had been making for him, he was almost asleep on his feet. Before he went, he admitted that he did not expect the patient to survive until the morning. She had lost so much blood before admission that, when they operated, she hardly bled at all. All we could do was to get blood into her as fast as we could. That and pray.

He put one of the X-rays taken in theatre up on the viewing screen, and although I had never been able to read an X-ray before, I could see a lot on that one. The area between her ribs and her hips was a mass of round white dots.

She had been wearing a wide leather belt with a large metal buckle, and there was a distinct gap, showing where the belt had been.

X-rays are passed through the body onto a photographic film. The thicker the tissue through which they pass, the lighter the image on the film. The white dots were solid pieces of lead.

I was curious to know how she had managed to get in the way of a blast from a shotgun. Dr. Piper merely said,

"So are the police. They don't even know her surname, but she had a bracelet on her wrist that had Veronica engraved on it. Hence, Veronica Smith."

As he left, he told me to expect a visit from the police. They would probably want to sit with Miss Smith until she woke up, if ever she did.

I took her blood pressure as soon as Dr. Piper had left. It was considerably lower than it had been ten minutes before. I stood feeling her pulse for several minutes, and it was gradually getting weaker. There was no doubt that she was going. I asked one of the juniors to 'phone the switchboard and ask Dr. Piper to come straight back.

He was back on the ward in four minutes. As soon as his bleep had sounded, he had come running. He had not even bothered to check which ward was calling him. He was too late to save her. He listened for a heart beat, then stood up and turned off the drip.

There is something horribly final about clamping off an intravenous infusion. I felt as if we were pulling a life raft away from a drowning man. I am very glad that I have never worked in an Intensive Care Unit and had to witness the switching off of a life support system.

I waited for Dr. Piper to pronounce the time of death, then drew the sheet over her face. She looked such a pretty woman. As we came out from behind the screens, there was a policeman walking down the ward. I felt a great deal of satisfaction that she had gone before he had arrived.

I don't know why, but I hate it when policemen sit at a bedside, especially when the patient is dying. However nice they may be, they somehow manage to take away the dignity of death.

I never found out how she had met with such a nasty accident, even the Bush Telegraph was silent on the matter. I did, however, find out why she had died. For some reason, the *Post Mortem* report found its way onto Sister's desk. A broken blood vessel had been missed during the operation. There had been so little blood in her body that many of the arteries had collapsed. As the new blood began to circulate, the artery opened and she bled to death. Had she lived, she would have been without most of her gut, and a large proportion of her stomach.

Despite knowing all that, I still felt responsible for her death. I had been in charge of the ward, and she had died. For the first time in my career, I wrote in the Kardex, the date and time of a death, listed those present and signed my name as witness. It is a task that I have repeated countless times since, but I have rarely felt so guilty as I did on that night.

My second night was not so traumatic, although there had been several operations that day, and the theatre patients all had blood drips. I had copied the habit, frowned on by Matron, of wearing my scissors tucked into my belt. During the night I "borrowed" from the clinical room a pair of artery forceps, and wore them next to my scissors. I had found that the clamps on the giving sets were not very effective at closing the tube completely. When expelling air, one needed a total closure, or the air continued down the tube.

All intravenous fluids, not just blood, came in glass bottles. To replace the empty bottle, one lifted it off the stand, removed the end of the set and placed it in the new bottle. The task was complicated by the short pipe that allowed air into the bottle. It was not easy to change the bottles without getting air into the giving set, or filling the airway up with fluid. Apart from the danger of air entering the patient's bloodstream and causing an air embolism, air in the tube slowed down the rate of flow, so it had to be removed.

Although Mr. Harris had shown me how to do this, I was far from happy about it. I had seen other nurses doing it, but it was really a job for the doctors. I debated whether or not to call the houseman, but eventually decided against it. Had I done so, the poor man would never have left the ward all night. It was a reasonably simple matter to clamp off the tube and expel the air.

Small amounts could be moved by flicking the tube and breaking the air bubble up into smaller ones that rose upwards to the bottle. If there was more than, say, three inches of air, the only solution was to wrap the tube round a finger and squash it. That way the air was forced out of the tube, and back into the bottle.

I was engrossed in the task of expelling air when Dr. Piper came to see the patient.

"The easiest way to do that is to change the set. I'll show you what to do."

I didn't tell him that his boss had already shown me what to do! I knew he was right; it was far easier to remove the tube from the canula in the patient's arm, fill a new set with fluid and reconnect it. I wasn't too bothered by the fact that it was not an approved nursing procedure. All that concerned me was the fact that I might move the canula from the vein into the surrounding tissues. Had that happened, no one would have thanked me for changing the set; I would have been in trouble for messing up the infusion.

I went off duty relieved that I had survived the last two nights, although I felt considerably older than I had at the beginning of the week!

I had three nights off duty to look forward to, two from the rota, and an extra one because of the carnival. I was due to see Matron at nine to finalise the plans for the float. I had my supper and sat in the sitting room to pass the time until then. At ten minutes to nine, Home Sister came in and told me that I was to return to Ward Six. Sister had sent for me.

Whatever she wanted, she would have to be quick, I thought. I wasn't going to keep Matron waiting. Sister informed me that I had filled in the temperature charts incorrectly, and that I was to rewrite the charts. I looked at the chart on the top of the pile and couldn't see anything wrong with it, and I said so.

Sister pointed out that I had linked the dots that I had put on the charts with straight lines. All the previous dots were linked with a half circle. She expected me to sit and copy out all the charts because I had spoiled the look of them. My reply was instantaneous; I didn't stop to think.

"Sister, if you want those charts changed, then you will have to do them yourself; either that, or leave them until Monday night when I come back on duty."

I left the office before she could recover from the shock. It must have been the first time anyone had stood up to her and her petty ways. I expected her to ring Matron and complain, but if she did, I never heard about it. Either, she knew she was wrong in calling me back to the ward for such a stupid reason, or else she did not want to admit that she had at last found a nurse that was not afraid of her.

Matron was in a good mood, and was anxious to know all about the plans for the float. I had asked permission for the hospital carpenters to make a set of rails to round the back of the lorry to give it the appearance of a play-pen. Matron had not only organised the rails, but had asked the carpenters to fit them. The lorry would be parked in the courtyard by midday, she told me, in case we wanted a rehearsal.

The last thing I wanted was a rehearsal. Matron would undoubtedly have seen us, and then we would have had to change our plans. I explained that we planned to depict life on a children's ward, and apart from nurses dressed to represent children, there would be two nurses in uniform on the float. Six nurses would walk beside the float with the collection boxes.

It all sounded innocent enough, and she said that she thought that we would make a stunning display. How right she was! Matron explained that she would not be able to wave us off, as she had been offered a place on the balcony of the Town Hall. That was the best news I had received for weeks. I had been a bit worried that she might have tried to stop us from leaving the hospital grounds when she saw the float.

As I left her office, she handed me an envelope.

"This contains two tickets to the Carnival Dance. One is for you, the other for the nurse that has done most to help. There are also two passes allowing you to stay out until the end of the dance."

When I checked, the passes stated,

"The holder of this pass has my permission to be exempted from the evening roll call. She is to report to the hospital no later than 3:00 A.M."

I was staggered. Never before had I heard of such a late pass being granted. I decided that she had only done it to save face. She would have looked jolly silly had we excused ourselves from the dance half way through, explaining that we had to be in bed by midnight.

I thought that it would be best to offer the other ticket to my room-mate, Sue. She had managed to persuade Ian, one of the male nurses, to take part. For that, she deserved a night out. The other point in favour of taking Sue with me was that we would both return together, instead of me waking her up in the small hours. I would never have heard the last of that!

I was a little concerned about the actual dance. Those attending were expected to appear in costume that they had worn in the parade. I was not too happy about that. It is one thing to make a fool of yourself within a group, another entirely when there are just two of you.

I had left the final preparations until the very last minute. Our costumes had been made by the ladies in the Linen Room at the Annex under the direction of Sister Children's. Although I had been consulted as to the theme and the number of costumes required, the final idea had been hers. She was stage managing the event. She was even coming to wave us off.

We had arranged to dress in our rooms, and meet at the float five minutes before it was due to depart. The fewer people that saw us, the better!

The first shock I had was when I saw Sue's "uniform." She was to be one of the nurses on the float, and I had assumed that she would be wearing her own uniform. Not so. The bodice part of her dress was unaltered, but the skirt was so short it only just covered her bottom. The apron was even shorter.

Once she was dressed, it was even worse. Not only were her dark blue uniform pants visible, but so were her stocking tops and suspenders! Even I was shocked. I could see someone getting into very serious trouble, and I had a fair idea who that someone was likely to be.

It was a very nervous group of nurses that gathered beside the lorry. Had it not been for Sister Children's, I'm sure none of us would have climbed onto the float. Eventually, we were all settled in position; all, that is, except Ian.

The driver had just announced that he could not wait any longer when a car drew into the yard. It contained Ian, and a collection of enormous Teddy bears.

He was wearing a white theatre gown, the type that is open all down the back, and he had tucked the gown into a towel that had been tied round him like a nappy. He had at least pinned the towel to the gown.

It struck me as Ian climbed onto the back of the lorry, that he had the best pair of legs on display that day! That was in itself a good thing, because he was showing far more leg than even the two "nurses." He was carrying a baby's bottle fitted with a teat, and the bottle was half full of a brown liquid that looked suspiciously like whiskey.

I had to know. How ever much he needed the Dutch Courage, there was going to be enough trouble as it was without one of the nurses getting drunk.

"Ian, is that whisky in that bottle?"

He looked hurt that I had even suggested it.

"Wally, that is not whisky in that bottle. May Flo strike me dead if I'm lying to you."

I should have asked what was, in fact, in the bottle; instead I accepted his word. It turned out to be brandy, and by the time we reached the balcony of the Town Hall, Ian was as drunk as a Lord. He had long since given up the fight to stay on his feet, and was sitting slumped against the bars of the play-pen.

As soon as he saw the mass of people on the balcony, he struggled to his feet, and pointed towards Matron.

"There she is; lets all bow to the old bat as we go past."

I protested, as most of our skirts were bordering on the obscene, even when we were upright. We settled on a compromise. He could bow; the rest of us would wave.

As the float drew level with Matron, Ian swept off his bonnet and gave a deep bow. Then, he stood up and blew her a kiss. I could cheerfully have murdered him on the spot, until I looked up and saw that Matron was laughing. I was staggered. She was pointing at us, and laughing her head off!

Ian must have been even more drunk that I realised. He turned to the crowd, and said,

"Three cheers for our beloved Matron."

We were left with no choice but to join in, although, amidst the cheers, I heard a voice saying,

"We're a bloody lot of hypocrites."

The crowd enjoyed it, and so did the local paper. They published a photograph of us, taken outside the Town Hall, that showed Matron in the background. The caption read:

"Local nurses show their admiration for Matron."

They could not really have said anything else I suppose. They could hardly have printed the truth:

"Male nurse makes a fool of himself whilst drunk."

Having made his bid for the title, "Creep of the Year," Ian returned to his former position and went to sleep. His set actually presented him with a badge that stated, "Matron's Pet." He had the last laugh though; he won the gold medal for the outstanding student of his year!

It was a very tired band of nurses that climbed down off the float when it returned to the hospital yard, but we all agreed that it had been worth the effort. We had no idea how much money we had collected altogether, but there had been over one hundred pounds thrown onto the float.

Sue and I had time for a short rest before setting off for the Town Hall, and the dance. We both felt fools walking through the town in our fancy dress. Most weekends, the town was deserted after six o'clock, but that night the streets were full of people, a large proportion of whom, or so it seemed, we had nursed.

I'm sure Matron had no idea what she was letting us in for, or she would never have given us the tickets.

As we entered the ballroom, a band of middle-aged men were doing their best to play pop songs. Their best was appalling. They must have been the only band in existence that could turn a Rolling Stones tune into a waltz.

I wasn't interested in dancing; I had caught sight of food. Dodging the dancers, I headed towards the buffet, and didn't leave it until I had satisfied my appetite. Even then, I was loath to leave so much glorious food, but Sue appeared and dragged me back to the fray. She said she was fed up with being proposition by old men in dinner jackets. I had the feeling that, had they been young men, I would have been left at the buffet.

There was a dearth of young men; there weren't all that many young women either. The room appeared to be full of balding, fat men, and their equally fat, blue-rinsed wives.

Poor Sue was having a very bad time. The sight of her suspenders was proving too much for the lecherous old sods. So many of them had pinged her elastic suspenders, that the tops of her legs were beginning to bruise. We both spent the evening being mauled about by supposedly upright members of the local community. I prayed that I would one day get the chance to nurse them, and get my revenge. I vowed that if ever I went to another dance at the Town Hall, it would be in a suit of armour!

We were not alone in our suffering. Two girls had arrived just after us, dressed as birds. They had sewn layers of feathers onto bikinis. Long before the end of the dance, they were walking around in just their bikinis, the feather having all been plucked off.

Sue and I stayed until the Mayor announced the total of the money collected. Our float had raised nearly three hundred pounds. We had collected in a couple of hours more money than each of us would earn in two years.

I did not realise how much wine I had consumed until we started to walk home. For some reason, I decided that it would be safer to walk along the white line in the middle of the road. I had only managed to walk a few feet, before I was removed from the centre of the road by a large policeman.

Sue, always at her best in an emergency, explained that I was afraid of being followed home by one of the councillors. The policeman kindly escorted us back to the hospital gates.

Sunday passed in a haze, but by Monday morning I had more or less recovered. All I had to show for the experience was a rash of small bruises on my backside. Sue took longer to recover; the tops of her legs were so bruised that she had to go off sick for a week!

Sue and I were summoned to Matron's Office. I had prepared a speech justifying the float. Before I had a chance to start, we were told to sit down, and offered coffee.

Matron wanted to know the names of all the people that had helped with the float. She wanted to see them, and thank them personally for the effort they had made. She even congratulated us on the theme.

Matron had heard about the problems that we had at the dance, and even that we had been escorted home. Instead of the expected telling off, she congratulated us on keeping our heads in a difficult situation.

It did not seem appropriate to tell her that it was not our *heads* that had been in danger!

CHAPTER TWENTY-FIVE

Three nights off had given me the much needed chance to catch up on my sleep. By the time I returned to duty on Monday night, I felt ready for anything!

On nights, one tended to become divorced from the rest of the hospital. We saw very little of the day staff, and gossip passed us by, so I was unprepared for the state of the ward.

Sister had been stricken by the latest 'flu bug, and had gone off sick. Three other nurses were also ill. Peters had simply walked out; she had been due for a week's holiday, and had planned to spend it preparing for her wedding. As soon as Sister took to her bed, Matron cancellled Peter's holiday.

This time, Peters had been pushed too far. I missed her; she was an excellent nurse. In her position, I would have done the same thing. She had already given in her notice, and was due to leave two days after returning from holiday.

Dennis had been left to manage the ward over the weekend with only five nurses, all of them students. By Monday evening, she looked exhausted. None of the day staff had been off duty for three days.

I was again senior nurse on night duty, so I took the report from Dennis, then left her in the office to catch up on her paper work.

The fact that there were so few nurses to look after the patients had made no difference to the surgeons; they had just carried on as usual. Seven patients had been to theatre that day, five of them for major operations. It had also been a busy weekend. There were now eleven patients that were very ill, all of them having drips.

I set the juniors to work, and then did a round of the ill patients. I did not like what I found. Even to my inexperienced eye, four of them looked terminal. The only bright point was that all four had relatives sitting with them. That at least meant that we would not have to sit with them. There was no way that I could have spared a nurse to sit and wait for any of them to die, even had I know which was going first!

I checked the drips, did the observations, then started on the medicine round. I had only just moved the trolley out of the office, when the 'phone rang. Casualty were sending up a head injury.

I hated head injuries; they were such an unknown quantity. One minute they could be fine, the next, gone. There was nowhere near the office for her either. The nearest I could manage was halfway down the ward. It looked as if it was going to be a busy night!

I was relieved to see that the head injury was conscious when she arrived. That was one problem less to worry about. We wouldn't have to keep on turning her to prevent pressure sores; she could turn herself. Having settled her in bed, and completed the admission forms, I recommenced the medicine round.

I managed to finish it without further interruption. Apart from the eleven ill patients, the only one to cause me concern was a young lady in the side ward. She had been admitted on Friday night with head injuries and a compound fracture of her tibia and fibula (lower leg.) She had come to us, rather than the Orthopaedic Ward, because her head injuries were so severe that the surgeons thought that they might have to operate.

Luckily, they were wrong. She had regained consciousness and had suffered no apparent lasting damage. When I went in to say hello to her, she looked very flushed, and was complaining of pain in her leg. The room smelt terribly of drains. That in itself was nothing strange. The sluice was next door to the side ward, and the drains were always getting blocked and "scenting" the room.

As I left the room, Dr. Patel entered the ward. For once I was pleased to see him. He was undoubtedly one of the best doctors in the hospital, but I had not forgotten the saga of the missing leech. I could never relax in his presence.

I was relieved to find that he too was worried about Elizabeth, and pleased, when he said he would see her first, before he went into the ward.

He opened the side ward door, then stopped and sniffed. He hurriedly closed the door, and said,

"Shit! We've dropped a monumental clanger."

Before I had the chance to ask what was wrong, he grabbed me and marched me out of the ward. Once we were out in the fresh air, he let go of my arm. Then he said,

"Who else has been in that room since you came on duty?"

I did not take kindly to being hauled off the ward. Rather than answer his question, I said.

"What the hell do you think you are doing? I am supposed to be in charge of the ward. I'm not going to be able to do a lot stuck out here in the yard."

Having made his apologies, he went on to explain his behaviour. The smell I had noticed was not the drains. It was the characteristic odour of *Clostridium Welchii*, an anaerobic spore forming bacilli, that caused Gas Gangrene. I felt myself go pale. I had heard enough about Gas Gangrene to know that we were in serious trouble.

I had no idea what to do; I was completely out of my depth. I think Patel was too, even he managed to look pale! I was dispatched back to the ward, to mount guard outside the side ward door. No one was to be allowed in there. Since I had already been in, I would have to treat the patient.

Patel explained that the bug, given the chance, would spread round the ward like wildfire. I was not to go near any of the other patients. Whatever happened in the ward, I was to have no part of it.

I felt a fool standing outside the side ward door, so I went inside and stood talking to Elizabeth. She told me that she had been riding pillion on her boyfriend's motorbike when they were hit by a car. She had fallen off, slid along the road, and ended up in a ditch. She had lain there for over an hour before the ambulance men found her.

Patel was right. As clangers go, it was monumental, not to say disastrous. I am ashamed to admit, that my first thought was not for the patient, but that the theatres would have to be closed and fumigated! That would give us a few days respite, no operations, perhaps even no admissions. With luck, they might make it last until the end of the week, and the end of my spell on nights!

What I did not appreciate was, that I too would have to be fumigated. I had only been in the room for a few minutes, when the door opened, and Patel stuck his head round.

"Sister is looking for you," he said.

He was right. Night Sister was standing outside the door, holding a large bowl. As I emerged, she put the bowl on the floor and backed away from me. She pointed to the bowl and said,

"Put the keys in that bowl of Lysol."

I did as I was told.

"Now, Nurse," Sister continued, "we have a slight problem. Doctor thinks that Elizabeth's leg might have become infected with *Clostridium Welchii*. He is going to see her, and explain that she will have to return to theatre for a further operation. You are to prepare her, but you are not to go into the ward. As soon as she goes to theatre, you are to remover all the bedding and the curtains and put them in a sack. The porters will leave you some sacks outside the door. As soon as that is done, you are to let me know. I will stay on the ward."

Great, I thought; a ward full of ill patients, and I'm to spend half the night changing curtains. By the time I had Elizabeth ready for theatre, I knew just how a leper must feel; everyone kept well out of my way.

A chair was placed outside the door, and all the things that I needed were placed on it. The only person that came into the room was Patel. I stood and listened to him explaining to Elizabeth that her leg had become infected, and she was to return to theatre for a further operation.

As she was only twenty, she was not able to sign her own consent form. That had to be done by her parents. Had she been twenty-one, he would have had to explain that he was probably going to amputate her leg below the knee.

Having disposed of Elizabeth to theatre, and stripped the room, I stood at the ward door until Sister saw me. I was told to go over to Home Sister's Office. Then the fun really started.

Home Sister took me up to one of the bathrooms. I was told to bath and wash my hair, to make sure that I was not carrying any of Elizabeth's germs. Sister ran the bath for me, and to my surprise, filled it almost to the overflow. I thought that I was, for once, going to be able to enjoy a bath. That idea was soon squashed. Sister tipped a vast amount of carbolic into the water, and waited for me to climb in. Then, she ordered me to submerge. I had to lay in the water with only my nose sticking out!

Once Sister was satisfied that I was as sterile as possible, I was allowed to emerge and dress in the clean clothes that she had collected from my room. All that remained was for me to gargle, in case I had swallowed any germs. Having been passed as germ-free, I was sent back on duty.

By then, it was nearly midnight. Night Sister had left the ward in the care of the juniors. To say they were pleased to see me would be an understatement. No one had bothered to tell them what was happening. They had merely been told not to go into the side ward. I explained that Elizabeth had developed something contagious, and been taken to theatre. Swearing them to secrecy, I sent them to their meal. I decided not to bother going for dinner, so I asked them to bring me back some sandwiches. I wasn't really hungry, and I couldn't face having to explain why I stank of carbolic.

Considering they were both in their first year, they had managed the ward very well in my absence. All the drips were still running, and no one had died.

That soon changed, in the hour that the juniors were at dinner, three patients died. Fortunately, two of them had their relatives with them when they went, and by sheer chance, I was at the bedside of the third. I was left with the problem of what to do with two sets of weeping relatives. There was not room for them all in the office. I took them into the kitchen, made them a pot of tea, and left them to their own devices.

I was consoled by the fact that, having had three deaths, there were unlikely to be any more that night. Like admissions, they always ran in threes.

Having rung the switchboard and asked them to find me a doctor to certify the deaths, I rang Night Sister, and told her that there had just been three deaths. I was rather surprised at her reaction. She said,

"What the hell are you doing over there, trying to empty the ward single handed?"

Then she dropped the bombshell.

"Have you informed the relatives?"

I explained that two lots had been present, so already knew. I was told, that as soon as the deaths had been certified, I was to 'phone and break the news to the other relative.

I was horrified. What on earth was I to say? I tried to persuade Dr. Piper that it would be better if he rang, but he refused. It was not, he maintained, his job.

To make matters worse, the notes informed me that the next of kin was the patient's husband. Since she had been in her seventies, I reasoned that he would not be very young. I prepared a speech, then picked up the receiver. My hand shook so much, that I had to have four attempts at dialling the number.

The 'phone only rang twice before it was answered. Instead of the elderly male voice that I had expected, it was answered by a young-sounding female. I took a deep breath to try and steady my voice, and introduced myself. I was saved the trauma of explaining why I was ringing. The voice said,

"Is it about Mum?"

That put paid to my carefully rehearsed speech. I asked if it would be possible to speak to her father, about she explained that he was asleep, and if possible, she would rather not wake him. Now I was stuck. I knew that we were only supposed to notify the next of kin of a death. I spent so long in thought that the girl realised my problem, and said,

"Has she gone?"

I replied that I was sorry to have to break the news over the 'phone, but yes, her mother had died. There was a brief period of silence. Then the line went dead.

I have since learnt that there is no easy way to break the news of a death, but, given the chance, I avoid having to do it over the 'phone. It is often very harrowing to see a person's grief, but at least, one can offer comfort and contact.

The rest of the night passed in a frenzy. It takes two nurses a minimum of half an hour to lay out a body; that was an hour and a half gone from the night. There were also the relatives in the kitchen to contend with; they looked as if they were settled in for the rest of the night.

We could hardly take the bodies to the Mortuary with them still in the kitchen. I explained that there was nothing for them to do until the morning, when they would have to return to collect any personal effects from the Hospital Secretary. I was very pleased to see them leave the ward.

I felt that I ought to spend some time with them. They were all very upset, but time was short enough as it was. I was torn between caring for the bereaved, and caring for my patients. It is a situation that I have never managed to resolve. One cannot be in two places at once.

By the time the day staff came on duty, I was both physically and mentally exhausted. I gave Dennis a report of all that had happened during the night.

She was not very pleased about Elizabeth, especially as she had been transferred to the Private Wing, straight from theatre. Dennis thought that it reflected on her ability to run the ward.

She was very angry that I had not asked the relatives if the bodies were to be buried or cremated, and informed me that I would have to 'phone them all and ask. I refused. It was bad enough having to break the news, without asking them what they wanted done with the bodies.

I do not know how nurses cope today, when they also have to ask permission for organ removal. I thank God that I have never been placed in such an awful position.

The rest of the week was comparative bliss. The ward had been closed to admissions, and the theatres for fumigation. By the end of the week, we only had fourteen patients, and they were all well on the road to recovery.

I was extremely happy to leave Ward Six for the last time. I had had more than enough experience of life's traumas.

I was now half way through my training. From now on, it was a downhill rush to Finals. Everyone I had spoken to had said that the last half of the three years went in a flash; that it was dangerous to put off revision until the start of the final year. From now on, one must study as much as possible.

The whole set agreed that from Block onwards, we would become model students. Before we turned over our new leaves, we decided to have a party. I managed to persuade one of the dining room maids to find us some food, and I collected enough money off the other five to buy two large bottles of cider.

I even managed to get permission from Home Sister to use our room for the party, on the basis that we would be well out of the way. Had we used one of the sitting rooms, members of other sets might have been tempted to join us, and noisy gatherings were very much frowned upon.

It was the first time we had all been together since we had taken our Prelims in February, and I was shocked to see how much the others had aged. They were probably thinking the same about me! We had all had roughly the same general experiences. We had all spent rather longer on the carpet of Matron's Office than members of other sets, and we were all weary, depressed and broke.

Why were we always the group that rebelled? Why was it that our particular set had refused to accept the outdated rules? Why was it always left to us to try and change things?

The thing that upset us most was not the work; it was hard, admittedly, but we had expected that. It was the way we were treated. On duty, we were given responsibility that we were really far too young and inexperienced to cope with.

Yet when off duty we had to suffer the indignity of being locked into the Home at ten-thirty every night. Night Sister even checked up on us to see that we were in bed. If we could be trusted to be responsible when it suited "them", why couldn't "they" leave us alone to run our own lives. We agreed that we would have had more freedom in a convent; there, we would have had our own rooms.

By the time we had drained the bottles, our depression began to lift, and we began to see the funny side of our lives over the last year and a half.

Beryl, having reached the advanced age of twenty-two, was feeling the restrictions of life in the Nurses' Home more than the rest of us, and she announced that she was seriously thinking of leaving. She had worked in a bank before starting her training, and had experienced life in the outside world. Although she enjoyed nursing, she could not take being treated as a child when off duty.

We all tried to make her change her mind, and stay, but without success. There was obviously more bothering her than she would admit. Eventually, she burst into tears and told us what was really wrong. Before starting her training, she had been considering getting married, but wanted to have some sort of career. Anxious to avoid getting pregnant before the end of her training, she had been to a Family Planning Clinic and had a Dutch cap fitted. She had found the cap that morning when moving rooms. It had lain so long, forgotten in its case, that it had perished.

Sister P.T.S. had told us always to look for the funny side in any situation; that if we didn't laugh, we would end up crying. As usual she was right, although it was often hard to find a funny side. Crying did not change anything, but laughter often did.

All the nurses I have ever met have the most atrocious sense of humour; perhaps they have developed it as a safety valve. The sight of Beryl crying her eyes out over a perished cap was too much for all of us; we dissolved into fits of laughter. What caused most amusement, was the fact that she had even considered that she might have the chance to use it.

Our laughter drew in other nurses and the small room became crowded. We were so engrossed in talking and laughing that we did not notice the time. For once, Night Sister had failed to knock on the door reminding us that it was ten-thirty, and time for lights out. Perhaps she had realised that it was more important for us to relax and forget about the troubles of the world than to sleep.

Helen, a small, usually very proper girl, was very drunk. She decided to recite her Pledge. Solemnly she stood with her hand on her heart and repeated Flo's words. As she did so, we were reminded of the fact that we too had made the same promises.

We were all agreed that we had kept most of our promises. In P.T.S., we had all been a little concerned as to whether or not we would be able to keep the first promise. We need not have worried; we had no choice but to remain pure; we were too tired to bother with men.

In eighteen months we had changed from young irresponsible children into mature women. We had seen birth, death, pain and suffering.

For some of us, the pain had been too much. Of the six that had given up, four had just found the conditions altogether too stressful, and had admitted defeat, one had been admitted to a psychiatric hospital after having a nervous breakdown, and one had been sacked after attempting to commit suicide.

Only the strong remained.